T0106524

When a murder case from the past heats up again, it's up to Marley McKinney to sort through a tall stack of suspects in the latest Pancake House Mystery...

Although it's a soggy start to spring in Wildwood Cove, the weather clears up just in time for the town to host an amateur chef competition. Marley McKinney, owner of The Flip Side pancake house, already signed up to volunteer, and chef Ivan Kaminski is one of the judges. But when Marley visits her landscaper boyfriend Brett at the site of the Victorian mansion that's being restored as the Wildwood Inn, she discovers something else pushing up daisies: human remains.

The skeleton on the riverbank washed out by the early-spring floodwaters belonged to eighteen-year-old Demetra Kozani, who vanished a decade earlier. While the cold case is reopened, Marley must step in when some of the cook-off contestants fall suspiciously ill. Stuck in a syrupy mess of sabotage and blackmail, it falls to Marley to stop a killer from crêping up on another victim...

Includes pancake recipes right from The Flip Side menu!

Books by Sarah Fox

The Literary Pub Mystery Series
Wine and Punishment

The Pancake House Mystery Series
The Crêpes of Wrath
For Whom the Bread Rolls
Of Spice and Men
Yeast of Eden
Crêpe Expectations

The Music Lover's Mystery Series
Dead Ringer
Death in A Major
Deadly Overtures

CRÊPE EXPECTATIONS

A Pancake House Mystery

Sarah Fox

LYRICAL PRESS
Kensington Publishing Corp.
www.kensingtonbooks.com

First Electronic Edition: May 2019
eISBN-13: 978-1-5161-0775-9
eISBN-10: 1-5161-0775-6

First Print Edition: May 2019
ISBN-13: 978-1-5161-0778-0
ISBN-10: 1-5161-0778-0

Printed in the United States of America

Chapter 1

A banner with bold lettering rippled in the breeze. It gave a snap now and again when a stronger gust tried to wrest it free of the table it was fastened to, but it remained in place, the thick paper refusing to tear. So far the banner had done its job, grabbing people's attention and directing them to the table where I sat with a stack of papers in front of me.

"Looks like we've got the makings of a great competition this year," Patricia Murray commented from the chair next to mine.

"I had no idea it would be this popular," I admitted, running my eyes down the list of names written on one of the papers.

I leaned back in my folding chair and stretched my legs under the table set up in the parking lot of Wildwood Cove's grocery store. It was early on a Saturday afternoon, and normally at that time of day I'd be at my pancake house, The Flip Side, closing up and tidying the restaurant. Today, however, I'd agreed to volunteer my time to help with registration for the Olympic Peninsula's annual amateur chef competition.

Each year, one of the peninsula's communities hosted the competition, and this time it was Wildwood Cove's turn. The event would take place over the following three weekends, and already several residents of Wildwood Cove and other towns had signed up. I'd been sitting at the registration table for two hours, and people were still arriving to put their names down for either the teen division or the adult category.

"I was worried with all the rain this year that most people wouldn't want to come out and participate," Patricia said. She owned a bed-and-breakfast three properties away from my beachfront Victorian, and she was also on the organizing committee for the amateur chef contest.

"We're definitely lucky the weather decided to change," I said before Patricia greeted the latest person to approach the registration table.

I'd spent many of my summer vacations in Wildwood Cove while growing up in Seattle, but I'd only moved to the seaside town permanently the previous spring and had never been present for the cooking competition. It sounded like fun, though, and I was eager to be involved with the community, so I hadn't hesitated about volunteering to help out when Patricia had asked me. My participation would be limited to assisting with registration, but I'd been assured that I was providing some much needed help.

As Patricia registered a teenage girl with dark hair even curlier than mine, I breathed deeply, enjoying the fresh air and the lack of rain. The peninsula had seen very little sunshine over the past two months, and the rainfall had been so heavy and persistent that the nearby river had flooded its banks, damaging some homes and causing a slew of problems. Now that we'd had a few days without any rain, the floodwaters were finally receding, allowing everyone to breathe easier, even though many people had a long road of cleanup and restoration ahead of them.

I sat up straighter when I noticed a fifty-something woman approaching the registration table. She had her light brown hair tied back in a bun, and she walked with careful steps. A man about her age followed along behind her and hung back when she reached the table. I greeted her and provided her with the registration form. Her name was Dorothy Kerwin, I noted as she filled in the form with her name, address, and the division she was entering. When she'd completed the form, I provided her with the booklet that every entrant received. It contained the rules and the event schedule.

"Hi, Dorothy," Patricia said with a smile when she'd finished registering the teenage girl. "How are you doing these days?"

"Better, thank you," Dorothy replied with a hint of a smile.

"Are you ready to go, Dot?" the man hovering behind her asked as he glanced at his watch.

"Sorry," she said to me and Patricia. "I'd better be on my way."

Despite the man's impatience, he didn't hurry Dorothy once they set off, one of her arms tucked into his.

"Had you met Dorothy and Willard Kerwin before today?" Patricia asked me once we were alone.

"No."

"The poor woman has been through a lot over the past year or two. She fell off a stepladder and broke her back, and then her twin sister passed away while Dorothy was still in the hospital."

"That's terrible," I said with a surge of compassion for the woman. "I think this is the first time she's participated in any community event since all that happened, so it's nice to see her getting involved."

I was about to agree with her when I caught sight of my boyfriend, Brett Collins, out of the corner of my eye. I smiled and waved as he approached, carrying two take-out cups from the local coffee shop, the Beach and Bean. The light breeze ruffled his blond hair as he reached the table.

"A coffee for you, Patricia," he said, setting one of the cups in front of her. "And a matcha latte for you, Marley." He handed the second cup to me.

We both thanked him. Since no one was waiting to be registered at that moment, I got up to give him a hug and a quick kiss.

"Did you get something for yourself?" I asked.

"Yep. A sandwich and a coffee. I put them in the truck."

"I'm guessing you have to head back to work now?"

"I do, but I should be done for the day in about three hours."

He was on his lunch break from his landscaping work at an old Victorian mansion that would soon be opening to guests as the Wildwood Inn. Brett ran his own lawn and garden business, and the new owners of the mansion had hired him to landscape and prepare the gardens before the inn's grand opening, which would be marked by a garden party later in the month. The mansion's owners, Lonny and Hope Barron, had spent the past several months restoring the Victorian and getting it ready for its new life as an inn.

"I'll see you at home, then," I said, leaning into him for another hug before reluctantly releasing him.

"Hello, everyone!" Brett's sister, Chloe, breezed over to us, her blue eyes bright.

She caught sight of the cups Patricia and I held. "Drinks from the Beach and Bean? That's where I'm headed."

"That makes more sense," Brett said.

"More sense than what?" Chloe asked.

"For a second there I thought you were here to register for the cooking competition."

"Why wouldn't that make sense?" Patricia asked as Chloe's smile morphed into a frown.

Brett slung an arm across Chloe's shoulders. "Because my kid sister couldn't cook to save her life."

"I can so cook," Chloe retorted, giving him a shove. She looked to me for support.

"You make good cookies," I said. "I know that much."

"You mean the ones *Jourdan* made for the Fourth of July barbecue?" Brett asked, referring to their cousin.

"Hey, I helped," Chloe protested.

"Right. I seem to recall that you spooned the dough onto the cookie sheets and Jourdan did the rest."

"I'm sure you can cook," I said to Chloe, wanting to placate her before things escalated.

"Of course," Brett said, trying to keep a straight face. "She can make toast, rubbery scrambled eggs, and pasta—as long as the pasta comes from a store and the sauce comes out of a jar." He addressed his sister. "And what about that time you tried to cook a family dinner and nearly burned down the house?"

Chloe's gaze hardened. "It was a tiny little fire, and I put it out right away."

I couldn't help but laugh, and beside me Patricia was struggling to contain a smile.

"You're no help, Marley," Chloe said, turning her frown on me.

"I'm sorry." I quickly took a sip of my latte to keep myself from laughing again.

Chloe grabbed a pen off the table. "Registration form, please," she said to me.

I glanced at Brett and then back at her before handing over a form.

"What are you doing?" Brett asked.

"Exactly what it looks like." Chloe wrote her name on the form. "I'm signing up for the competition."

"Hasn't the town seen enough disaster lately with all the flooding?"

Chloe pressed the pen so hard against the paper that I was surprised when it didn't tear. "Just you wait. I'm going to make you eat your words."

"They'll probably taste better than your scrambled eggs."

Chloe threw the pen at him. He caught it right before it smacked him in the face.

Chloe passed me the completed form, and I gave her a booklet.

"You'll see," she said, swatting her brother's arm with the booklet before storming off, heading in the direction of the coffee shop.

"Brett," I said, "you shouldn't tease her like that."

"But it's so fun," he said with a smile.

I shook my head, and he wrapped his arms around me.

"I've got to run," he said in my ear. "See you later."

After giving me a quick kiss, he left for his truck, parked on the street. A group of three teenagers arrived to register for the youth division, so

Patricia and I kept busy for the next several minutes. Two adults registered after that, but then we had another lull. Patricia's cell phone rang, and she got up from the table, walking a few steps away before answering the call. While she was still occupied, Logan Teeves arrived and asked to register. Logan was seventeen and lived next door to me with his dad, Gerald. He'd dated Patricia's daughter, Sienna, for a while, and although they'd broken up, they were still friends.

"I didn't realize you liked cooking," I said as Logan filled out the registration form.

He shrugged and brushed his fair hair off his forehead. "My dad doesn't cook, so we'd always be eating takeout and frozen dinners if I didn't learn." He shrugged again. "It's kind of fun."

"Well, I think it's great that you're entering." I handed him a booklet. "Good luck."

Logan wandered off, and Patricia returned to the table, dropping into her seat with a worried frown on her face.

"What's wrong?" I asked.

"That was Sid Michaels on the phone."

"The owner of Scoops Ice Cream?"

Patricia nodded. "He was supposed to be one of the judges for the competition, but now he has to make an unexpected trip to San Francisco. He's not sure when he'll be back, but he thinks he'll be gone at least two weeks."

"So now you need another judge," I surmised.

"As soon as possible. Would you be able to step in, Marley?" she asked.

"I could," I said slowly, "but I don't eat meat."

"Right. And that would be a problem, especially for the first challenge."

On the opening day of the competition the contestants would be cooking main course dishes, with the dessert challenge the following week.

Patricia swiped away a strand of dark hair that the breeze had blown across her face. "How about Ivan? Do you think he'd be willing to step in?"

"To be honest, I'm not sure." Ivan Kaminski was The Flip Side's talented chef. He was a wizard in the kitchen and more than qualified to take on the role as judge for the competition, but he wasn't the most social man, and I wasn't sure how he'd feel about taking part in the event. "I could ask him, though."

"Would you?" Patricia said with obvious relief. "That would be fantastic."

"When do you need a definitive answer?"

"As soon as you can get one?"

I pulled my phone from my pocket. "I'll send him a text now, and if I don't hear back from him today, I'll talk to him about it in the morning."

"Thanks, Marley. That's a huge help."

I really wasn't sure how Ivan would respond to the request, but I decided to do my best to convince him to help with the judging, even if it did put me in direct line of one of his intimidating scowls.

A few minutes later I received a curt text message in response:

We'll talk tomorrow.

I didn't share the reply with Patricia, not quite knowing what to make of it. At least he hadn't said no outright, but I wasn't entirely sure what to expect in the morning.

Chapter 2

When I left for The Flip Side the next day, the few clouds overhead were tinged with pink and the sun was creeping its way up over the eastern horizon. I set off on foot, walking along the beach toward town and enjoying the peace and quiet of the early morning. Other than the gentle lapping of the waves against the shore and the occasional call of a bird, there wasn't a sound to be heard. Breathing in the fresh, salty air, I couldn't help but be in a good mood. I loved walking to work, and over the past few months I'd driven more often than I'd made the trip on foot. Between the cold, dark weather of winter and the incessant rain in March, I hadn't had many opportunities to enjoy the beauty and tranquility of Wildwood Beach.

Once I'd left the sand for the paved promenade that ran along the front of the pancake house and other beachfront businesses, I fished my keys out of my tote bag and had the right one ready when I reached The Flip Side. As usual, Ivan and his assistant, Tommy, had arrived before me, and the light from the kitchen spilled out through the pass-through window into the dim dining area. I flicked on the overhead lights and dropped off my tote bag and jacket in the office before heading for the kitchen.

"Good morning," I greeted as I pushed through the swinging door.

I received a cheerful hello from Tommy and a nod from Ivan. The chef was in the midst of slicing up a log of dough with cinnamon and sugar swirled inside. Even though the maple pecan sticky rolls weren't cooked yet, my mouth watered at the sight.

"Isn't there someone else who can judge the competition?" Ivan asked, tearing my attention away from the sliced dough.

"The amateur chef competition?" Tommy asked.

Ivan gave a grunt of confirmation.

"Sid Michaels from Scoops Ice Cream was supposed to be on the judging panel, but he's had to leave town unexpectedly, so Patricia's in a bit of a lurch," I explained. "She'd really appreciate it if you could help out, Ivan."

He spared me a brief glance, his dark eyes settling on me only for a second before he returned to his work. A year ago I would have been intimidated standing there before the muscular, tattooed chef, but I now knew that beneath his burly, imposing exterior was a good heart.

"The competition starts next Saturday afternoon," he said as he sliced the last piece of dough in half. "I'll be working."

"If you leave right after we close, you'll be able to make it in time."

"I'll still have work to do after closing."

"I can handle the cleanup and next day's prep," Tommy offered. "I don't mind staying a bit later than usual."

"Thanks, Tommy," I said with a grateful smile.

Ivan glared at us before placing the sliced sticky rolls in a baking dish and passing it to Tommy. He wiped down the counter next, all the while leaving me in suspense.

Finally, his eyes met mine again.

"I'll help with the judging."

I couldn't stop another smile from spreading across my face.

"Thank you, Ivan. Patricia will be so relieved."

I hurried out of the kitchen and fetched my phone from the office so I could text Patricia the good news. With that done, I started my workday, and an hour later the first customers had arrived, hungry for breakfast.

"This weather is a welcome change, isn't it?" Eleanor Crosby said as I delivered a plate of blueberry crumble pancakes to her.

"That's for sure," I said, sliding a plate of marzipan pancakes in front of her dining companion, Marjorie Wells. "Did either of you have any trouble with flooding?"

"Not us, thank goodness," Marjorie replied. "But my nephew had a couple of inches of water in his crawlspace."

"I'm sorry to hear that," I said. "So many people have been left with a mess to deal with."

Eleanor took a sip of her coffee. "At least the river level's going down now."

I agreed that was a good turn of events and left the ladies to eat. While the aftermath of the flooding was a hot topic of conversation that morning, many diners were also chatting about the amateur chef competition and the upcoming garden party at the Wildwood Inn.

"Brett's working on the gardens up at the inn, isn't he?" Gary Thornbrook asked.

He was having breakfast with his buddy Ed, as he did at least twice every week. Ed and Gary were The Flip Side's most frequent customers, and they rarely strayed from their usual selection from the menu—blueberry pancakes with bacon and sausages on the side.

"He is," I said as I topped off Gary's coffee. "It's a lot of work for him, especially since he's got all his regular clients to deal with as well. He's thinking of hiring someone to help him, at least part-time."

"He's done well with his business," Ed said.

"He has," I agreed with a rush of pride. Before moving on to the next table with the pot of fresh coffee, I paused and asked, "Are you two going to the garden party?"

"If we can still fit into our suits," Gary said with a laugh, patting his generous stomach.

I smiled and continued on to the neighboring table.

The last diners of the day left the restaurant shortly after two o'clock, and I locked the door behind them, flipping the "open" sign to "closed." Leigh Hunter, The Flip Side's full-time waitress, untied her red apron from around her waist. Patricia Murray's daughter, Sienna, did the same with her apron. Sienna was seventeen and still in school, but she worked at the pancake house on the weekends.

"Did you know that Logan's entering the amateur chef competition?" I asked Sienna.

"Yep. He's a really good cook. He got into watching cooking shows about three years ago, and now he can make some really amazing stuff."

"I hope he does well in the competition," Leigh said.

"He will," Sienna said with confidence. "My friend Ellie Shaw's entering too. She didn't really want to, but her mom thought she should."

"Why didn't she want to?" I asked.

"She's kind of shy. I don't think she likes the idea of cooking in front of an audience."

"Maybe she'll forget anyone's watching once she gets cooking," Leigh said.

"I hope so. She's really talented, especially with desserts." Sienna headed for the break room to fetch her jacket, and soon she and Leigh had left the pancake house for the day.

Talking about cooking made me wonder if Brett would be finished work by dinnertime. I sent him a text message asking him how things were going. I tidied up the pancake house while waiting for his response. It came about half an hour later. He figured he'd have to work until six o'clock, but he hoped he wouldn't have to stay at the inn any longer than that.

Hungry? I wrote in another text. *I can bring you a snack.*

I love you, was his quick response.

Smiling, I finished up my remaining tasks and grabbed a can of soda from the kitchen before heading out. I walked to Marielle's Bakery and picked up two doughnuts and half a dozen chocolate chip cookies. From there, I set a course for home. The Wildwood Inn sat on the outskirts of town, and making the trip on foot would have taken a while, so I decided to make a quick stop at home to pick up my car.

After checking on my cat, Flapjack, and Brett's dog, Bentley, I set off in my hatchback. When I reached my destination, I followed a long driveway toward the beautiful white Victorian mansion and continued along the branch that led around the house to the large detached garage, built in the same style as the inn. I parked my blue hatchback next to the cube van Brett used for his lawn and garden business.

With the paper bakery bag and soda can in hand, I wandered around the garage until I could see clear to the back of the inn's property. An expanse of green lawn stretched from the mansion to a white gazebo—a new addition, Brett had told me. Beyond the gazebo, flagstone pathways wandered around numerous flower beds. Brett had been working hard to add some color before the garden party. He'd already transplanted numerous types of flowers in a variety of hues and would add more over the coming days. Some of the flower beds farther back in the garden were home to recently planted rosebushes, which would bloom in a few weeks' time.

As soon as I started across the lawn, I spotted Brett near the back of the property, working away at one of the last flower beds, only a stone's throw from the woods that bordered the garden. There was a small cottage in the back corner of the lot, but I couldn't see anyone else around. The garden was peaceful, the only sound the chirping of birds in the trees.

I followed the flagstone pathway past the flower beds, raising a hand in greeting when Brett looked up and saw me approaching.

"I come bearing food," I said as I reached him.

He grinned and drove the spade he was holding into the soil so it would stand upright on its own. "Best news I've heard all day."

I glanced around the garden. "You've made a lot of progress since the last time I was here. It looks great."

"I need to work at a couple of other sites this week, but hopefully this job will be done in the next two weeks." He pulled off his work gloves and tucked them into the back pocket of his jeans. "How was your day?"

"Great. Everything went well at The Flip Side. A lot of people were talking about the garden party. They're going to love what you've done here."

"Hopefully Lonny and Hope will love it too," he said.

"They will," I said without any doubt. "They like what you've done so far, right?"

"So far so good," he confirmed.

I held up the paper bag and can of soda. "Your snack."

"Thank you. You're the best."

"I can't say I was disappointed to have a chance to see you before tonight."

He grinned. "I'm definitely not disappointed either."

He led me to a stone bench at the end of the garden that faced the flower beds, the mansion visible in the distance. I sat with him and snacked on one of the doughnuts while he devoured the other one along with a couple of the cookies. When I'd finished eating, I rested my head against his shoulder.

"It's so peaceful here," I said, listening to the birdsong coming from the woods behind us.

Brett took a long drink of his soda. "It's definitely a nice place to work."

I raised my head. "Speaking of which, I should probably let you get back to it."

He eyed the rosebushes sitting in pots near one of the flower beds, waiting to be transplanted. "Another two hours or so and then I'll be heading home."

I got to my feet and set the paper bag on the bench. "I'll leave these here in case you want more."

Brett set down his soda can as he stood up. He took my hands, pulling me in close. "Thanks for stopping by, Marley."

He gave me a lingering kiss that I reluctantly pulled away from.

"See you later."

I was about to set off along the garden path when something small and black streaked toward the tree line. I spun around to follow its progress.

"A kitten!" I exclaimed. "Did you see that?"

The tiny black cat paused at the edge of the woods, its green eyes wide, one ear twitching while the rest of its body remained frozen.

"Does it belong to Lonny and Hope?" I asked.

"I don't know," Brett said. "I caught a brief glimpse of it earlier today, but that's the first time I've seen a cat around here."

I took a careful step toward the kitten. It dashed beneath a bushy fern and hunkered down, out of sight except for the tip of one black ear.

"It looks way too tiny to be out here on its own," I said.

"We can take it up to the house and see if that's where it belongs. If we can catch it, that is."

As if it had heard Brett's words, the little kitten darted out from its hiding place and zipped away, deeper into the woods.

"Catching it might not be possible, but I don't want to leave it in the woods. Maybe we can at least get it to run back this way."

"We can try," Brett agreed.

We moved off in opposite directions, planning to circle around into the woods and hopefully herd the kitten back to the garden. I tried to move quietly as I entered the woods, not wanting to scare the cat farther into the forest. Despite my efforts, twigs still snapped under my feet and the underbrush rustled as I picked my way through the trees.

I could hear rushing water somewhere nearby and realized we were close to the Wildwood River. My concern for the kitten shot up. Although the water level was on its way down now, the river was still higher than usual and could be dangerous for anyone who got too close to the slippery, unstable banks. I didn't want the kitten going anywhere near the water.

As I moved deeper into the forest, the dirt beneath my feet became soggier. Through the trees, I caught sight of the river, still swollen and muddy, hurtling its way toward the ocean. I swept my gaze from left to right, desperately seeking out any sign of the kitten.

"Can you see it?" I called out to Brett when he came into view. We were almost to the river now, and I had to talk over the sound of the rushing water.

"Not yet," Brett called back.

At the sound of his voice, something moved slightly a few feet away. I peered at a small, hollowed-out cavity at the base of an old tree. It was dark inside the hole, but I was certain I'd seen movement. I crept closer to the tree, moving slowly and cautiously.

I was about to crouch down in front of the hole when the kitten darted out of the hollow tree. I dropped to my knees and grabbed at the kitten, ending up flat on my stomach, my arms outstretched ahead of me. A fallen tree branch poked at my ribs, cold moisture was seeping through my jeans, and I had a face full of ferns, but I also had a wriggling kitten in my grasp.

"Are you okay?" Brett asked as he hurried over to me.

"I caught it!" I said through the ferns.

I couldn't see too well, but I heard Brett reach my side. One of his hands brushed against mine.

"I've got it. You can let go now."

I released my firm but gentle hold on the cat and climbed to my feet, brushing pine needles and clumps of mud from my clothes. I smiled at the sight of Brett holding the little kitten against his chest, but when I reached down to brush a clod of mud from my knee, my smile slipped away.

"Brett..."

"Are you hurt?" he asked with concern.

I shook my head and stepped back before pointing at the ground.

Next to the patch of ferns I'd landed in, a partial human skull poked out through the mud.

Chapter 3

I couldn't tear my gaze away from the skull, even though the sight of it sent an uncomfortable chill creeping up my spine. The empty eye sockets gaped at me, and everything around me suddenly seemed more sinister—the shadows, the rustling of leaves, the roar of the nearby river.

I shivered.

"Are you okay?" Brett asked.

I nodded.

The kitten let out a squeak of a meow. Finally, I managed to look away from my unsettling discovery. The little cat was a welcome distraction. He'd struggled at first but was now settled against Brett's chest. I didn't know why I'd started to think of the cat as male, but I figured I had a fifty percent chance of being right.

I marked the location of our find with one of Brett's work gloves, sliding it over the end of a spindly tree branch. We gave the partially exposed skull a wide berth, even though we'd already trampled over the surrounding area. When we emerged from the woods, Brett handed me the kitten and pulled his phone from the pocket of his jeans.

"I'll call Ray," he said, waking up the device.

Ray Georgeson was the sheriff of Clallam County and Brett's uncle.

I held the little kitten close to me, and he settled in my arms with a purr. He seemed too comfortable with me to be feral, so I thought there was a good chance he belonged at the mansion.

"I'll take you up to the house soon," I told the kitten as I half listened to Brett's side of the conversation with his uncle.

He was only on the phone for a minute before he hung up.

"Ray is on his way, but he's in Port Angeles so he'll be a while. Deputy Mendoza might be able to get here sooner, though." Brett tucked his phone back in his pocket and picked up the bag of cookies. "He wants us to wait up at the house."

"We can ask where this guy belongs while we're there," I said, running my hand over the kitten's black fur, his purr growing louder in response.

As we walked along the flagstone path, I tried unsuccessfully to stop a shiver from working its way up my spine. "I guess that skull's been there a while."

"It must have been," Brett agreed. "And it might have stayed there a lot longer if not for the flood."

I knew what he meant. The skull was located within the area that had flooded recently, and had likely been exposed as a result of the river water flowing over it and carrying away the top layer of dirt.

"Do you think there's a chance that whoever it is died accidentally?" I asked, trying to hold on to that hope, even though it already seemed like a faint one.

"I guess a homeless person could have been camped out in the woods and died there without anyone knowing," Brett said. "But then..."

"The skeleton wouldn't have been buried," I finished for him.

"Although, maybe it was the passage of time or an animal that buried it. We don't know for sure that there's a full skeleton. It could just be the skull."

"And it could be from some ancient burial ground."

"Could be."

We fell silent, all the possibilities running around and around in my head. We passed by the garage, and Brett set the bag of cookies on the hood of my car before approaching the back of the mansion. Three steps led up to a large covered porch that stretched the entire width of the house.

Still holding the kitten, I glanced down at my muddy clothes. "I'd better stay here."

I waited at the base of the steps while Brett scraped some mud from his boots and climbed up to the porch. He knocked on the back door, and several seconds later a petite woman with straight brown hair opened it. I guessed that she was in her late twenties. Although I'd never met her, I'd seen her from a distance before and knew she was one of the owners of the house, Hope Barron.

"Hi, Brett," she said with a smile. "How's the garden coming along?"

"Really well," he replied, "but we came across a problem in the woods." He gestured my way. "Have you met my girlfriend, Marley?"

"No." Hope smiled and waved at me.

I waved back, holding the kitten against me with one arm.

Hope shifted her gaze back to Brett. "What kind of problem in the woods?"

"Marley and I went into the forest to catch the kitten...and found a human skull."

Hope's eyes widened. "Are you sure it's human?"

"Unfortunately."

She shook her head, her eyes still wide. "I... What does this mean?"

"Someone from the sheriff's department will be here soon to take a look at the skull. We'll see how things go from there. Does your property extend all the way to the river?"

Hope shook her head again, clearly still shocked. "It ends at the tree line." She opened her mouth to say something more but then closed it, as if at a loss for words.

The kitten squirmed in my arms, and I decided it was a good time to change the subject. "Is this your cat?" I asked.

"No," Hope replied. "But it's probably the same one I've seen around here a few times. The first time I saw an older cat too—the kitten's mother, I assumed—but she was killed by a car two days ago."

Sadness pressed against my chest. "That's terrible."

"It is," Hope agreed. She pointed to food and water dishes on the porch. "I put out some food, hoping I'd be able to catch the little guy, but clearly you've had more luck."

"Did the mother have any other kittens that you know of?" Brett asked.

"No, I only ever saw the one. I figured someone probably decided they didn't want them anymore and dumped them here."

A rush of anger joined my sadness. "I don't know how anyone could do such a thing." I kissed the kitten's head. "That would explain why this one seems used to people, though." I stroked his fur and looked up at Hope. "Do you want to keep him?"

"I can't, unfortunately. Lonny and I decided to keep the inn pet-free in case any guests have allergies. If I managed to catch it I was going to take it to the animal shelter. Do you want to take him home?"

"We could," I said with a glance at Brett. "I'm not sure what my cat will think."

"We can give it a try," Brett said.

I smiled and stroked the kitten's fur. "Did you hear that? You're coming home with us."

The sound of an approaching vehicle wiped the smile from my face, reminding me of why Brett and I were up at the house.

"I'll go put this little guy in my car for now," I said.

"And I'd better go phone Lonny." Hope disappeared into the house.

Brett came down from the porch and headed around the side of the mansion. As I reached my car, I saw a sheriff's department cruiser slow to a stop in front of the Victorian. Brett crossed the driveway to meet Deputy Mendoza as she climbed out of the vehicle.

"Hopefully I won't have to leave you alone too long," I said to the kitten as I set him down on the front passenger seat of my car.

My tote bag was also on the seat, and the kitten immediately batted at the straps. I opened the window a crack and shut the door. I stayed there a moment, watching him pounce on my bag, before I joined Brett and Deputy Mendoza at the front of the Victorian mansion.

Brett had already explained the situation to Mendoza, and the deputy was now speaking into her radio. Several minutes later, another sheriff's department cruiser followed the long driveway up to the house and parked behind Mendoza's vehicle.

"I understand you found a skull in the woods," Ray Georgeson said once he'd climbed out of his cruiser and had said hello. His gaze settled on me.

"It happened totally by chance," I said.

I had a habit of getting involved in murder investigations and had found dead bodies in the past. It wasn't a habit Ray approved of, but he refrained from commenting on that for the moment, and Brett told him how we'd come upon the discovery.

"And you said the skull is partially buried?" he asked.

"Yes," I said. "It was probably the floodwaters that uncovered it."

Ray took off his hat and ran a hand through his brown hair before replacing it on his head. "Mendoza and I will go take a look."

We gave him general directions and told him about the glove I'd used to mark the location of the skull. As the sheriff and deputy headed around the back of the mansion, Hope came out the front door. Brett and I chatted with her for a few minutes, and then we all wandered around to the back gardens. Ray and Mendoza had yet to emerge from the forest, so I decided to go check on the kitten.

When I peeked in through the car window, I saw the little black cat curled up on the driver's seat, sleeping. Brett came up behind me and looked over my shoulder.

"Sound asleep?" he asked.

"Looks like it. He's so cute." I leaned back, resting against Brett's chest.

He wrapped his arms around me, and we watched the kitten sleep.

Out of the corner of my eye, I noticed movement at the edge of the woods. Ray and his deputy were on their way back toward the house. We met up with them as they approached, but they didn't have much to say other than that they'd be calling in more resources.

"Do you think there's a full skeleton buried there?" I asked.

"No way to tell yet," Ray replied. "We won't start digging until we've got the right people out here to do it."

It quickly became clear that those people wouldn't arrive anytime soon. After a few more words with Ray, I decided to head home. Brett was allowed to keep working in the garden, so I left him to transplant the remaining rosebushes.

The kitten woke up as soon as I opened the car door, and I picked him up and moved him over to the passenger seat. He dug his claws into the upholstery and stretched before climbing on top of my tote, nearly tumbling off when he tried to peer inside the bag.

"You're a goofball," I said to him, giving him a scratch under his chin.

He leaned into my touch, closing his eyes in bliss. I tucked the paper bag of leftover cookies inside my tote and buckled up.

As I drove, the kitten went back to exploring my bag, managing to poke his head inside, but otherwise not getting up to too much mischief. He was adorable, and I was already falling for him. I hoped Bentley and Flapjack would take to him as quickly as I had.

When I pulled into my driveway, I spotted my friend Lisa Morales's sedan parked in front of my blue-and-white Victorian. I parked next to her car and caught sight of her sitting in one of the white wicker chairs on the covered porch. She waved to me as I got out of my car.

"Sorry," I called out. "I expected to be home earlier. Have you been waiting long?"

I couldn't bring myself to mention the skull, so I kept that to myself for the moment.

"Only a couple of minutes," she replied, coming down the porch steps toward me. "Don't worry about it. I was enjoying this gorgeous spring weather."

"It's a nice change, isn't it?" I reached back into the car and scooped the kitten into my arms as he pounced on the seat I'd just vacated.

"Aw, a kitten!" Lisa almost melted right in front of me. "Where did it come from?"

"He's a stray. I found him up at the Wildwood Inn while I was visiting Brett."

Lisa couldn't take her eyes off the black cat. "Can I hold him?"

I passed the kitten over, and he immediately snuggled against Lisa, purring away.

"He's so adorable," Lisa gushed. "Are you keeping him?"

"Maybe. I'm pretty sure Bentley will accept him, but I don't know how Flapjack will feel about having another cat in the house. He's still getting used to Bentley living here full-time." I fetched my tote bag from my car and led the way up to the front door. "I was going to cook, but that was when I thought I'd be home earlier. Should we order takeout?"

Lisa had arrived for a movie night, something we tried to do together once a month. Chloe was supposed to join us as well.

"Takeout would be great. I've been craving Chinese food all week."

"Then that's what we'll order." I unlocked the front door but paused with my hand on the doorknob. "Maybe I should go in first so Bentley doesn't scare the kitten half to death."

I knew that as soon as I opened the door, the dog would come charging into the foyer to greet me.

Lisa kept the kitten cradled close to her chest. "Good idea. We'll wait out here for a moment, won't we, little guy?"

I smiled, knowing Lisa had now fallen for the kitten as much as I had.

I left them out on the porch and entered the house. As expected, I heard a clattering of claws on the hardwood floors, and Bentley raced down the hall toward me, his tail wagging. I kicked off my green Converse sneakers, leaving them by the door, and crouched down to greet the dog.

"Hey, buddy, did you miss me?"

Bentley wagged his tail so hard that his whole body wagged with it. I laughed, and he gave me several sloppy kisses on the cheek.

Flapjack made a more sedate entrance, padding along the hallway and sitting down just inside the foyer, flicking his tail as he waited for me to go greet him.

"I brought someone home for you to meet," I told him as I picked him up and kissed him on the top of his orange head.

Flapjack closed his eyes briefly as I stroked his fur.

"Be nice, okay? He's just a little guy."

Flapjack made no promises, but since Bentley had calmed down, I set the tabby on the floor. Crossing my fingers, I opened the front door, hoping my cat would welcome a new member to our family.

Chapter 4

I held on to Bentley so he wouldn't charge the kitten when Lisa set him on the floor. I didn't expect Bentley to deliberately hurt the black cat, but he was an exuberant dog and many times larger than the kitten, so there was always a chance he'd cause accidental harm to the little guy. Flapjack sat on the floor, his tail giving the occasional swish as he eyed the cat in Lisa's arms.

"Let's hope this goes well," Lisa said, gently setting the kitten down.

Bentley tried to bolt from my arms, but I held on tight.

Flapjack stood up slowly, his amber gaze fixed on the newcomer. The kitten had his front paws slightly splayed in a wide-legged stance. His ears twitched, but he otherwise stood frozen, looking first at Bentley and then at Flapjack.

The orange tabby moved toward the kitten, stopping when he was about six inches away. Then he flicked his tail and let out a long, loud hiss.

The kitten literally jumped. When he had all four paws on the floor again, he arched his back and hissed in return. Flapjack mirrored the kitten's stance and raised an orange paw.

Lisa came to the kitten's rescue, quickly sweeping him up off the floor and into her arms. He squirmed until he'd turned around enough to keep an eye on Flapjack.

I released my hold on Bentley, disappointment rushing in to replace the hope I'd been harboring. Bentley dashed across the foyer and sniffed Lisa's legs. She reached down with one hand and gave him a pat on the head. Flapjack turned his back on all of us and gave a dismissive flick of his tail before stalking off down the hallway.

"That didn't go so well," I said, frowning at Flapjack's retreating form.

"It took him time to warm up to Bentley, right?" Lisa said. "Maybe he just needs more of a chance to get used to having another cat around."

"Maybe." I took in the sight of the kitten snuggled up against Lisa. "Or, maybe he's destined for another home."

Surprise registered on Lisa's face when she caught my meaning. "My home?"

"Why not? You've been thinking about getting a cat."

She'd mentioned the possibility a couple of times over the past few months.

Lisa nuzzled her face against the kitten's head. Even from a few feet away, I could hear the kitten purring. Lisa smiled, and I could see in her face that she was falling head over heels.

"You'd be okay with that?" she asked. "I can tell you already love him."

"So do you. Besides, I'll still get to see him whenever I'm at your place."

"That's true." She gave the kitten a kiss. "Would you like to come home with me?" she asked him. "Auntie Marley can come visit you anytime."

Still purring, the kitten stretched his neck so he could touch his nose against Lisa's.

My grin became almost as bright as Lisa's. "I think that decides it."

"Thank you, Marley. I really do love him already."

"I can see that. And I'm so happy for both of you."

Lisa shifted the kitten in her arms and ran a hand over his black fur. "I'll need to take him to a vet to get checked out. He probably needs his shots, and I want to make sure he's healthy. Plus, I'll need to go buy food, a cat bed, toys, a litter box...."

I laughed. "Tomorrow. In the meantime, I'll send you home with some food, and I've got an extra litter box you can borrow for the time being."

"Then we're all set," Lisa said to her new family member. "Now, how about dinner?"

When we arrived in the family room at the back of the house, a perturbed Flapjack stalked off, heading for the second floor. I was sorry he was unhappy but I knew it was only temporary, and his departure allowed Lisa to let the kitten run free and eat some dinner while I took Bentley out in the yard for a few minutes. When I brought the dog back in, Lisa kept the kitten in her arms. Neither of them seemed unhappy with that arrangement.

I received a text message from Chloe, letting us know that she was on her way to my place, so I phoned in our food order while Lisa settled on the couch. We'd determined that the kitten was indeed a boy, and Lisa had already started mulling over possible names.

"Max… Lucky…" Her gaze fell on an astronomy book Brett had left out on the coffee table. "Orion!"

The kitten let out a meow, his green eyes gazing up at Lisa as he did so.

"I think he approves," I said with a smile.

Lisa beamed at the kitten. "Then that settles it. Hello, Orion."

He bumped his head against Lisa's chin and purred.

Chloe arrived minutes later and showered attention on Orion.

"Have you decided what you're going to make for the first round of the competition?" I asked as she scratched the kitten under his chin.

"Not yet. No matter what I try to make, it'll probably be a disaster."

"Don't say that," I protested.

"Marley's right," Lisa said. "Stay positive. I'm sure you'll do great."

Chloe didn't look the least bit convinced, but our food arrived at the front door at that moment. As I paid the delivery guy, Brett pulled up in his work van and parked next to my car.

"That smells good," he said, relieving me of the bag of takeout once he'd given me a kiss. "Chinese food?"

"Yes, and I made sure to order your favorite."

"Chicken in black bean sauce? I'd better hurry up and grab a shower, then. I don't want to miss out."

"I'm sure Lisa and Chloe won't eat it all. But yes, go on so the food will still be hot when you get back down here."

He took a moment to say hi to Lisa and his sister, and to fuss over Bentley. Then he disappeared upstairs. Lisa, Chloe, and I set the food out on the kitchen table, and I got out plates and poured drinks. Lisa had left Orion on the couch, and he was now balancing his way along the back of it. Bentley had followed Brett upstairs, so the kitten was free to roam. He pounced on some imaginary foe, lost his balance, and had to leap down onto the arm of the couch to save himself from falling. From there he hopped to the floor and swatted at the little red ball I'd dug out of Flapjack's stash of toys. The ball rolled across the floor, and Orion went skittering after it, making us all laugh.

Once Brett had joined us at the table, I finally told Lisa and Chloe about the skull we'd found in the woods while catching the kitten. Somehow it was easier to talk about the disturbing discovery with Brett at my side.

"Ugh," Chloe said with a shudder. "I would have freaked out. Was it just a skull? Not an entire skeleton?"

"The skull is all we saw," Brett replied, "but we don't know what else is buried with it, if anything."

"Do you think it's from an ancient burial?" Lisa asked.

"We really don't know," I said. "I guess we'll have to wait and see."

"Tassy James was found in the woods," Lisa said. "Maybe this is another of her killer's victims."

Tassy James was a young woman who'd gone missing decades ago, her remains discovered only recently.

"We don't know that there were any other victims," I pointed out.

"And this skull is a long way from where Tassy's remains were found," Brett added.

Chloe had stopped eating. "Do you think…?"

"Think what?" I asked, worried by the way some of the color had drained from her face.

"The party in the woods wasn't far from the mansion," she said, addressing her brother, her blue eyes worried.

Brett set down his chopsticks. "Let's not jump to conclusions. Ray will tell us more when he can."

"What conclusions?" I asked, feeling lost. "And which party?"

Understanding dawned on Lisa's face. "*That* party?"

"Which party?" I asked again.

"It was about a week or so after my high school graduation," Chloe explained, her face still pale. "A bunch of people from my class had a party near the river."

"And what happened?" I asked, knowing something must have.

"One of my classmates—Demetra Kozani—was never seen again after that night. She left the party and that was it. She just disappeared."

"But we don't know that she disappeared from Wildwood Cove," Brett said.

"We don't know that she didn't."

I knew I was still missing something. "Where else would she have disappeared from if she was last seen here in Wildwood Cove?"

"No one knew she was missing until several weeks had passed," Lisa explained.

Chloe picked up the story. "She was planning to leave the next morning to head for New York City. She'd been telling everyone for months how she was going to be a model in New York after finishing high school. Everyone assumed she'd gone on her way."

Brett snagged a piece of chicken with his chopsticks. "She didn't have any brothers or sisters. Her mom had moved to Arizona, so Demetra was living on her own for several months. It was only when her mom hadn't heard from her for a while and couldn't get in touch with her that she got worried and raised the alarm."

"Even then, most of us figured she was in New York and too caught up in her new life to keep in touch with anyone," Chloe said. "She always made it clear she thought she was better than the rest of us."

The sharp edge to Chloe's last words surprised me.

"But to not even keep in touch with her mom..." I said.

Lisa reached for her glass of water. "That's why the police finally looked into it, but no trace of her was ever found. She still had clothes and other belongings at the house her mom owned here in town, but everyone figured she wouldn't have taken too much with her."

"She planned to hitchhike from here to Seattle," Chloe said. "So she wouldn't have wanted too much baggage. She was going to get a job in Seattle for a few weeks to earn the money she needed to get the rest of the way to New York."

"So one theory was that she'd hitchhiked with the wrong person," Brett said. "But there was never any evidence of that, or anything else."

Chloe poked at her food with her chopsticks but didn't seem interested in eating anymore.

I reached over and squeezed her arm. "I'm sorry, Chloe. That must have been difficult for everyone who knew her."

Chloe nodded, her eyes fixed on her plate. "Maybe it's not her." She didn't sound optimistic.

I set down my chopsticks and pushed back my chair, wanting to dispel the somber mood that had fallen over us. "How about we get the movie started and eat dessert while we watch?"

"Good idea." Lisa stood up, and Chloe soon followed.

We cleaned up the dishes and leftover food and settled on the couch with generous slices of double chocolate cake. Brett took a slice with him when he disappeared into the office at the front of the house so he could catch up on some invoicing for his business. Bentley followed at his heels, and Orion stayed in the family room with the rest of us.

We'd picked a romantic comedy to watch that night, and I was glad for the lighthearted choice. It was nice to see Chloe smiling again, and Orion's presence helped to get us all in good spirits. He spent the first half of the movie playing with Flapjack's bouncy ball on the couch, scampering over our laps to get to the toy, then back the other way when one of us tossed it again. After about an hour of those antics, he settled on Lisa's lap and fell fast asleep.

Once the movie was over, I helped Lisa load her car with the cat supplies I was giving her, and then she set off for home with her new housemate. Chloe left as well after stopping by the office to say goodbye to her brother.

As I locked the door behind her, Brett emerged from the office.

"Done working for the night?" I asked.

"Yep. Did you have fun watching the movie?"

"We did. And I think it helped to cheer Chloe up."

"That's good." A dark cloud seemed to pass over his blue eyes.

"Do you think the skull really could be Demetra's?" I asked.

"The place where she was last seen alive isn't far from where we found it."

I took that as a yes. "Were she and Chloe close?"

"No." Brett ran a hand over the back of his neck. "Not at all. They didn't get along."

That struck me as odd. "I've always thought Chloe was the type of person to get along with pretty much everyone."

"She is," Brett said as we headed up the stairs to the second floor, Bentley charging ahead of us. "But Demetra was an exception. She had a mean streak, and Chloe was often one of her targets. When Chloe was in middle school, she came home crying more than once because of something Demetra had said or done. Things got a bit better in high school, but Demetra was still a thorn in her side at times. Still, if the skull is Demetra's, Chloe will be upset. As much as she didn't like Demetra, she never would have wanted her to come to any harm."

"I don't doubt that for a second."

We reached our bedroom and found Flapjack on the bed. I spent a few minutes cuddling him, and it seemed he'd forgiven me for bringing Orion into his home.

With my cat happy again, I got ready for bed, and as I brushed my teeth, I couldn't shake the feeling that the skull was indeed Demetra's.

Chapter 5

It wasn't until the end of the week that word got out that an entire skeleton was found in the woods near the Wildwood Inn, and that it had officially been identified as the remains of Demetra Kozani. I heard the news from the first customers who arrived at The Flip Side that Saturday morning for an early breakfast. I texted Brett with the information right away, wondering if Chloe already knew. He wrote back to say she was probably still asleep. He was getting ready to leave for work but was going to stop by the house Chloe rented from him to make sure she heard the news from him rather than through the grapevine.

All morning long, the diners at the pancake house talked about Demetra and speculated about how she'd ended up buried in the woods. It was clear that most people didn't think it was an accident, no matter how much they would have liked to believe that scenario. I could tell many of the townsfolk were hoping that if someone had killed Demetra, the culprit was a random stranger passing through town. I supposed that was possible, if that person had been roaming the woods at night. Considering the location of the skeleton, though, I had to wonder if someone who attended the party knew more about the last moments of Demetra's life than he or she had ever let on.

Still, I tried not to get ahead of myself. The cause of death hadn't been made public knowledge, and I was one of those people holding on to the hope that Demetra had somehow died accidentally. It was a very slim hope, though.

Around noon, Brett and Chloe showed up at the pancake house for lunch. While Chloe sat down at a free table by the window, Brett joined me in the office.

"Is Chloe all right?" I asked as soon as we were alone.

"She's a bit shaken up. That's why I decided to take a long lunch break to spend some time with her. I didn't want her sitting at home alone while she's feeling down."

"Does she have any idea who might have wanted to kill Demetra?"

"I don't know. I didn't want to ask her that, especially since we haven't heard for certain that she was murdered."

"But you think she probably was," I said, reading his expression.

"It seems most likely."

"It does," I agreed.

Brett took my hand and gave it a gentle squeeze. "Join me and Chloe for lunch?"

The pancake house wasn't overly busy at the moment, so I agreed and sat with him and Chloe after I'd stopped by the kitchen. Soon I was digging in to a plate of French toast stuffed with blueberries and cream while Brett ate bacon cheddar waffles and Chloe tried the marzipan pancakes. We never minded eating breakfast foods for lunch, especially when Ivan was the one cooking.

"It's hard to be in low spirits when eating such good food," Chloe said after she'd sampled her lunch.

"So you're feeling better?" I asked, hopeful.

"A bit, yes. It's just hard because if Demetra was murdered, I could know her killer. So many of my classmates were in the woods that night." She frowned at her plate. "And my last words to Demetra weren't exactly nice."

"*She* wasn't exactly nice," Brett pointed out. "Not that I like to speak ill of the dead, but she wasn't known for her kindhearted nature."

"That's true, but..." Chloe shook her head. "Never mind. Let's talk about something else."

"Are you still going to participate in the cooking competition today?" I asked her.

"Of course. It'll be a good distraction." She pointed a stern finger at her brother. "And don't you bother saying anything."

Brett held up both hands as if in surrender. "I wasn't going to."

"Yeah, right." She sent him a withering glare as he fought to hide a grin.

"What are you planning to make?" I asked, hoping to prevent any further feuding between the siblings.

"Chicken Parmesan. I've got all the steps and ingredients memorized. That's all I need, right?"

"Should be," I said.

Brett was unsuccessfully fighting a grin again. When Chloe's eyes narrowed, he mimed zipping his lips. Chloe shook her head, but I could tell she wasn't truly mad.

We chatted about other subjects as we finished up our meals, and I got back to work after they left the pancake house, Brett heading back to his own job and Chloe setting off to run some errands before attending the competition. Brett was hoping to finish work early enough to watch Chloe compete. He'd promised he'd be there to support her, not to make fun of her, and I knew that was the truth. He only ever took his brotherly teasing so far, and Chloe and I both knew he wanted her to do well in the competition.

As planned, Ivan left The Flip Side shortly after closing. I helped Tommy in the kitchen for a while, and then we set off together to check out the cooking contest. Chloe wouldn't be competing for a couple of hours yet since the teen division would go first, but I still wanted to be there from the beginning so I could cheer on my neighbor Logan Teeves.

It only took a few minutes for us to walk to the grocery store on Main Street. A large tent had been set up in the parking lot, the two longest sides open to the air. There were several cooking stations beneath the canopy, and a long table with three chairs behind it sat on a raised platform. I figured that was where the judges would sit and watch the contestants as they worked.

Out in the open air, bleachers had been set up for the spectators. People were already claiming seats, so I headed that way while Tommy stopped to talk to some friends. Sienna waved to me from the second row, and I climbed up to take the empty seat on her right. Sitting on her left was the girl with the corkscrew curls I'd seen registering for the competition the week before. Today her hair was pulled back into a long braid.

"Hey, Marley," Sienna said as I sat down next to her. "This is my friend Ellie Shaw. Ellie, this is Marley McKinney. She owns the pancake house."

"You're competing today, aren't you, Ellie?" I asked once we'd exchanged hellos.

She nodded and bit her lower lip, not looking too excited at the prospect. Sienna patted her friend's arm. "She's a little nervous."

"A lot nervous," Ellie corrected her.

"You'll do great."

"Try to enjoy yourself," I said. "That's the most important thing."

"My mom thinks *winning* is the most important thing." Ellie stood up before Sienna or I could say anything in response to that. "I'd better go get ready."

"Good luck," we called after her.

She sent a nervous but grateful smile our way and headed for the tent.

"I really hope she does well," Sienna said.

"How come her mom is so worried about winning?" I asked.

"Partly because of the cash prize for the winner and partly because she thinks it will look good on Ellie's résumé and college applications."

"Is Ellie planning to go to culinary school?"

"I don't think so, but I guess it's another accomplishment to add to her list."

Down at the base of the bleachers, a balding man stepped up to a microphone. He tapped the mic and said, "Hello? Can everyone hear me?"

A squeal of feedback had me wincing along with many of my fellow spectators.

The man moved the microphone and its stand behind the large speaker before trying again. "Hello, everyone, and welcome to the Olympic Peninsula's seventh annual amateur chef competition!"

I clapped along with the rest of the audience.

"For those of you who don't already know, I'm Bruce Hannigan, though most people call me Coach Hannigan. I'm glad I have the chance to help out with this great event, and I'm happy to see so many people here to enjoy the competition."

He grinned at the growing crowd. "I'd like to thank this year's sponsors and all the volunteers who have made this event possible." He smiled at a woman with short, curly hair who was taking his photo. "Those volunteers include photographer Amy Strudwick, who has graciously given up her Saturday afternoon to document this event." He gestured to the judges. "And of course our esteemed judges. Allow me to introduce Marielle Ryskamp of Marielle's Bakery."

Marielle waved at the crowd from the judges' table, her round cheeks pink as she smiled brightly.

"And Quaid Hendrix, renowned food blogger," the MC said next.

A tall, muscular man wearing his brown hair in a short ponytail raised a hand to acknowledge the smattering of applause, but he didn't so much as crack a smile. He appeared on the brink of boredom, and I wondered if he considered himself above the whole competition.

"And last but not least," Coach Hannigan continued, "Ivan Kaminski, chef at The Flip Side pancake house right here in Wildwood Cove."

Sienna and I applauded loudly, and even the rest of the crowd seemed more enthused by his introduction than Quaid's.

"Now I believe our first group of teen contestants is ready to get started, so let's get cooking!"

When the audience's clapping had tapered off, Bruce Hannigan introduced the first round of teen competitors. Ellie and Logan were both in the first group of six contestants. As the teenagers took up their positions in front of their respective cooking stations, Coach Hannigan explained that they'd have thirty minutes to prepare their entrée. For this round, they'd been allowed to bring ingredients from home and to plan what they would cook.

After making sure that all the contestants and judges were ready to begin, the MC stepped back from the microphone and blew a whistle while hitting a button to start a large digital clock counting down from thirty minutes. The time passed quickly, friends and family cheering on the competitors while Coach Hannigan read brief contestant bios from note cards.

A couple of the teens in the tent appeared on the verge of panic, their moves rushed and frantic. Ellie seemed tense but in control, her expression focused and determined. She looked up from her work only a couple of times to check the clock.

Logan didn't seem quite as intense as Ellie, but he was still focused, and he moved about his station with more ease and confidence than I'd ever known the quiet teen to show.

When time ran out, Coach Hannigan blew his whistle again and the competitors stepped back from their cooking stations. One by one, as the coach called their names, they carried their dishes up to the judging table where Marielle, Quaid, and Ivan each sampled the food before making notes on their clipboards.

A second group of teens went through the thirty-minute challenge before Patricia Murray collected the score sheets from the judges and consulted with another woman I recognized from the competition's organizing committee. A few minutes later, Patricia handed a sheet of paper to Bruce Hannigan, who approached the microphone once again. He announced the names of the teenagers who'd made it through to the next round of competition.

Sienna let out a loud cheer when Ellie's name was announced, and another one when Logan was mentioned. I clapped along with the rest of the spectators, happy to see a relieved smile on Ellie's face.

Since there was going to be a short break before the first group of adults competed, I got up to stretch my legs while Sienna hopped down from the bleachers and rushed off to hug Ellie and Logan. I caught sight of Chloe near the edge of the tent and headed her way. She kept twirling a strand of her long blond hair around one finger, and nervousness shone clearly in her blue eyes.

"All set?" I asked her.

She nearly jumped at the sound of my voice. "Oh, hi, Marley." She closed her eyes briefly. "What am I getting myself into?" She sounded like she was teetering on the verge of panic.

"Relax," I told her. "This is just for fun. There's no reason to freak out."

"But I'll make a fool of myself in front of everyone."

"No, you won't."

"Maybe I should back out," she said as if she hadn't heard me.

"Nonsense," a gruff voice said from behind us.

We both spun around, startled.

Ivan glared at us. I couldn't blame Chloe for shrinking back in the face of his intense gaze. I was tempted to do so myself, and I was used to Ivan's daunting ways.

"Don't give up without a fight," he counseled Chloe.

"But I can't cook," she said, her voice little more than a whisper.

"Nonsense," Ivan said again.

Before Chloe could come up with another response, Ivan strode away, skirting past a group of teens so he could get to the small table set up with coffee and tea for the judges and contestants.

I put a hand on Chloe's shoulder. "Ivan's right. You should give it a try. What's the worst that could happen?"

"I could set the tent on fire."

"That's not going to happen." When she opened her mouth to contradict me, I added, "And even if it does, the tent's well stocked with extinguishers."

To my relief, Chloe smiled. "I'm glad you're here, Marley."

"So am I," Brett said, appearing from behind me and resting an arm across my shoulders.

From beneath the canopy, Patricia read off names of the next competitors. When she called out Chloe's name, Brett gave his sister a gentle shove.

"Go on, Chloe. You can do this," he said.

"Since when do you think that?" she asked.

"Since always." He gave her a nudge. "Go on."

She looked anything but confident, but with a last uncertain glance over her shoulder, she walked toward the tent.

Chapter 6

When the next round of competition got under way, I could see the fear on Chloe's face, even from where I sat on the bleachers. Despite her lack of confidence, however, she didn't panic. When the whistle blew, she set about preparing her chicken Parmesan with hurried but not frantic movements. I held Brett's hand as I watched and realized after a few minutes that I had a tight grip on his fingers.

I loosened my hold. "Sorry about that."

He smiled at me. "I'm nervous for her too."

"It looks like she's doing all right." I hoped that appearance wasn't deceiving.

We fell silent, not speaking for the rest of the round. Hope Barron was competing too. She seemed calm and collected, moving around her station with confidence.

When the whistle blew to end the round and the contestants lined up in front of the judges' table, I couldn't help but tighten my grip on Brett's hand again.

Chloe was third in line to take her dish to the table. She at least appeared to have finished making her chicken Parmesan. Hopefully she'd remembered all the ingredients. I knew she wouldn't take it lightly if the judges reacted badly to her dish.

Brett and I watched in tense silence as the first contestant in line approached the judges' table. I recognized her from the registration day as Dorothy Kerwin. All three judges tasted her dish—I couldn't see what it was from my vantage point—and then she picked up her plate and retreated to stand behind her fellow contestants. The next competitor went through the same process before it was Chloe's turn.

The judges kept to their routine of not saying a word as they sampled Chloe's chicken Parmesan. When she'd taken her plate away from the table, the judges spent a moment making notes on their clipboards before turning their attention to the next contestant.

Soon all the dishes had been sampled, and Chloe came to join us on the bleachers to watch the next two groups of competitors in her division.

"How do you think it went?" I asked her as she sat down next to me.

Chloe shrugged. "I didn't start a fire, and the chicken was cooked. That's better than I was expecting."

"No matter what happens, you did great," Brett said.

"Thanks. I doubt I'll make it through to the next round, but I'm glad I didn't quit."

Once the last round of the competition had ended, it took a few minutes for Patricia to tally all the scores. When she handed a piece of paper to Coach Hannigan, everyone on the bleachers sat up straighter and fell quiet.

"We're now ready to announce the names of the contestants who've made it through to the next round of competition," the MC said into the microphone. "Congratulations first to Dorothy Kerwin."

As I clapped, I noticed Dorothy's husband, Willard, sitting below me and to my left. Gone was his bored expression from the week before. Now he was smiling as he applauded enthusiastically.

"Also moving on to the next round are Hope Barron and Mikey Soldado."

Bruce continued to announce several more names, none of which were familiar to me.

"I'm sorry, Chloe," I said, putting an arm around her shoulders and giving her a squeeze.

"That's all right. I knew I wouldn't make it to the next round. I'm really not any good at cooking."

"I'm proud of you for giving it a go, Chloe," Brett said. "And I shouldn't have teased you."

"Isn't that what big brothers are for?" Her smile let us know she wasn't bothered.

The crowd was slowly dispersing around us. We got up from the bleachers as the judges left their table and headed for the refreshments set out for them.

"I'm going to talk to Ivan for a moment," I said, before leaving Brett and Chloe.

I smiled at Marielle as I approached the refreshments table. I didn't know her well, but I made regular visits to her bakery for bread and the

occasional treat. Ivan was in the midst of filling a mug with coffee from
the urn on the table.

"Thanks again for stepping in to help with the judging," I said to him.

He acknowledged my words with a brief nod before taking a sip of coffee.

"You won't mind doing it again next weekend?" I asked, hoping for
Patricia's sake that he wouldn't refuse.

"I don't mind," he said, much to my relief. "It wasn't so bad. Tell Chloe
her chicken Parmesan was good. It's just that other dishes were better."

"She'll appreciate you saying that."

"We should really be getting paid for this," a man's voice said from
somewhere behind me.

Ivan's dark eyes flicked toward a spot over my shoulder, and I turned
around to see that the speaker was Quaid Hendrix. He was in conversation
with Marielle as they both drank coffee.

"There's no room in the budget to pay us," Marielle said in a pleasant
voice. "Besides, I don't mind volunteering my time."

Quaid let out a snort. "But that crud we had to sample! We should be
getting hazard pay. I hope no one makes something with coconut next
week. I can't stand the stuff."

Marielle frowned, but Quaid didn't seem to notice. He also didn't
notice that he'd drawn attention from others around him. Along with me
and Ivan, several family members of contestants who'd made it through
to the next round were nearby. I wasn't sure if Dorothy Kerwin's husband
had heard Quaid's comments, but I suspected Logan's dad, Gerald, and
Ellie's mother, Judith Shaw, had caught his words.

Fortunately, Quaid didn't say anything more, instead refilling his
coffee mug.

The competitors who'd made it through to the next round were gathered
around Patricia, who was giving them some instructions for the next week.
The contestants' family members hung around, waiting.

When Patricia finished up, everyone went their separate ways.

"Good job, Logan," I said as the teenager passed by me on the way to
meet up with his father.

"Thanks." He mumbled the word but looked pleased.

"See you in the morning, Ivan," I said before going off in search of
Brett and Chloe.

I found them just outside the tent. Chloe was in conversation with Hope
Barron, but my attention didn't stay on them for long. I was too distracted
by the fact that Quaid Hendrix was approaching Brett.

"You're the gardener out at the Wildwood Inn, right?" Quaid said.

I hung back so as not to interrupt.

"In a way," Brett replied. "I'm doing some landscaping before the opening."

"I was a gardener there, back in the day," Quaid said. "That was a stepping-stone job, of course. I had bigger and better things waiting for me."

Brett's eyebrows shifted up a fraction of an inch, but he gave no other indication that he knew Quaid's words were meant as an insult.

Without saying anything more, Quaid strode away, coffee mug still in hand. I watched him go as I moved to stand next to Brett.

"What a guy," I said, my voice matching the cold glare I was aiming at Quaid's retreating back.

Chloe shuddered as she joined us. "Ugh. I can't stand him."

"He insulted Brett," I told her.

"Don't worry about it." Brett put an arm around my shoulders. "He doesn't bother me."

"I wish I could say the same." Chloe frowned in Quaid's direction as he disappeared into the thinning crowd.

"You know him?" I asked.

"Not well but still more than I care to. He lived in Wildwood Cove back when I was in school. He hit on me more than once when I was a teenager and he was in his late twenties. He always creeped me out."

A crease appeared between Brett's eyebrows. "You never mentioned that before."

"It wasn't a big deal, and it wasn't like I was the only one. He was always hitting on girls my age."

Brett was about to say something when we were all distracted by the approach of Brett and Chloe's uncle, along with Deputy Mendoza.

"Chloe," Ray said after we'd all exchanged greetings, "how are you doing?"

"You mean since hearing about Demetra? All right, I guess."

"Are you able to answer some questions for Deputy Mendoza?"

Chloe's gaze shifted back and forth between her uncle and the deputy. "About Demetra?" When her uncle nodded, she asked, "Why can't you ask me the questions?"

"We're related. It would be better for you to talk to Mendoza."

"She's not a suspect, is she?" I asked, unable to keep a note of incredulity out of my voice.

When Chloe's eyes widened with fear, I regretted saying anything.

"We don't have any suspects at the moment," Ray said. "We're talking to everyone who was at the party on the night Demetra was last seen, or at least those we're able to locate."

Some of the fear had left Chloe's eyes, but she still seemed tense. "Can Brett stay with me?" she asked her uncle.

"Sure. That's not a problem."

Mendoza moved closer to the empty bleachers, and Brett and Chloe followed her. I hung back, and Ray excused himself, approaching Hope next. Judging by Ray's demeanor as he spoke with Hope, I figured he was talking to her in an official capacity. Maybe she was part of the same graduating class as Chloe and Demetra.

I sat down at the end of the lowest tier on the bleachers, several feet away from where Mendoza was questioning Chloe. I hadn't intended to eavesdrop, but I could hear the conversation from where I sat.

"I don't know what I can tell you that I didn't say when I was questioned ten years ago," Chloe said.

"We just want to go over everything again to be thorough," Mendoza said. "And to see if you remember anything differently now that we know Demetra's dead."

Chloe rubbed her arms as if chilled, even though the sun was shining down its warmth on us. "I can't think of anything that I didn't remember before. Like I said back then, I left the party before Demetra did. Anything I know that happened in the woods after that is secondhand from people who stayed later than I did."

"I understand you had a fight with Demetra at the party, a fight that almost became physical."

"Demetra was making a show of hitting on my boyfriend."

Mendoza consulted her notebook. "Your boyfriend was Justin Archer?"

"Yes. I know now that Justin wasn't worth fighting over, but at the time it upset me. And I'm pretty sure that's what Demetra wanted. I told her to get away from Justin, and she laughed in my face. Then she said something about me being scared of competition because everyone knew who Justin would rather be with. Meaning her, of course."

"And then what happened?"

"I left. Justin came after me, but I told him to leave me alone. He hadn't exactly fended off Demetra's advances. So he went back to the party and I went home. Whoever said the fight almost got physical was exaggerating."

"Is this really relevant?" Brett asked. "Chloe left before Demetra did, by at least an hour, right?" He directed his last question at his sister.

She nodded. "That's what everyone else said—that she stayed long after I left."

"We just want to make sure we have a full picture of what happened that night," Deputy Mendoza said. "Do you know where Justin lives now?"

"I haven't kept in touch with him. We broke up the day after the party and went our separate ways. A couple of years ago I heard he was living in Vegas, but I don't know if he's still there."

Mendoza jotted something down in her notebook. "All right. Thank you."

"That's it?" Chloe sounded relieved.

The deputy nodded. "But if you think of anything else—anything at all that might be significant—please let us know."

Mendoza set off to join Ray, who'd wrapped up his conversation with Hope. I got up from my seat and joined Brett and Chloe.

"Are you okay?" Brett asked his sister, giving her shoulder a squeeze.

"Yes," she said, but her demeanor was anything but relaxed.

"Why don't you come over to our place for dinner?" I suggested. "We're going to make pizza."

Some of the tension eased out of Chloe's shoulders, and she smiled. "Homemade pizza? I won't turn down that offer."

The three of us fell into step with each other, following Main Street northward, closer to the ocean.

"Demetra must really have been a piece of work," I said to Chloe as we walked. "I've never known you to even come close to fighting with someone."

"I wish I hadn't let her get to me. That's exactly what she wanted." Chloe sighed. "I couldn't stand her, and yet I feel bad saying that now that I know she's dead."

"It's terrible that she's dead, but your feelings toward her are completely understandable," Brett assured his sister.

"If someone as easygoing as you had a problem with Demetra, I'm guessing others did too," I said as we turned right onto Wildwood Road and headed for the edge of town.

"Oh yeah." Chloe shook her head. "Even her best friend couldn't stand her at times."

"Sounds like Ray and his deputies will have a long list of suspects to work their way through."

"Most likely," Chloe agreed. "I just hope my name doesn't end up on that list."

Chapter 7

"That won't happen," Brett said to his sister. "There's no reason you'd be a suspect. You left the party earlier than Demetra and went straight home. Mom and Dad confirmed that ten years ago."

"That's true," Chloe said. "I guess I can't help but find this whole situation unsettling."

"I can't blame you," I said.

The three of us were walking side by side, but we fell into single file when we heard a vehicle approaching from behind. I expected the dark blue pickup truck to drive on past us, but it slowed to a stop and the driver lowered the window. I didn't recognize the man behind the wheel, although it quickly became clear that Brett and Chloe did.

"Hey, Lonny," Chloe greeted as she approached the truck with her brother. "And Hope," she added when she got closer.

When I reached Chloe's side I spotted Hope sitting in the passenger seat.

"Hey, guys." Lonny rested one arm on the window frame.

"I don't think you've met my girlfriend, Marley." Brett put an arm around me. "Lonny is Hope's husband. He works at the garage in town."

"Oh, with Zach," I said.

"That's right." Lonny smiled at me. He was a good-looking man with tousled brown hair and dark eyes.

"He fixed my car once," I said.

"Then it was in good hands. Zach's the best mechanic around."

Hope nudged his arm. "Tied for the best."

Lonny grinned again, but then his smile faded away. "I guess you've all heard about Demetra."

"Hard not to," Brett said. "The whole town's been talking about the news."

"It's so sad." Hope leaned over Lonny to get closer to the open window. "After so many years of not hearing a word from her, I figured she was most likely dead, but I never would have thought she was still here in Wildwood Cove. I always guessed she'd run into trouble while hitchhiking her way to Seattle, or somewhere between Seattle and New York."

"That's what I thought too," Chloe said.

Everyone fell silent, the only sound around us the rumble of the truck's engine.

"Anyway," Lonny said after a moment, "Hope and I are off to see my folks for dinner, so we'd better get going."

"Congratulations on getting through to the next round of the competition," I said to Hope.

She smiled, her gray eyes happy. "Thanks. I'm having a lot of fun with it."

Brett, Chloe, and I stepped back from the truck and waved as Lonny put it in motion.

"So they knew Demetra too?" I asked once we'd resumed walking along the grassy verge at the edge of the road.

"Yes," Chloe replied. "Hope was in our year at school, and Lonny's a year older. They've been together since Hope was sixteen. I think that's so sweet."

"Were they at the party after your graduation?"

"Hope was," Chloe said.

"Are many of the people who were at the party still here in Wildwood Cove?"

"Several, right?" Brett said to his sister.

Chloe nodded. "We weren't a big group. I think there were maybe a dozen or so of us there when the party started. A couple of people moved to Port Angeles or Port Townsend and there are some who, like me and Hope, went away for a few years before coming back home. My ex Justin left for good, though. So did the Olafson twins. They're both in California now. But they're the sweetest girls you'd ever meet so I'm sure they had nothing to do with Demetra's death." She bit down on her lower lip. "What's the chance that she was killed by a stranger?"

Brett and I shared a glance.

"Most people are killed by someone they know," I said. "But it's always possible there was someone else out there in the woods that night."

"Demetra was better at making enemies than friends, though," Brett reminded us.

Chloe frowned. "So you think it was someone at the party. I can't imagine any of my classmates murdering her. Not even Justin."

"There has to be a story there," I said.

"Not really. It's just that he was a total loser. I don't know what I was thinking at the time."

"Neither do I," Brett said. "I was relieved when you broke up with him."

"Really? You never said you disapproved at the time."

"I figured that would make you stay with him longer."

A hint of a smiled appeared on her face. "At that age? You're probably right." Her expression became thoughtful. "Of course, Tyrone was ticked off that night, and he always had a temper. It got him in trouble on the field from time to time."

"Tyrone?" I said. "Field?"

"The baseball field," Brett filled me in. "Tyrone Phillips was the star of the team back then."

"And he was Demetra's boyfriend," Chloe added. "Until graduation, at least."

"What about at the time of the party?" I asked.

"That's why he was ticked off. Demetra dumped him a few days before that."

We were all quiet for a few seconds.

"That doesn't sound good, does it?" Chloe said, breaking the silence.

"No," I agreed.

"But Tyrone was questioned several times years ago," Brett said. "He was the obvious suspect when it was discovered that Demetra had gone missing. Nothing ever came of it."

"But back then they didn't have the body," I pointed out.

"True."

We turned off Wildwood Road and followed the long driveway through a stand of fir trees toward the blue-and-white Victorian. I'd inherited the beachfront home the previous spring, and Brett had moved in with me a few months ago. It still put a big smile on my face to think of the house as *our* home rather than just mine.

As soon as we opened the front door, a big ball of curly golden fur came barreling down the hall toward us.

"Did you miss us or something, Bentley?" I asked with a smile as the dog wagged his tail so fast that it was almost a blur.

We all took turns getting down on his level and giving him a hug and a pat, with Bentley doling out plenty of licks in return. When things had settled down, Flapjack wandered into the foyer. I scooped him up into my arms and kissed the top of his head.

"How are you doing, Jack?"

He purred in response, his eyes closing to mere slits. His engine revved up even more when Chloe gave him a scratch under the chin.

We all headed for the family room and kitchen at the back of the house. I opened the French doors that led out to the back porch, and Bentley charged outside and down the steps. While he sniffed around the yard, looking for the best place to relieve himself, I set Flapjack on the porch railing and filled my lungs with fresh, salty air while my gaze roamed over the ocean view.

As familiar as it was, I never got tired of the beautiful seascape that stretched out beyond the house. The tide was out at the moment, wet sandbars exposed to the sunshine that was fading as the evening headed toward nightfall. Now that spring had arrived in Wildwood Cove, I would soon resume one of my favorite pastimes—heading out at low tide to see all the creatures in the tidal pools.

As I stood at the railing, Brett came up behind me and wrapped his arms around me.

"Enjoying the view without rain for a change?" he asked.

I leaned back against him. "Yes. I'll never get tired of it."

"Just like I'll never get tired of the view I've got right now."

I tipped my head back to see him looking down at me.

"That's very sweet," I said with a smile.

"And very true."

Bentley bounded up the porch steps and nosed his way between us, forcing us apart.

"I think he's trying to tell us it's time for dinner," I said with a laugh.

Bentley trotted into the house, and we followed close behind him. Flapjack hopped down from the porch railing and joined us inside before I shut the doors.

"Are you two lovebirds ready to cook or what?" Chloe asked from the kitchen.

"Definitely." I washed my hands at the kitchen sink. "I'm getting hungry."

"Are you going to help?" Brett nudged his sister's arm with his elbow.

"Of course. It's about time I learned to cook."

"Ivan wanted me to tell you that your chicken Parmesan was good." I flipped through my file of recipes and pulled out the one for my favorite pizza dough.

"Really?" Chloe's skepticism was written all over her face.

"I swear that's what he said. And Ivan doesn't hand out compliments easily."

"So I'm not a total disaster in the kitchen?" Hope had replaced her skepticism.

"Not anymore, at least," Brett said.

Chloe gave him a shove that failed to knock him off balance.

We got to work on the pizza dough and then focused on the toppings. Chloe grated cheese while I chopped up vegetables, and Brett rummaged through the cupboard for a can of pizza sauce. Sometimes I made my own sauce, but we were all too hungry to wait around for that tonight.

Once the pizza was in the oven, we set the table and I got drinks for everyone. Even though we talked about other things while we prepared our dinner, Demetra's death had remained on my mind. The crime had taken place a long time ago, but that didn't mean I was any less curious about it. Unsolved mysteries had a way of preying on my mind until they had some closure. That had led me into trouble on a few occasions in the past, but it had also driven me to clear innocent people of suspicion.

"Chloe, when you said Tyrone was ticked off on the night of the party, how mad are we talking about?" I asked.

"I remember him sulking, just staring at the campfire and drinking beer. Somebody told him to cheer up or something, and he almost blew up. Hope managed to calm him down. But if looks could kill, Demetra and Justin would have dropped dead when they were flirting in front of everyone. I thought Tyrone would really lose it that time, but somehow he kept quiet. I was the one who lost it."

I handed her a can of soda and set another on the table for Brett. "And he was still at the party when you left?"

"Yes."

Brett popped open his drink. "He left the party before Demetra, though, right?"

"That's what I heard from everyone else."

I poured a glass of sweet tea for myself as the oven timer went off. "Do you know how long it was between the time he left and when Demetra left?"

"Not exactly," Chloe said. "No one was a hundred percent sure about the timing of everything that night, but I think I remember someone saying it was no more than half an hour. And no one could confirm what time Tyrone got home."

Brett retrieved the pizza from the oven. "So he could have hung around in the woods and confronted Demetra after she left the party?"

"It's possible. And he probably would have had time to bury her body without anyone else coming along because all the others stayed at the party for another hour or so."

"Does he still live in Wildwood Cove?" I asked.

"No. He's in Seattle now. He got a baseball scholarship to some college back east, but he lost it after he flunked several classes. I don't think he ever finished college or played baseball again. Last I heard he was working for a towing company."

I took three plates down from the cupboard while Brett sliced the steaming-hot pizza. "Did the sheriff focus on anyone else as a possible suspect during the original investigation?"

"Not as far as I know." Chloe took the plate Brett offered her. She drew in a deep breath of pizza-scented air as she headed for the table. "This smells so good."

"But Demetra's best friend was questioned several times, wasn't she?" Brett handed me a plate and then loaded up the last one for himself.

"She was, but more to get information about Demetra. I don't think anyone ever suspected her of anything."

"Demetra is a nice name," I commented as I grabbed some napkins to take to the table.

"It's Greek," Chloe said. "Demetra was born in Greece, but her family moved here when she was two or three. It *is* a nice name. Too bad she didn't have a personality to match. Her mom was always such a nice lady, but her husband walked out on them when Demetra was seven or eight. Maybe that had something to do with how Demetra turned out."

"Some people must have liked her," I said. "She had a best friend and a boyfriend."

"But even those relationships were rocky at times."

We sat down at the kitchen table.

"Who was Demetra's best friend?" I asked once we were settled.

"Chrissy Mazurek. She owns a clothing boutique here in town."

I took a bite of hot pizza and quickly followed it with a sip of iced tea. "She and Demetra didn't always get along?"

"They were competitive with each other, although they pretended not to be. It's not the sort of friendship I'd ever want with anyone."

"Maybe that competitiveness went too far?"

"Maybe, but like Brett said before, Demetra was good at making enemies." Chloe set down the remains of her pizza. "I don't want to think about it anymore. It's too awful. I was never good friends with Chrissy or Tyrone, but I don't want to believe either of them could have hurt Demetra. I don't want to believe *anyone* I went to school with is capable of murder."

I understood how difficult it was for Chloe to picture any of her former classmates as a killer, but from the sounds of things, Ray and his deputies would have plenty of suspects to investigate.

Chapter 8

However many suspects the sheriff's department was looking into, Ray and his colleagues kept that information to themselves. Although the town was still preoccupied with the discovery of Demetra's remains and the fact that she was most likely murdered, the talk about the case waned as the days passed. The subject still came up now and then at the pancake house later in the week, but by then most people were more focused on flood damage, the amateur chef competition, and the weather, which thankfully stayed nice throughout the week.

On Saturday afternoon, Ivan left the pancake house at his usual time. Since there were fewer people taking part in the cooking competition this round, it was starting an hour later than the week before. I spent a few minutes wrapping up some tasks in the office, but then I too headed for the competition site.

I wandered toward the tent, ducking out of the way as Amy Strudwick snapped some photos of the setup. I met up with Ivan and noticed Patricia speaking with Marielle and Quaid. She smiled and waved at us, but then she hurried off, a clipboard in hand. I admired her knack for organizing events and her dedication to the town. There were few community functions in Wildwood Cove that she wasn't involved in.

I met up with Ivan and Marielle said a cheery hello to us as she came over our way. Quaid, however, ignored us. I wasn't bothered by that, and I didn't think Ivan was either.

"I'm going to grab a cup of coffee," Marielle said, her gaze drifting toward the refreshments table where coffee and tea were once again available for the judges and contestants.

Quaid held out a black travel mug. "Get me some while you're at it."

Marielle frowned at his lack of politeness, but after a brief hesitation she took the travel mug and headed for the coffee urn.

Quaid's phone rang, and he stepped out from beneath the tent, putting the device to his ear.

"Charming," I said.

Ivan heard me and gave a grunt of agreement. "He needs to learn some manners."

"That's not likely to happen anytime soon."

I told Ivan I'd see him later and claimed a spot on the bleachers, where a dozen or so others had already gathered. I spent a few minutes on my phone, reading text messages from Lisa and smiling at the collection of adorable photos she'd sent me of Orion. The vet had declared him to be in good health, and he was settling into his new home, causing plenty of chaos and making Lisa fall more in love with him every day.

After sending a message in reply, I returned my attention to the scene before me. It appeared as though most of the competitors had arrived now, several of them lingering near the refreshments table. Willard Kerwin was there with his wife, and Judith Shaw was hovering near Ellie, talking almost constantly. Mrs. Shaw stood out in the crowd of casually dressed people. She wore a gray pantsuit with a silk blouse and pearls. Her straight blond hair was sleek and perfectly styled. I didn't know what she was saying to her daughter, but whatever it was only seemed to be making Ellie nervous. She kept tugging at her apron and retying it, as if she couldn't keep her hands still. An African American man I guessed was her father settled a hand on her shoulder, and she smiled up at him, finally appearing to relax at least a bit.

I smiled myself when I noticed that Marielle hadn't made Quaid's coffee a priority. She'd left his mug on the table while she mingled with a couple of people I recognized from the competition's organizing committee.

Amy was still snapping photos of the people hanging around inside the tent. Quaid finished up his phone call and turned around, bumping into Amy.

"Watch it, would you?" he practically snarled before storming away.

Amy shot a glare his way but then got back to taking pictures.

"Could I have all the judges over here, please?" Patricia called out from the far side of the tent.

Marielle handed Quaid his mug and they headed over to Patricia, Ivan falling into step behind them. Quaid took a big gulp of coffee and nearly choked when he swallowed it down.

"This tastes like slop!" he groused, his complaint loud enough to be heard halfway across the parking lot. "Seriously, we volunteer our time for this and we can't even get a decent cup of coffee?"

Chloe sat down beside me as Quaid tossed the rest of his coffee into a bush growing at the edge of the parking lot.

"Is he having a tantrum?" she asked, her eyes on Quaid.

"Sounds like it."

Patricia was busy attempting to placate the judge. Quaid still had a scowl on his face, but he'd quit complaining. Patricia waved Amy over her way and soon had the judges gathered in front of a tree growing in a narrow strip of garden at the far edge of the parking lot. Amy took several photos of the judges, and then everyone returned to the tent.

Bruce Hannigan conferred with Patricia for a moment and then approached the microphone. "Ladies and gentlemen, the first round of competition will begin in fifteen minutes. If any competitors have not yet checked in with Patricia Murray, please do so now."

"What sport does he coach?" I asked Chloe.

"High school baseball. Or he used to, anyway. He's retired now, but everyone still calls him Coach Hannigan." She picked up the purse she'd set between us on the bench. "Want to make a quick run to the Beach and Bean?"

"Sure," I agreed.

The trip there and back took less than fifteen minutes, and the competition had yet to get under way when we returned. The first round of competitors had assembled in the tent, and Amy was getting some shots of them as they took their places at their stations.

For this round, the contestants would be making desserts. They'd all decided beforehand what they would make and—as with the first round—had been allowed to bring their own ingredients. Since there was only one group of competitors left in each division, both Ellie and Logan were participating in this round.

The bleachers had grown more crowded so we decided to not waste any time grabbing a couple of seats. Before I could follow Chloe up to the third row, Patricia called out my name. As soon as I saw her face, I knew something was wrong.

"What is it?" I asked when she hurried over to me. I'd never seen her so stressed.

"The first round of competition is supposed to start right now, and Quaid's in the grocery store's washroom, vomiting."

I glanced toward the judges' table. Sure enough, Ivan and Marielle were the only ones there.

"Stomach flu?" I guessed.

"That or food poisoning. I called his wife and she's coming to pick him up, but now I'm short one judge. No one's using any meat ingredients in this round, so would you be able to step in? Hopefully Quaid will be back next week."

"Sure, I can. I'm no expert, though."

"You don't need to be. Let your taste buds guide you."

"All right. No problem."

Relief smoothed out the worry lines on Patricia's face. "Thank you so much, Marley."

I took a few seconds to explain to Chloe what was happening, and then I walked with Patricia over to the judges' table. She explained the scoring sheet to me as we went, and by the time I sat down next to Marielle I knew what I was supposed to do.

"Looks like I'm joining you today," I said to my fellow judges.

"Quaid's sick?" Ivan asked.

"Apparently." I scooted my chair closer to the table. "His wife's going to pick him up and take him home."

"You mean somebody actually married the guy?" Marielle said.

I shouldn't have smiled, under the circumstances, but I couldn't help myself. "Hard to believe, right?"

When I glanced Ivan's way, I thought I detected a hint of amusement on his face, though it was hard to tell with him. His expression never varied much from his intimidating glower.

Over at the microphone, Coach Hannigan introduced the competitors and announced the start of the first round. The whistle blew, and Ellie, Logan, and their fellow teen chefs jumped into action. I glanced over the score sheet one more time and then settled in to watch the teenagers while sipping the vanilla steamed milk I'd picked up at the coffee shop.

Amy made her way around the tent, taking photos of the teens in action, never getting in their way. The time seemed to pass quickly—even more so for the contestants, I guessed—and the whistle blew again. The teenagers stepped back from their stations. Some looked pleased, others worried. Ellie Shaw fell into the latter category.

When instructed to do so by Patricia, the six teenagers picked up their dishes and stood in a row before the judges' table. Everyone had managed to finish and plate their desserts, some more artistically than others. My mouth watered at the sight of all their creations, and I figured that was a good start.

Ellie was up first with her coconut macadamia squares. She'd drizzled chocolate on the plate to help with the visual appeal, and the taste exceeded the nice presentation. The bar had a delicious shortbread base and was topped with macadamia nuts and coconut in chewy caramel. The whole thing was topped with dark chocolate, and my first taste left me wanting more. I snuck in a second bite but then I had to fill out my score sheet and move on to the next contestant's creation. It crossed my mind that the teen was lucky Quaid wasn't on the judging panel that day, considering how he felt about coconut, but in my mind she fully deserved a spot in the final round of competition that would take place in a week's time.

Logan impressed me with a chocolate soufflé that tasted heavenly, and a fourteen-year-old girl named Cherise had whipped together the most amazing double chocolate mocha brownies. After my fellow judges and I had finished tasting all of the dishes, Ellie, Logan, Cherise, and a boy named Vincent were the ones to nab spots in the next round. The other desserts tasted good but didn't stand out as extraordinary, and one boy's mousse hadn't set properly.

After a short break, the adult division's competition got under way. Again, when it came time to test the dishes, my mouth watered with anticipation. The first woman who brought her dessert to the judge's table looked embarrassed, probably because the filling had oozed out of the Swiss roll she'd made and had pooled on the plate. I knew next to nothing about baking, but I guessed that the cake had been too warm for the filling, causing it all to melt out. The flavors were still great, but the unfortunate presentation took the dish out of contention for the top four spots.

Dorothy Kerwin had a better result. Her pistachio cake made it hard for me not to dive in and finish off the entire sample. The same was true of the red velvet crêpes made by a woman named Cynthia. Hope's chocolate toffee bars landed her a spot in the top four, and a man in his twenties also made the cut with his scrumptious frosted pumpkin cupcakes.

"Thanks so much for helping me out," Patricia said to me after the competition had wrapped up for the day.

"Believe me, it was my pleasure," I assured her. "I got to taste some great food."

"I'm so glad you enjoyed it." Patricia's phone rang in her hand. "Sorry. I should get this."

"No worries," I said. "I'll see you around."

Patricia wandered away with her phone to her ear. I remained in place, searching the bleachers for Chloe. Most of the spectators had dispersed, and I couldn't see Brett's sister in the stands.

Dorothy and Willard Kerwin, Ellie Shaw and her parents, and a couple of other competitors had gathered around Amy as she showed them some of the pictures she'd taken. I noticed Lonny Barron heading for the tent to meet up with Hope. I said a quick hello to him as he passed by and then pulled out my phone, deciding to text Chloe to see if she was still around.

Before I could send a message, a man standing nearby turned around and almost crashed into me.

"Sorry," he said quickly, dodging around me and heading for the street.

I did a double take and stared hard at him, but all I could see now was the back of his head.

"It can't be," I said as the man disappeared around the front of the grocery store.

A strange hum of confusion and excitement rushed through my bloodstream. I broke into a run, slipping past a small group of people to reach the sidewalk. It only took me seconds to get there, but I was too late. The man was already gone.

Your eyes were playing tricks on you, I told myself.

There was no other explanation.

And yet I couldn't shake the feeling I'd seen my father walking down the street.

My father who'd died before I was born.

Chapter 9

"Marley!"

The sound of Chloe calling my name startled me out of the confused fog that had settled over me.

She held up a cloth shopping bag. "I popped into the grocery store for a moment to pick up a few things. Mac and cheese is my favorite meal, so I figure that should be what I learn to make next."

I tried to keep up with what she was saying, but the words seemed to blur together.

"Marley? Are you okay?" Chloe asked, regarding me more closely.

"Yes," I said quickly. "Sorry. Making mac and cheese is pretty straightforward, so I'm sure you'll do fine."

"I hope so. Want to hang out with me while I cook? You can be my official taste tester."

I couldn't get the image of my father's look-alike out of my mind. All I wanted to do right then was track him down.

"Can I take a rain check?" I asked. "I've got something I need to do this evening."

"Did I scare you off by offering to cook for you?"

"Not at all," I said honestly. "I'll definitely take you up on the offer another time."

"All right. It's probably best that I have a trial run first anyhow."

"You'll do fine," I told her again as I took a step backward. "See you later."

I set off along the sidewalk at an easy pace, but I couldn't hold back for long. Breaking into a jog, I circled around the block, keeping my eyes peeled for the man with wavy brown hair whom I'd seen minutes earlier.

I peeked through the front windows of stores and eateries, but after nearly twenty minutes of searching, I'd still had no luck finding him.

Unsettled and dispirited, I altered my path and headed home. I couldn't help but cheer up when I got there. As soon as I stepped in the front door, my welcoming committee was there to give me an enthusiastic greeting. Bentley bounced around me until I told him to sit so I could give him a big hug. He planted a sloppy kiss on my face and shook out his curly golden fur, his tongue lolling out of his mouth while he smiled his best dog grin.

As soon as Bentley calmed down, Flapjack moved in for his turn. He rubbed against my legs, purring, as I took off my sneakers and left them by the front door.

"How was your day, guys?" I asked once I had my cat in my arms.

With his motor still going full tilt, Flapjack bumped his head against my chin.

We made our way to the family room, and Bentley trotted over to the French doors that led out to the porch. I set Flapjack down and opened the doors so Bentley could go outside and do what he needed to do. Flapjack padded his way into the kitchen and sat down in the middle of the floor, his amber eyes gleaming with expectation.

"Right," I said, getting the message loud and clear. "Dinner."

Bentley came bounding into the house at the sound of that word. I returned to the French doors, pausing to take a quick look at the ocean. The tide was out, slowly creeping its way up the beach. A man and woman walked hand in hand across a wet sandbar, a golden retriever trotting along ahead of them. The beach was otherwise deserted.

Although I was tempted to leave the doors open to allow the fresh sea breeze to sweep through the house, the air had cooled since the early afternoon and had a slight chill to it now, a reminder that spring was still in its early weeks. I decided on a compromise, shutting the doors and opening the kitchen window a few inches.

Flapjack gave an impatient meow and sat at my feet, almost on my toes. Bentley joined us in the kitchen, his tail wagging. Taking the hint, I got busy preparing their dinners and soon had two happy animals digging into their food, Bentley in a corner of the kitchen and Flapjack in the laundry room where his canine housemate couldn't sneak in and gobble up his food.

With my four-legged friends taken care of, I opened the fridge and surveyed the contents, trying to decide what Brett and I could eat for dinner. Nothing seemed appetizing, probably because I'd filled up on food samples in the afternoon while judging the competition. It also didn't help that I was too distracted to think much about meal preparation.

I gave up for the time being and shut the fridge. Flapjack emerged from the laundry room, through his cat door, and sat on the kitchen floor, licking his paw before swiping it across his face. When I headed for the family room, he followed me, taking up a perch on one end of the couch before resuming his grooming routine. Bentley curled up on the rug, and I grabbed a photo album from a shelf along one wall before joining Flapjack on the couch.

I couldn't stop thinking about the man I'd seen in town. Of course he couldn't be my father, but...

But what? I asked myself.

I had no answer to that question but still felt compelled to open the album.

The pages held pictures from before I was born. My mom had put the album together and had given it to me when I was a teenager. On the very first page was a studio portrait of my dad, taken when he was in his midtwenties, along with another picture of him in jeans and a T-shirt, grinning and squinting into the sun as he leaned against a Mustang convertible. The third and final photograph on the page showed my dad together with my mom, their arms around each other. I knew from the stories my mom had told me over the years that these photos were from around the time of their engagement, but at the moment all my attention was focused on the pictures themselves, rather than the stories behind them.

My hair was the same color as my dad's had been, although mine was curly while his had been wavy. We also had the same gray-blue eyes. I hadn't managed to see the eye color of the man I'd spotted in town earlier, but everything else seemed about right—the face shape, the hair, the nose. If my dad hadn't died so young and had the chance to age by another thirty-five years after the photos were taken, wouldn't he have looked just like the man I'd seen that afternoon?

Yes.

I flipped through the rest of the pages in the album, a few more of which showed my dad, sometimes on his own and sometimes with my mom, who by the end of the album was clearly pregnant. They'd planned to get married shortly after I was born, but my father died from an undiagnosed heart problem before I ever arrived.

He's dead, I reminded myself.

But what if he's not?

I snapped the album shut as soon as the question popped into my mind.

"Impossible," I said out loud.

Bentley raised his head, a question in his brown eyes.

"It's all right, buddy," I assured him. "I'm just thinking crazy thoughts."

I heard the sound of a key in the front door at the same time as Bentley did. In a flash, he was charging down the hall to the front of the house. I shoved the photo album back onto the shelf and followed after him, arriving in the foyer in time to see Brett giving Bentley an enthusiastic greeting of pats and tummy rubs.

I had to wait my turn, but the greeting Brett gave me was worth it.

"You'd think you missed me or something," I said once we broke apart.

"Always." He kissed me again, this time on my forehead. "I'll grab a quick shower before dinner."

"What do you want to eat?" I asked as he headed up the stairs to the second floor, Bentley on his heels.

"Whatever you feel like," he called over his shoulder.

I leaned against the banister. "I don't know what I feel like."

He paused at the top of the stairs. "In that case, spaghetti."

That sounded good to me, and for the first time since I'd arrived home, I felt the tiniest rumbles of hunger in my stomach.

By the time Brett appeared in clean clothes, his blond hair damp, I already had the tomato sauce bubbling away on the stove.

"Smells good," he said with appreciation. He wrapped his arms around my waist as I stirred the pot. "Sorry I took so long. I missed a call from Lonny while I was in the shower so I called him back when I was done."

I leaned into him. "Everything all right?"

"Everything's fine. He and Hope just wanted to add a few more mature plants to the list of ones I'm going to pick up for them."

I reluctantly pulled away from him so I could put a pot of water on the stove for the pasta. "They really want the garden party to be perfect, don't they?"

"They do, but I get it. The party will kick off their business, and they've put a lot of money, time, and effort into the inn."

"But they're not being... What would the equivalent of a bridezilla be in this situation?"

"Whatever it would be, no, they're not. They're great clients to work with."

I turned on the burner under the pot of water before facing Brett. "That's good, especially since you're spending so much of your time working for them these days."

He pulled me into his arms. "I'm sorry. I know I've been busy lately."

"I'm not complaining, but I'm glad you're home now."

"So am I."

By the time he finished showing me how happy he was, the water was boiling away madly on the stove. I added the pasta and managed to finish getting our dinner together without further distractions.

While we ate, I told Brett about my day and my unexpected stint as a judge.

"I guess I should feel sorry for Quaid," Brett said, "but somehow that's hard to do."

"He's not the most charming guy, is he?" I said.

Our conversation shifted away from Quaid. As we finished up our meal, I considered telling Brett about the man I'd seen near the competition site that afternoon. I was on the brink of saying something when I stopped myself. After all, the man couldn't have been my father and I didn't want to sound crazy.

Before I had a chance to carry my dirty plate to the kitchen, Brett picked it up and piled it on top of his.

"You did the cooking, so I'll do the cleanup," he said.

I leaned back in my chair, my stomach pleasantly full. "I knew there was a reason why I love you."

"Only one?" Brett said as he set the plates in the sink.

"More like a million and one."

The lopsided grin I loved so much made an appearance. "I wouldn't mind hearing each one of them."

"Maybe later," I said with a smile.

"That's good motivation to get these dishes done."

I stayed seated for another minute or so, but then I grew restless.

"You're supposed to be relaxing," Brett said when I got up and grabbed a cloth so I could wipe down the kitchen counters.

"I'd rather help get this done so we can relax together."

"I guess I can't argue with that plan."

I finished wiping down the quartz countertops and rinsed the cloth out at the sink. I dried my hands with a tea towel while Brett loaded the last of the dishes in the dishwasher and added some soap. As I watched him start the appliance on its wash cycle, a big smile spread across my face. I knew I probably looked goofy, but I couldn't help myself. My heart was about to explode with happiness in that moment.

"What?" Brett asked when he caught sight of my expression.

"It's so perfect."

He quirked an eyebrow. "The way I arranged the dishes in the dishwasher?"

I stifled a laugh. "No. This." I made a sweeping gesture with my arm. "You and me, here together, doing mundane domestic things like cooking and cleaning. It's perfect. So much more perfect than I ever thought it could be." My smile faded, a hint of uncertainty creeping in to replace some of my happiness. "Does that sound dumb?"

Brett took hold of my hands. "Not at all. I know what you mean. And it is. Perfect." He pulled me closer and folded me into his arms.

I rested my cheek against his chest. "So it hasn't been a disappointment in any way?"

"Living here with you? Of course not. Like you said, it's even better than I imagined it would be."

I tipped my head back so I could see his face. "Did you imagine it? Before I asked you to move in?"

"I did." He rested his chin on the top of my head. "Because you and me, we belong together."

"We do," I agreed.

"Like whipped cream and pumpkin pie."

"Like whipped cream and pumpkin pie crêpes," I amended.

"Mmmm." The sound rumbled in his chest. "Now you're making me hungry."

"You just ate," I reminded him. "How can you possibly be hungry?"

"There's more than one type of hunger," he said, kissing me below my left ear.

"In that case," I said with a smile, "I'm famished."

Chapter 10

After I'd finished work on Sunday, Brett and I put together a quinoa salad. We were having dinner with his parents, and I'd promised to bring a dish to contribute. Not long after we got the salad made, we were in Brett's truck and heading into town. Instead of going straight to Brett's parents' house, we made a detour to pick up Chloe. She lived in the house Brett owned and had done so for a few years now. Since Brett had moved out, she'd been searching for a roommate but hadn't yet found the right candidate.

Chloe was waiting on the front porch when we pulled into the driveway. She was carrying a covered bowl, which she set on her lap once she was seated in the back of the truck's cab.

"What have you got there?" I asked once we were on the move again.

"Fruit salad," Chloe replied. "I figured it was a safe choice because there's no cooking involved and my dad can eat it."

"I'm sure it will be delicious," I said.

Frank, Brett and Chloe's dad, had suffered a heart attack a few months earlier. He was still going through the rehabilitation process, and he tired more easily than he used to, but he was recovering well. He was on a strict healthy diet now, though, one his wife was making sure he stuck to.

"Is that the quinoa salad you brought to the barbecue last year?" Chloe asked, leaning forward to check out the plastic bowl in my lap.

"It is."

"Yum. I didn't even know I liked quinoa until I tried your salad."

"I'm glad you like it," I said. "It's one of my favorite dishes to make."

Brett slowed the truck to a stop at an intersection and waited as a pedestrian crossed the road.

Chloe leaned forward again. "Hey, isn't that Tyrone?"

The pedestrian stepped up onto the sidewalk on our right.

"It is!" Chloe tapped her brother on the shoulder. "Pull over."

"Hold on," Brett said. He turned the corner before guiding the truck to the curb.

Chloe hopped out of the vehicle, leaving the fruit salad on the seat.

"Tyrone!" she called out, waving when he turned around.

He didn't smile when he spotted Chloe, but recognition flashed across his face and he headed our way.

"Tyrone, as in the baseball player and Demetra's boyfriend?" I asked quietly, getting out of the truck to join Chloe.

"The one and the same," she whispered. "I haven't seen him in years."

I studied Tyrone as he covered the last few feet of distance to reach us. He was fairly tall, with an athletic build, despite his baseball career ending nearly a decade ago. He had dirty blond hair and a scruff of stubble on his jaw.

Chloe smiled when he reached us. "I didn't know you were in town. Where are you living now?"

He had yet to return Chloe's smile. "Seattle still."

"Do you remember my brother, Brett?"

Brett hadn't left the truck, but the passenger side door was open and he raised a hand in greeting. Tyrone acknowledged him with a nod.

"And this is my brother's girlfriend, Marley. Marley, this is Tyrone Phillips."

"Nice to meet you," I said.

He nodded again and stuffed his hands into the pockets of his jeans. "How've you been?" he asked Chloe.

It sounded like he was asking more out of politeness than interest.

"Good, but it was tough to hear about Demetra, of course."

"Yeah, it's crappy news." He freed one hand from his pocket to scratch at the stubble on his jawline. "That's why I'm here."

"The sheriff wants to talk to you?" Chloe guessed.

His voice took on an edge. "No more than anyone else. My mom thought I should show my face here. It's not like I don't know that some people suspect me of hurting Demetra. Mom thought I'd seem less suspicious if I came back here. I don't think it'll change anyone's mind, but if it'll make her happy..." He shrugged and backed away from us. "Anyhow, I should get going."

"It was good to see you again," Chloe said, but she was speaking to his back by then.

"Not the friendliest guy," I commented as we got back in the truck.

"He never was, if I remember right," Brett said, pulling away from the curb.

"No, he wasn't," Chloe confirmed. "I wonder if it's true that Ray's no more interested in questioning him than any of the rest of us who were at the party that night."

"Would Ray tell you if you asked him?" I knew he wouldn't want me asking, since he didn't like my tendency to get involved in his investigations.

"Probably not. He never shares all that much about his work. And since this is a murder investigation, he'll likely be more tight lipped than usual."

I didn't doubt she was right about that.

"Do you think Tyrone could have killed Demetra?" I asked. "I know you said before that it's possible, since he doesn't have an alibi and might have had a motive, but what does your gut instinct tell you?"

"I want to say there's no way anyone I know or used to know could be a killer, but that's what everyone wants to be able to say, right? Doesn't make it true." She fell silent for a moment. "He could have done it. I've always felt a bit uneasy around him. Maybe because he's not very personable, or maybe because I know about his temper. Out of everyone who was at the party that night, he's the one I have the least trouble picturing getting violent."

"How tall was Demetra?" I asked, thoughts turning around in my head.

"Not as tall as me," Chloe said. "Maybe five foot five?"

A little bit shorter than me, then.

"You're thinking Tyrone easily could have overpowered Demetra," Brett said with a glance my way.

"Yes. Of course, we don't know how she died, but at this point he seems like a solid suspect to me."

"I wish I could say otherwise," Chloe said, "but I'd have to agree."

Chapter 11

Dinner at the Collins house was a relaxed and happy affair. Mostly we chatted about Frank's rehabilitation progress, the pancake house, Brett's business, and Chloe's job as a teacher. There was no mention of murder or human remains during the meal, and I was glad about that. Those topics might have put a damper on the evening, and I knew it troubled Chloe to think about her former classmate's death.

After we'd finished up the meal with Chloe's fruit salad, Frank settled in a comfy armchair in the living room for a bit of a rest while Brett, Chloe, and I cleared the table.

"Mom, you go sit down with Dad," Chloe said once we'd transferred all the dirty dishes from the dining room to the kitchen.

"Nonsense," Elaine said as she opened the dishwasher. "I invited you over here. You shouldn't have to do all the work."

"We don't mind," I said as I set a stack of plates on the counter. "And the three of us will make short work of it."

Brett put an arm around his mom's shoulders and guided her toward the living room. "Go and relax, Mom. We'll take care of everything in here."

"If you insist." She smiled over her shoulder at me and Chloe. "Thank you."

As predicted, it didn't take long for the three of us to get the dishwasher loaded and the kitchen cleaned.

"Do you mind if we stick around a while so I can play some chess with my dad?" Brett asked as I washed my hands after wiping down the countertops.

"Of course not."

A phone rang somewhere nearby, the sound muffled.

"That's mine," Chloe said, grabbing her purse from a nearby chair and digging through it. When she checked the screen of the device, surprise registered on her face. "It's Kyle."

"As in Deputy Kyle Rutowski?" I asked.

She nodded as she answered the call.

Although I was curious to know why the deputy was calling Chloe, I figured it might be a personal call and none of my business. Brett and Chloe had grown up with Kyle in Wildwood Cove. I didn't know if Chloe hung out with Kyle at all these days, but I guessed from her reaction that it wasn't common for him to call her. Still, I decided not to be nosy and followed Brett to the living room.

I settled on the couch, and Brett produced a chessboard from a cabinet. He and his dad were pulling up chairs to a small table when Chloe appeared in the doorway, a hint of anxiety creating a furrow across her forehead.

"Kyle's coming over in a few minutes," she announced to the room.

"Kyle Rutowski?" Elaine asked.

Chloe nodded.

"I'm guessing it isn't a social visit," Frank said.

Chloe sank down on the couch beside me. "No. He says there's something he wants to show me. It's got something to do with Demetra, but he didn't say anything more than that."

"Hopefully it's just something routine," her mom said.

The doorbell rang before Chloe could say anything more.

"That was fast," Frank said.

Chloe got up from the couch. "He said he was nearby."

She headed for the foyer to answer the door, and we heard a murmur of voices before she reappeared in the living room, Kyle right behind her. Dark-haired and of average height, Kyle was close in age to me and Brett. He was in uniform, his face serious, although he gave us a brief glimpse of a smile as he greeted everyone.

Once we'd all said hello, he held up a small plastic evidence bag. "I'm wondering if you've ever seen this before," he said to Chloe.

She took the bag from him, studying its contents closely.

"What is it?" I asked, unable to keep my curiosity in check.

"A ring." Chloe held the bag up to the light, and for the first time I noticed a small object in one bottom corner. "Gold, with what looks like a ruby. And an inscription. It's hard to read but I think it says 'always.'" She glanced at Kyle. "Is it a real ruby?"

"We haven't confirmed that yet."

She took another moment to study the ring before handing the bag back to the deputy. "I've never seen it before. Was it Demetra's?"

"That's what we're trying to find out."

"But it was found with her remains?" I guessed.

"It was."

"So she was wearing it when she died?" Chloe asked, sounding puzzled.

"We're not sure about that."

"I don't know...." Chloe still seemed perplexed.

"What is it?" Kyle asked.

"It's a nice ring," Chloe said. "If Demetra owned something like that, she would have flaunted it. Even if the ruby's not real, she probably would have told everyone it was. And I definitely don't remember her ever wearing a ring like that."

That probably left Kyle with more questions than answers, but he kept his expression neutral and didn't let on to what he was thinking.

"I appreciate you taking the time to have a look at it," he said to Chloe before addressing the rest of us. "Sorry to interrupt your evening."

"No apologies necessary," Elaine said, getting up from her chair. "How's your mother doing these days?"

"She's doing well, thanks," Kyle said as Elaine walked him to the front door.

Their conversation faded away, and a moment later we heard the sound of the door closing.

"It's so strange," Chloe said, still standing in the same spot when her mom returned to the room. "Demetra was such a show-off. She wouldn't have kept quiet if that ring was hers. And the inscription makes me think it could be an engagement or wedding ring. She definitely wouldn't have kept it to herself if someone had proposed to her."

"What if it happened right before her death?" I said.

"You mean someone proposed to her and then killed her right after?" Brett asked, sounding doubtful.

"That does seem unlikely," I conceded. "Unless she turned him down and that threw him into a rage."

"You're thinking of Tyrone," Chloe said. "And, unfortunately, that could be possible. Demetra had already dumped him. If he proposed to her, she probably wouldn't have left it at a simple no."

"You think she might have laughed in his face?" Elaine asked, sounding shocked.

"That was her style, Mom. You remember what she was like."

"Yes, I do," Elaine said sadly. She put a hand to her daughter's back. "How about we focus on something more pleasant? Why don't I show Marley some old photos?"

Brett groaned. "Mom, please. You'll bore Marley to the point of insanity."

"Oh, hush," Elaine said, heading to a shelf lined with albums and large books.

"I don't mind," I said to Brett. "I'd love to get a glimpse of your childhood."

We'd first met when I was spending the summer in Wildwood Cove at age fifteen, but his younger years were, for the most part, an unknown to me.

"You say that now," Brett said as he moved a chess piece on the game board, "but give it time and you'll be begging for me to get you out of here."

"I doubt that."

Brett appealed to his sister. "Chloe, come on. You don't want Mom embarrassing you either."

With a smug smile, Chloe returned to the couch, leaving room for her mom to sit between us. "I'm not embarrassed by Marley seeing childhood pictures of me. I'm not the one who ran around the house at age three wearing nothing but a Superman cape."

Brett thumped his forehead to the table, making the chess pieces shake.

I laughed. "Don't worry, Brett. I'm sure you were adorable."

He muttered something under his breath but went back to playing chess with his dad, studiously ignoring the rest of us.

Sitting between me and Chloe, Elaine opened the photo album. It started with pictures from the day of Brett's birth when he was a tiny red-faced bundle. A cranky one, judging by his expression in all the pictures.

We went through the album page by page, all three of us laughing when we reached the pictures Chloe had mentioned. I saw Brett shake his head across the room, but he refused to look our way.

"That's the cutest bumblebee I've ever seen," I said when we reached photos of Brett getting ready to head out trick-or-treating for the first time.

Elaine turned another page.

"And that might be the cutest photo of all time." I pointed to a picture of a six-year-old Brett holding a newborn Chloe. His blond curls were longer than they were now, and fluffy. He had a giant smile on his face as he gazed adoringly down at the bundle in his arms.

"He couldn't help but be thrilled to have a baby sister like me," Chloe said with a grin.

Brett nearly choked. "At that point I didn't know what I was in for."

Chloe rolled her eyes. "Please."

I laughed, knowing their banter was good natured.

"Check," Frank said from across the room.

"Oh, man." Brett stared at the board for a moment before making a move. Frank moved one of his pieces next. "Checkmate."

Brett sat back in defeat. "I was distracted."

"Sure, son," his dad said with a smile.

I knew Brett wasn't really upset, and a second later he was grinning as he got up and clapped his dad on the shoulder. "Good game."

It was nearing nine o'clock, and I was usually early to bed and early to rise. Frank appeared to be fading, too, his face weary. We quickly wrapped up our visit and piled into Brett's truck. After dropping Chloe off, we headed along Wildwood Road, toward home.

"I do plan to get revenge, you know," Brett said.

"For the photos? Come on, it wasn't that bad. You were such a cute kid. Not that I ever doubted that, considering how you turned out."

"I'm enjoying the flattery, but that doesn't change my mind. I'm going to have a chat with your mom and ask her to bring some photo albums the next time she comes for a visit."

"You might want to rethink that plan," I warned as he turned into our driveway. "I'm an only child. My mom took *lots* of pictures of me when I was little. She'll have you trapped for hours."

Brett parked the car in front of the house. "I doubt it'll be that long."

I put a hand on his arm. "Trust me. *Hours.*"

Even in the darkness, I didn't miss the apprehension that flashed across his face.

"Think about all that time wasted," I said. "Hours that could be spent doing other things."

A grin appeared on his face. "Such as?"

"I'll leave that up to your imagination."

"Which happens to be running wild."

"I don't doubt it," I said, matching his grin.

He took my hand. "How about we don't waste *this* hour?"

"You're right. Why sit here in the truck when we could be going for a romantic walk on the beach?"

"That wasn't quite what I had in mind."

"I know. But Bentley needs a walk."

"True."

"And this night has more than one hour."

"Now you're talking."

We both grinned as we got out of the truck.

"And I suppose a walk won't be so bad if I can steal a kiss or two," Brett said when he met me around the front of the vehicle.

"I'm sure Bentley will return them with great enthusiasm."

Brett took my hands and leaned in close so he could whisper in my ear. "Don't tell Bentley, but I much prefer your kisses."

I went up on tiptoes and pressed my lips to his before saying, "Your secret's safe with me."

Chapter 12

I slept later than usual on Monday morning, getting up just in time to see Brett off as he left for work. He took Bentley with him, much to the dog's excitement. Bentley loved to hang out with his favorite human, and most of Brett's clients didn't mind if he brought his canine companion along. He'd run the idea past Lonny and Hope, and they'd assured him that Bentley was more than welcome on their property.

That left me and Flapjack at home. After eating breakfast, I wandered out onto the back porch with my cat in my arms. The morning breeze was cool but refreshing and filled with the smell of the sea.

"What do you think, Jack?" I asked as I set the tabby on the porch railing.

He sat down and gazed out at the ocean, his tail flicking back and forth.

"Is it crazy that I'm tempted to walk around town to see if I can spot the man who looks like my dad?"

Flapjack's amber gaze turned my way. He blinked before giving his tail another flick and getting up to stalk off along the railing.

"Okay, you're right," I conceded. "That would be a little bit crazy."

Still, the temptation didn't disappear.

I rested my forearms on the railing, enjoying the way the breeze lifted my hair from my shoulders. Tempted or not, I needed to be realistic. The man couldn't be my father. If I did get a better look at him, I'd probably see that the resemblance wasn't nearly as strong as I thought.

"I should focus on something else," I said out loud.

Flapjack ignored me this time. His attention was focused on a little chickadee perched on the clothesline, out of his reach, fortunately.

I fished my phone out of the pocket of my hoodie and sat down in one of the porch chairs. Chloe had probably arrived at the Port Angeles school where she worked as a second grade teacher, but her class wouldn't have started yet. I sent her a text message, hoping she might see it before she got busy with her students.

Any more info about the ring? I wrote.

After waiting a couple of minutes without any response, I went indoors to make myself a cup of tea. When I returned to the porch, Flapjack had left the railing to explore the yard. I sat down again and sipped my tea, enjoying the fact that I didn't have anything pressing to take care of that day. All I wanted to do was enjoy the weather, my tea, and the sound of the ocean waves crashing against the shore. I only managed that for a few minutes, however.

My mind was restless, refusing to stay idle. Thoughts about my father tried to resurface, but I pushed them away. I really needed to focus on something else.

Fortunately, my phone chimed on the arm of the chair, signaling that I'd received a reply from Chloe.

I heard through the grapevine that Kyle showed it to Tyrone but he said he'd never seen it before.

My fingers tapped against the arm of the chair. The case had awakened my curiosity, which wasn't the least bit surprising. Unsolved mysteries had a way of lodging in my mind, refusing to leave me at peace until I had answers to all the questions that had taken up residence in my head. If Tyrone had lied when he said he'd never seen the ring before, would something in his body language have given him away? No doubt Deputy Rutowski was used to detecting lies.

But it wasn't as if the deputy would tell me about his conversation with Tyrone, and I definitely didn't want to approach Tyrone himself. Not on my own, anyway. After hearing the stories about his temper, I figured it was safer to stay away from him. Still, the thought of letting the matter rest, of trying to forget about the investigation into Demetra's death, almost left me twitchy.

My phone chimed again.

Maybe Chrissy would recognize the ring, Chloe had written. *She was closest to Demetra, aside from Tyrone.*

In which case, Rutowski had likely paid a visit to her as well.

She lives in town, right? I asked Chloe via another text.

Yes. She owns the clothing boutique on Pacific Street.

A moment later, she sent another message. *Are you going to talk to her?*

Maybe, I replied. *Or will you?*

*Not today. I have a meeting after work and I don't have Chrissy's
number. We were never really friends.*

She followed that up with, *Gotta go. Bell's about to ring.*

I stayed in my chair until I finished my tea, but by then I knew any
further relaxation was a lost cause. I needed to pick up a loaf of bread at
the bakery at some point, and I figured it couldn't hurt to stop by Chrissy
Mazurek's clothing boutique on my way. It might turn out to be a pointless
detour, but it wouldn't take much time out of my day.

I found Flapjack sitting in a patch of sunlight on the grass. He didn't
protest when I picked him up and carried him inside. I set him down on
the kitchen windowsill—one of his favorite spots to rest—and he hunkered
down, his gaze on the world beyond the glass.

I decided to take advantage of the mild weather and walked into town.
Although I'd never been inside the clothing boutique, I'd walked past it
many times over the past year and knew it was situated between a hair
salon and a flower shop. When I left Wildwood Road for Pacific Street,
I found myself glancing left and right, searching the faces of the other
pedestrians making their way through the heart of town.

Stop it, I chastised myself as soon as I realized what I was doing.
Whoever he is, he's not your dad.

Despite my scolding, I couldn't stop myself from keeping an eye out
for the man I'd seen the other day. I wasn't surprised when I didn't spot
him. Since I'd never seen him before the weekend, he'd probably just been
passing through town and was most likely long gone by now.

I stopped outside the flower shop to admire the colorful bouquets on
display in the front window. I was tempted to buy some bright gerbera
daisies to take home to add color and cheer to the house, but I decided to
leave that for another time.

Tearing my attention away from the flowers, I entered the boutique next
door. A bell tinkled overhead as I entered the shop, and a woman with
plenty of frizzy blond hair smiled at me from behind the counter near the
back of the store.

"Good morning," the woman greeted. "Let me know if I can help you
with anything."

I thanked her and wandered between two circular clothing racks. The
small shop smelled faintly of perfume, a scent that was vaguely flowery
but not, I suspected, as nice as the natural flower smell the neighboring
store would offer. Still, it wasn't unpleasant, and the soft lighting and
instrumental music playing quietly in the background gave the boutique
a calm and classy atmosphere.

I figured it was a safe bet that the woman behind the counter was Chrissy Mazurek. She appeared to be the right age, anyway. I didn't yet know how to raise the subject of the mysterious ring with her, so I decided to browse through the shop to give myself some time to think.

As I flipped through a selection of flowing, summery dresses, I couldn't help but feel a bit out of place in my worn jeans and hoodie. I glanced over at the woman I assumed was Chrissy. She wore a cashmere sweater and understated gold jewelry, but I noted with relief that she wasn't looking down her nose at me. She wasn't paying attention to me at all, her eyes instead focused on the screen of the computer at the checkout counter.

Since I only dressed up on rare occasions, I didn't expect to have any real interest in the boutique's stock, so I was surprised when I came across an emerald-green dress that caught my fancy. It was a simple dress, but cute.

I took the hanger off the rack and ran my hand down the fabric. The color was gorgeous. With the garden party at the Wildwood Inn coming up in a few weeks, I'd have a reason to wear it. But did I *need* it? I already had a couple of nice dresses in my closet that I'd worn only a handful of times.

Maybe the better question was whether I could afford it. I flipped over the price tag, and my eyes nearly popped out of my head. I *could* afford it, but it was definitely pricey.

"Found something you like?" The shopkeeper came out from behind the counter to approach me.

"I'm just admiring this dress," I said, holding up the garment.

"That color would look great on you. Would you like to try it on?"

"Oh..." I hesitated.

"There's a change room in the back."

She was already heading that way, so I followed, still holding the dress.

"Here you go," she said, opening the door to a cubbyhole of a room with a stool in one corner and a full-length mirror on the wall. "Let me know if you need anything else."

"Thank you." I shut myself in the room and met my own gaze in the mirror. I still hadn't figured out how to broach the subject of the ring, but maybe I'd have a better chance of getting information if I seemed like a potential buyer rather than just a browser.

I kicked off my sneakers and traded my jeans, hoodie, and T-shirt for the emerald-green dress. It had three-quarter-length sleeves—perfect for spring—and a form-fitting bodice with a jewel neckline. Below the defined waistline was a cute, slightly flared bell skirt. It was short without being *too* short.

It was definitely different from anything else I owned, and I was already falling in love with it. But was it right for the garden party?

Maybe I needed an opinion from someone else.

I took out my phone and snapped a picture of my reflection in the mirror. I sent it to Brett along with a text message.

For the garden party. What do you think? Yes or no? Be honest.

I sent the same photo and message to Lisa.

Turning in a slow circle, I watched my reflection. It really was a cute dress. But I'd spent money on a dress only a few weeks earlier, one I wore to my mom's wedding in Seattle. Did I want to fork out more cash on another dress so soon?

My phone chimed. Brett had replied to my message.

Definite yes.

I smiled, but I still wasn't quite convinced. What if he was just being nice?

Another chime signaled a reply from Lisa.

So cute! Buy it!

Okay, so maybe I could feel my arm twisting.

I allowed myself another few seconds to admire the dress before slipping out of it and getting back into my jeans and hoodie. With the dress over my arm, I left the change room for the main part of the store. I was about to step around a mannequin wearing a bold flower-print dress so I could head for the checkout counter when I heard an unfamiliar female voice.

"Hey, Chrissy. What is it with this ring I've been hearing about?"

Instead of continuing on toward the counter, I stayed behind the mannequin and pretended to study the skirts and tops hanging from the racks along the back wall of the store. Maybe I wouldn't have to find a way to bring up the subject of the ring after all.

"Have you seen it?" Chrissy asked.

"No," the other woman replied. "But I heard a deputy showed a ruby ring to Tyrone, one they found with Demetra's remains."

"He showed it to me too," Chrissy said. "I don't get it, though. If Demetra had a ring like that, I would've known about it. She only owned costume jewelry."

"I also heard it might have been an engagement ring."

"That's what I thought. But Demetra definitely wasn't engaged."

"Everyone would have heard about it if she was."

"Exactly," Chrissy agreed.

That fit with what Chloe had said the night before.

I carefully peeked around the mannequin. The woman talking to Chrissy was leaning casually against the checkout counter. She had short, curly brown hair and wore denim capris with a white shirt and a red cotton scarf.

Amy Strudwick, the photographer from the cooking contest, I realized.

"So maybe the ring belonged to whoever killed Demetra," Amy said.

I saw Chrissy shudder before I resumed my feigned study of the clothing on display.

"It's still hard to believe she was murdered," she said. "I hope the killer's not anyone we know."

"If it is, my money's on Tyrone."

"He always did have a nasty temper. I hear he's in back in town."

"And not cooperating with the police."

"He never was all that bright," Chrissy said. "Not cooperating makes him seem guilty."

"The sheriff should have played to Tyrone's ego if he wanted information. That was always the best way to get past his surliness."

"I thought you never really had much to do with him."

"I didn't," Amy said. "But that's what I always heard about him."

"Well, it's definitely true."

"I wonder…" Amy said slowly.

I peeked around the mannequin again, eager to hear Amy's next words, but before she could say anything more, the hanger from the green dress slipped out of the garment and clattered to the floor.

Chapter 13

I stooped over to pick up the hanger, and when I straightened back up, both women had their eyes on me. Amy regarded me with curiosity, but Chrissy smiled.

"How did it go with the dress?" she asked.

"Great," I said. "It fits perfectly and I love it."

"I should go, Chrissy," Amy cut in. She pulled a business card out of her purse and set it on the counter. "My number's on the card. Keep me posted?"

"Sure, Amy. It was good to see you."

"You too."

With one last glance my way, Amy left the shop.

"Sorry, I couldn't help but overhear," I said as I set the dress on the counter. "You knew Demetra? You must be from the same class as Chloe Collins."

"That's right. How do you know Chloe?"

"Her brother's my boyfriend."

"Lucky. He's easy on the eyes," Chrissy said as she punched buttons on the cash register. She told me the total for the dress, and I pulled out my credit card. As I tapped it against the card machine, I glanced at the business card still sitting on the counter.

Amy Strudwick, Photographer, it read. Below that it listed a Port Townsend address.

"So if you know Chloe, do you know if she's been questioned by the cops recently?" Chrissy asked.

"She was shown a ring last night and asked if she recognized it, but she didn't."

"I was asked about it too."

"Really?" I didn't let on that I'd heard that part of her conversation with Amy.

"I didn't recognize it either. Receipt in the bag?"

"Yes, please."

She tucked the slip of paper in with the dress and passed me the bag. "Have they asked Chloe anything else?"

"Like what?"

Chrissy shrugged and tapped a long, bright red fingernail against the counter. "I don't know if you've heard about this, but Chloe never liked Demetra. And on the last night Demetra was seen alive, Chloe completely snapped and almost attacked her."

"But she didn't."

Chrissy reached beneath the counter and produced a pack of gum. "Not at the party, but who knows what she did after that?"

I struggled to keep myself from sounding defensive, but didn't entirely succeed when I said, "She has an alibi. She went straight home."

Chrissy unwrapped a piece of gum. "Did the cops confirm that?"

"Yes."

"Hmm. I guess that's lucky for her." She almost sounded disappointed.

"Do *you* have an alibi?"

Her eyes took on a hard glint, one that was decidedly unfriendly. "I was Demetra's best friend," she said as if that answered my question. She glanced at the bag in my hand. "Enjoy the dress."

"I will. Thank you."

Since she'd clearly dismissed me, I left the boutique, armed with my new dress and the knowledge that Chrissy also hadn't recognized the ruby ring.

* * * *

Instead of heading home, I texted Lisa to ask if she wanted to meet for an early lunch. I wandered toward Main Street as I waited for a response and was nearly at the law office where Lisa worked when my phone chimed.

Sure. Give me five minutes, she'd written back.

I resisted the temptation to cross the street and pass the time by browsing through Timeless Treasures, my favorite antiques shop. After spending money on my new dress, I didn't want to be tempted by any other potential purchases that day. Instead, I stayed on the east side of the street and wandered along the sidewalk, checking out the displays in the other shop windows.

"Marley!"

When I heard Lisa call my name, I turned and saw her waving at me from outside her office.

"Do you mind if we get some takeout and eat it at my place?" she asked once I'd reached her. "I like to go home and check on Orion during my lunch breaks."

"Of course I don't mind. I wouldn't pass up a chance to see the cute little guy."

A big smile lit up Lisa's face. "He really is adorable, isn't he?"

"Extremely."

Lisa told me tales of Orion's latest kitten antics as we waited for our food orders at a small Chinese restaurant one street over from her workplace.

"I can't wait to give him a cuddle," I said once we'd paid for our food. "And I'm so glad you were able to give him such a good home. He's one lucky kitten."

"I'm lucky too. He's so loving, especially considering that he was probably dumped by his previous human. And he makes me laugh every day. I've never had a pet before, and I didn't realize how much they can change your life for the better."

"They definitely do that."

When we reached Lisa's house and she opened the front door, we didn't have to wait more than a second or two to see Orion. He came skittering down the hallway as soon as he heard us arrive. I quickly shut the door so he wouldn't have a chance to escape.

Lisa scooped the kitten up with one hand as she set her container of take-out food on the small foyer table. "Hello, cutie. What have you been up to while I've been gone?" She held the kitten up so they were nose to nose and then planted a kiss on the top of his head. "Someone's here to see you."

She passed me the kitten, and he snuggled up against my shoulder, his purr rumbling away. My heart melted.

"He's grown since the last time I saw him," I said as I stroked his sleek black fur. "Haven't you, little guy?"

Since Lisa only had an hour off work, we settled down to eat after another minute or two of fussing over Orion. We laughed as the kitten kept us entertained during our lunch, chasing a ball around the dining room, pouncing on it whenever he got close to it and occasionally somersaulting over the toy.

"What does Ivan think of Orion?" I asked as we were finishing up our chow mein.

Lisa had started dating Ivan over the winter. It wasn't a match I ever would have predicted before they started spending time together, but things seemed to be going well for them.

"He adores him," Lisa said. "And Orion loves him back. You should see them together. Orion likes to perch on Ivan's shoulder. And he looks even tinier than usual when Ivan holds him."

I could picture that. Ivan was such a big, burly guy. Orion probably wasn't much bigger than one of his hands.

"Before we go," Lisa said as we finished off the last of the food, "you have to show me the dress."

"You already saw the photo," I reminded her.

"I still want to see it in person," she insisted.

I retrieved the bag from the foyer and held up the garment to show her.

"Oh, my gosh! That color!" she said as she fingered the green fabric. "The picture didn't do it justice."

"The color is the first thing that caught my eye." A hint of doubt squirmed its way into my mind. "Do you think it's right for the garden party?"

"Of course. Why wouldn't it be?"

"I guess I figured I'd wear one of my sundresses or something."

"It'll be perfect," Lisa said. "And Brett won't be able to keep his eyes off you."

"He did seem to like the picture," I said with a smile.

I tucked the dress back into its bag, and we cleaned up our take-out containers. After Lisa had set out fresh water for Orion, we both gave him one last cuddle and kiss before leaving the house.

"So," Lisa said once we were walking back toward Main Street, "how are things with you and Brett now that you've been living together for a while?"

"Great," I said, smiling again. "He's the first boyfriend I've ever lived with, and of course it's taking some adjusting for both of us, but things are going really well. I love having him there with me. It just feels...*right.*"

I glanced Lisa's way and saw that she was grinning at me.

"What?" I asked.

"I'm so happy for you. The two of you are perfect together."

"I can't argue with that. I'm so glad I ran into him again after so many years."

Up until the previous spring, I hadn't seen Brett since we were teenagers. I'd had a crush on him all those years ago, and when he walked into The Flip Side last March, I found out right away that he still gave me butterflies. Luckily, the attraction had been mutual.

"It was meant to be," Lisa said.

"I think you're right about that." I realized I was fingering the seahorse pendant I wore around my neck, something I often did when I thought about Brett. The necklace had been a gift from him on my birthday, and I wore it almost every day.

We'd reached Main Street, so I said goodbye to Lisa and she returned to work while I headed for the bakery to pick up a loaf of bread. The place was busy, with three people in line ahead of me at the counter and another half dozen patrons seated at the small tables off to the left, enjoying coffee or tea with their baked goods.

Marielle's assistant, Rachel, was serving the customers when I arrived, but by the time I was second in line, the bakery owner had appeared from the back.

"I can help you over here, Marley," Marielle said, waving me over to the second cash register at the other end of the counter. As was typical, her dark hair was tied back and her cheeks were flushed pink. "What can I get for you?"

"A loaf of sliced multigrain, please," I requested. "And a package of biscotti."

I'd recently discovered that her chocolate-dipped biscotti was delicious, especially when paired with a cup of orange pekoe tea.

Marielle fetched the loaf of bread and a package of half a dozen biscotti. "Anything else?" she asked as she set the items on the counter.

"That's all for today, thanks."

"I hear Quaid has fully recovered," she said as she punched buttons on the cash register. She glanced at the other customers and lowered her voice. "Unfortunately. I was hoping you'd get to judge with us again on the weekend."

I lowered my voice to match hers. "He's not exactly Prince Charming, is he?"

"More like a frog that will never turn into a prince," Marielle said. "Except that's insulting frogs, which isn't fair."

I smiled. "There's only one round of the competition left to go."

"That's a relief, though I've enjoyed everything else about it. Quaid's the only dark cloud on that horizon."

"Was it the stomach flu?" I asked. "I hope there's not one going around."

"I'm not sure what it was. It seemed to be short lived, though. Apparently he was up and about the next day. I think it's lucky he fell ill before he tasted any of the contestants' food that day."

"You think he would have blamed them for food poisoning otherwise?"

"I could see him doing that," she said.

"So could I."

I paid Marielle for my purchases and took a moment to chat with an elderly man who sometimes ate at The Flip Side with his wife.

"Rachel, can you take care of things for a bit while I run an errand or two?" Marielle asked, removing her apron.

"Sure thing," Rachel replied.

Marielle grabbed a red cardigan from the back and pulled it on as she headed for the door. I followed her out onto the sidewalk and waved as we set off in opposite directions. The sun was shining, lending pleasant warmth to the day and making me glad to be outdoors. I didn't make it far along the street before I stopped to talk to another acquaintance—Mr. Gorski, the owner of Timeless Treasures. He was on his way to get a sandwich from the bakery, so we didn't talk for too long, but I assured him he'd see me at his shop someday soon.

When I was on my way again, I decided to walk along the beach instead of the road, so I followed an unpaved pathway that would take me down to the ocean. The path stretched between a stand of trees and a building, out of reach of the sun's rays. I picked up my pace as I passed through the shade, eager to get back out into the sun, but I slowed down again when I heard a murmur of voices behind the chirping of the birds in the trees.

At first I wasn't sure where the voices were coming from, but then I spotted a flash of red between the trees. Someone was standing with their back to me, mostly hidden by branches and undergrowth. A woman, I realized by the sound of her voice, although I couldn't make out what she was saying. She was talking with a man, one I didn't recognize until he turned his head slightly. Then I realized it was Coach Hannigan.

If I'd seen them out in the open, I wouldn't have thought twice about it, but it struck me as odd that they were in among the trees, keeping their voices low, as if worried they might be overheard. Almost without conscious thought, I was taking my steps carefully now, trying to make as little noise as possible as I followed the pathway. I had the distinct feeling that they didn't want to be disturbed, and I was hoping I could make my way down to the beach without them noticing me.

I'd almost reached the end of the path when Coach Hannigan's voice floated toward me on the breeze.

"People respect me. I don't want my good name dragged through the mud."

The woman said something in response that I couldn't make out.

"Good," Hannigan said. "Keep it that way."

They parted ways then, the baseball coach striding through the trees toward the pathway and his companion heading for Wildwood Road. I hurried down to the beach, reaching the sand seconds later. When I glanced back over my shoulder, I saw Hannigan walking briskly in the other direction, heading toward town.

As I strolled along the water's edge, I enjoyed the salty, fresh air and the comforting rhythm of the ocean waves breaking gently against the shore. But although I tried to clear my mind as I walked, I couldn't rid myself of the thought that the meeting I'd witnessed was a strange one.

Chapter 14

I spent the next morning in Port Angeles, doing some shopping and picking up some fabric samples from a home renovation store. When I'd inherited my beachfront Victorian, I'd also become the owner of all its furnishings, including some beautiful antiques. The only problem was that some of the pieces had worn, faded, and outdated upholstery. I'd already reupholstered an antique slipper chair, but there was a settee and matching wingback chairs in the living room that still needed attention.

At the moment, the pieces of furniture were covered in rose-pink fabric. I wanted to change that to a color more my liking, but I wasn't yet sure what I wanted to go with. I was hoping that by taking fabric samples home, the decision would become easier. It would also allow me to get input from Brett. He was more interested in building and renovating than decorating, but I still wanted his opinion.

Once I'd finished running my errands and had the samples stashed in my car, I returned home, but only long enough to drop off my purchases. Bentley had gone to work with Brett again that morning and I was going to stop by the Wildwood Inn to see them. I was curious to know what the interior of the old mansion looked like now that Lonny and Hope had finished the renovations. Brett had mentioned my interest to the owners the day before, and they'd offered to give me a tour. Maybe while I was there I'd get some ideas for my own house.

I followed the long, winding driveway through the trees and up past the stately Victorian. Brett's work van was parked near the detached garage, and I pulled up behind it. The back doors of the van stood open, giving me a view of several potted plants that were no doubt waiting to be transplanted into the garden. Once out of my car, I peeked into the van for a better view of the plants. I spotted some pansies, winter heather in shades of pink and white, English daisies, and a few flowers I couldn't name.

Leaving the driveway, I wandered toward the back garden, going in search of Brett before I sought out Lonny and Hope. This time Brett was much closer to the house, working in a flower bed only a stone's throw from the Victorian's back porch. Bentley, lying in the grass, spotted me first. He jumped up and barreled across the lawn to meet me.

"Hey, buddy," I said, giving him a pat as his tail wagged.

I had to be careful not to trip over him as he bounced around me while I tried to get closer to Brett.

"Hey," Brett said in greeting as I approached. "How was your morning?"

"Good," I replied, watching as he transferred English daisies from a plastic pot to the hole he'd prepared in the flower bed. "I got everything done that I needed to do in Port Angeles. How are things going here?"

Brett dusted dirt from his work gloves before removing them and tucking them into the back pocket of his jeans. "Moving along well." He stepped away from the edge of the flower bed so he could give me a kiss. "What do you think?"

Bentley settled at our feet as we surveyed the large yard. I could tell that Brett had made good progress since my last visit. The flower beds were now bursting with color, dozens of blooming plants filling the plots that were previously empty.

"It's beautiful," I said. "I'm impressed."

"Fortunately, Lonny and Hope seem to be too."

"That's good news. How much do you have left to do?"

Brett nodded toward the one remaining bed without flowers. "I need to put in some plants over there, and tomorrow I'll be picking up the water feature they ordered. Hopefully it won't take long to get it installed."

"Where's that going?"

He pointed to the flower bed closest to the back porch. "Right over there. Hope wants to be able to hear the water while she's relaxing on the porch swing."

"That sounds like paradise."

Brett settled an arm across my shoulders. "You want a porch swing and a water feature? We could make it happen."

"Maybe a porch swing, but we've already got a water feature with the ocean on our doorstep."

"Good point. I don't think any fountain could live up to that." He wiped the back of one hand across his forehead, leaving a small smear of dirt by his temple. "Have you seen Lonny or Hope yet?"

"Not yet. You were first on my list to visit."

"I'm glad to hear it," he said with a smile.

Bentley jumped up and nudged my knee with his nose.

I gave him a pat on the head. "Okay, the two of you tied for first."

I brushed the dirt from Brett's temple and gave him a quick kiss. "But I'll go look for them now and let you get back to work."

"Stop by again before you head home?"

"I will," I assured him.

I gave Bentley one last pat before crossing the lawn. He whined at first, wanting to follow me and stay with Brett at the same time, but when Brett spoke to him in a low voice, he settled down. I glanced over my shoulder before heading around the side of the house and saw him lying down at the edge of the flower bed, resting his head on his paws.

I could have tried knocking on the back door, but since I didn't know Lonny and Hope well, I felt more comfortable going around the front. There was no porch swing on this side of the house, but there was some nice white wicker furniture with colorful seat cushions. The inn's future guests would have a beautiful view of the front garden whenever they chose to sit out there with a cup of coffee or a book to read.

The inn wasn't right on the beach, but the property was private and peaceful. Hopefully it would become a popular place for visitors to stay. The Barrons had put so much work into the place and they seemed like such a nice couple that I wanted their business venture to succeed.

When I knocked on the front door, I heard footsteps approaching and a second later Hope opened the door and smiled at me.

"Hi, Marley. Come on in."

I thanked her as I stepped inside the foyer. My attention was immediately drawn to the impressive, curving staircase across the spacious entryway. The dark wood of the stairs and banister gleamed in the sunlight streaming in through the open door. When Hope closed it, I noticed small beams of colored light shimmering on the stairway and on the rug that covered much of the foyer floor. I turned and looked up. I'd been so focused on the porch and its furniture when I approached the house that I hadn't noticed the stained-glass window above the door.

"That's beautiful," I said, my gaze still transfixed on the stained glass.

The window featured red climbing roses with verdant green foliage and little birds perched here and there among the flowers.

"I love it too," Hope said. "It's not original, unfortunately, but I can't be too sad about that, considering how nice this one is."

"It really is gorgeous."

As I removed my sneakers, I took in the rest of the spacious entryway. An antique desk sat off to the left, a computer and phone sitting on top of it along with a vase of bright flowers. On my right was a mahogany bench with an ornately carved back and legs, and when I glanced up I noticed a crystal chandelier.

"Brett tells me you've been renovating your home too," Hope said as she led me into a room off to the right of the foyer.

"We are. Slowly. It's Victorian too, although not nearly as grand as this one."

"This is a lot of house," Hope said. "Much more suited as an inn, I think."

"I'm sure people will love staying here."

We were standing in the middle of a large parlor. Like the foyer, it was furnished with antiques and featured lots of gleaming wood. A beautiful bay window let in plenty of natural light, and a green tiled Victorian fireplace created a feature in the middle of one wall.

I soon discovered that the rest of the rooms in the inn were as beautiful and as tastefully furnished as the parlor. Hope led me through a library—well stocked with books—a dining room, and a small office. The kitchen was at the back of the house with a view of the garden where Brett was still at work. As I'd done with my house, Lonny and Hope had updated the kitchen with modern appliances, but they'd managed to work in several charming features like plank flooring, glass-fronted cabinets, and crown molding.

Also at the back of the house were a conservatory and a second living room. Lonny and Hope intended the latter for their own private use. They'd also added a small powder room as part of their personal quarters. A back stairway provided access to the master suite, but Hope led me to the front staircase to get to the second floor.

All the guest rooms were stunning and luxurious, with four-poster beds and pretty views out every window. When we reached one of the bedrooms at the back of the house, I brushed aside the sheers hanging over one of the windows and took in the sight of the garden stretching out beyond the house.

"We're so pleased with the work Brett has done with the garden," Hope said, crossing the room to stand beside me.

"I know he's enjoying the project. And everything looks beautiful." I recalled something Brett had told me when he'd first accepted the job at the inn. "Your aunt used to own this place, right? Are you from Wildwood Cove originally?"

"I was born in Denver, but I moved here when I was three. My mom wasn't able to look after me so my aunt and uncle raised me. This is the house I grew up in. I've always loved it." She gazed around the room with a smile on her face. "My aunt and uncle ran a bed-and-breakfast together, but once my uncle died my aunt didn't keep the business going much longer. I attended college back east, and then Lonny and I spent a few years overseas. When we came back, my aunt was more than ready to downsize. At first the plan was to help her clean out the house and get it ready to sell, but I didn't want to let the place go. Luckily, Lonny got on board with the idea of running an inn, so we bought the property from my aunt, and here we are."

"You should be proud of all you've done. The place looks amazing."

Hope beamed at the compliment. "Thank you. It's definitely been a labor of love."

My gaze landed on the small cottage at the back of the property, near the forest line. "The cottage is so cute. Are you going to use it for guests?"

"Yes. I'm hoping it'll be popular with honeymooners and such."

"I'm sure it will be." I let the sheer curtains fall back into place and followed Hope out of the room. "Have the police finished with the scene out in the woods?" I asked as we descended the front staircase to the main floor.

"Yes, thank goodness. As of yesterday. They combed the woods and our entire property, though I don't know what more they thought they'd find after so many years. It's been unsettling for us, but it must be far worse for Mrs. Kozani." Hope shuddered as she reached the bottom of the stairs. "It's frightening to think of something so terrible happening so close by, even if it was a long time ago."

"The party took place near here, didn't it?"

"It did." She paused in the foyer. "Will you join me for a glass of lemonade?"

"I'd love to. Thank you."

Hope shifted the conversation back on topic as she led me to the kitchen. "It was supposed to be one last celebration before we all went our separate ways. No one ever guessed it would be the end of life for one of us. Of course, we didn't even know something had happened to Demetra until her mom contacted the police."

"From what I've heard, most people figured she'd started a new life in New York City."

"I was one of those people."

In the kitchen, Hope retrieved a jug of lemonade from the fridge and poured two tall glasses. She handed one to me and suggested we sit out on the back porch. I readily agreed.

"I can't even imagine what Mrs. Kozani must be going through," Hope said once we were sitting comfortably in wicker chairs that matched the ones I'd seen out front. "What she must have gone through for the past ten years."

"It's incredibly sad," I agreed. "Does she still live in Arizona? I heard she moved there before Demetra disappeared."

"I think that's where she's living. She still has a house here in Wildwood Cove, but she doesn't come back very often."

Bentley trotted up the steps to the porch and nuzzled my hand with his nose. I stroked his curly golden fur, and he rested his chin on my knee.

"He's so cute," Hope said with a smile, dispelling some of the melancholy that had settled over us. "And speaking of cute animals, how's the kitten doing? Did you end up keeping him?"

"My friend Lisa took him in." I set my glass of lemonade on a small table and produced my phone so I could show her some pictures of Orion.

We laughed at the more amusing of the photos and chatted about other lighthearted subjects until we'd finished our lemonade. While Hope took the empty glasses inside, I spent a minute or two with Brett before saying goodbye to him.

When Hope returned from the kitchen, she walked with me to my car. "It was nice having you over for a visit, Marley. We should do this again sometime."

"I'd love to come back," I said. "And Brett and I should have you and Lonny over to our place sometime. Maybe once the garden party is over?"

"That sounds great."

I paused by my car, my mind tracing back to the discovery I'd made in the woods during my last visit to the inn. "Quaid Hendrix mentioned that he used to work here as a gardener."

Hope made a face. "That's true, unfortunately."

"You're not a fan?" I guessed.

"Definitely not. Although, maybe I shouldn't be saying that. Are you friends with him?"

"No way. I only met him recently, and he didn't make a good impression."

Hope seemed relieved by my answer. "I always found him creepy, to be honest. I felt like he was leering at me whenever he was around."

"From what I've heard, that was a habit of his. Maybe it still is. He certainly isn't pleasant to spend time with."

"He lived in the cottage while he worked here," Hope said. "I did my best to steer clear of him, but it was a relief when he quit and moved off the property."

A series of lightbulbs lit up in my mind. "Was he living in the cottage ten years ago?"

"He was. And, you know, I can't help but wonder: Did Quaid have something to do with Demetra's death?"

She'd voiced the very same question that was running through my head.

Chapter 15

I was about to climb into my car when Hope shaded her eyes and peered past me down the driveway. I heard the rumble of an approaching vehicle and turned to follow her line of sight. When I spotted a sheriff's department cruiser slowly making its way up the winding driveway, I exchanged a glance with Hope.

"Maybe they're not done with the scene in the woods after all," she said, a trace of apprehension behind her words.

We said nothing further as the cruiser pulled to a stop next to my car. When Deputy Devereaux got out of the vehicle, he removed his hat and left it on the driver's seat.

"Afternoon, Hope, Marley," he said as he made his way around my car to reach us. He knew me from previous investigations, including the one following the death of my cousin Jimmy.

"Afternoon," Hope returned. "Are you heading out into the woods again?"

"No, we're finished out there. It's you I came to see."

The barest hint of surprise showed on Hope's face before it disappeared. "What can I help you with?"

Devereaux presented the same evidence bag I'd seen at the Collins house. "I was wondering if you could identify this."

Hope took the clear plastic bag from him, her eyebrows drawn together. When she noticed the ring in the corner of the bag, she held it up to the sunlight. "I'm not sure I understand why you're asking, but I've never seen this before."

"It was found with Demetra's remains," I said. Then I winced and looked to the deputy. "Should I have kept quiet about that?"

"No, that's fine," Devereaux assured me. "I was about to say that myself."

"I was there when Deputy Rutowski showed it to Chloe," I explained to Hope when she glanced my way.

She took another moment to study the ring, but then handed it back to the deputy with a shake of her head. "It still doesn't look familiar. Do you think it belonged to Demetra, or to her killer?"

"We don't know at this point," Devereaux said.

"I don't know if that ruby is real, but either way, Demetra would have shown it to everyone if it was hers. I don't remember her having any jewelry that nice."

"That's what Chloe said." I turned my attention to Devereaux. "Have you found out yet if the ruby is real?"

"It is. I confirmed that this morning."

"Sorry I couldn't be of more help," Hope said.

"That's no problem," Devereaux assured her. "How about Lonny? Is he around?"

"He went into town for some groceries. Do you want me to call him and ask how much longer he'll be?"

"No need," the deputy said. "I'll show him the ring another time."

"I doubt it'll do much good, though I'm sure he'll be happy to take a look. He knew who Demetra was, but that's about it. I don't think he ever spent any time with her."

"I figured as much," Devereaux said. "Thanks for your time." He returned to his cruiser. "Enjoy the rest of the day," he said to both of us before climbing into the vehicle.

We waved once he'd turned the cruiser around and was heading down the driveway.

"Strange," Hope said after the deputy's car was out of sight.

"About the ring?"

Hope nodded. "I really don't think it was Demetra's. But how likely is it that it would have been buried with her if it belonged to the killer?"

"I guess if it was a loose fit, it's not all that far fetched, especially if there was a struggle of some sort."

"True." We turned our backs on the driveway, staring across the property to the woods.

"So does that mean Demetra was killed by a woman?" Hope asked. "That was definitely a woman's ring."

"It's possible," I said. "Or maybe someone gave that ring to Demetra shortly before she was killed."

Hope's eyes widened. "Someone like Tyrone?"

"Chloe and I were wondering about that the other night."

Hope frowned, her eyes still fixed on the tree line. "I don't know. Tyrone's always had a temper, but he was never violent, as far as I remember. I always thought his bark was far worse than his bite."

"Maybe he was pushed too far."

"It's possible," she conceded.

"How about Chrissy or any of the other girls who were at the party that night? Did any of them own a ring like that?"

"Not that I recall."

"There's an inscription that says 'always,' so Chloe and I thought it might be an engagement or wedding ring."

"Could be, but none of the girls from my class were engaged that summer, at least not that I know of. I don't think any of them got married for at least a couple of years. I was the first to get engaged and married."

"When did that happen?"

Hope smiled, her eyes lighting up with the memory. "New Year's Eve. The one after graduation. We got married six months later."

"I guess you've got an anniversary coming up soon, then."

"We do. I can't believe it's been nine years already." Her smile grew brighter. "I love him even more now than I did back then."

"Sounds like you have an amazing relationship."

"We do. We've had our rough spots, of course, but we worked through them and came out stronger on the other side."

Across the garden, Brett spotted us and waved before grabbing a spade and driving it into the soil.

"How about you and Brett?" Hope asked. "How long have you been together?"

"A year."

"If he makes you smile like that, things must be going well."

I realized she was right—I had a big smile on my face. "I'm very lucky."

"I'm sure he is too."

The sound of another approaching car drew our attention back to the driveway. This time Lonny pulled up next to my car in his dark blue truck.

He raised a hand in greeting and called out through the open window, "Hey, Marley."

I returned the greeting as he got out of the truck.

"You just missed Deputy Devereaux," his wife said.

"Oh? I thought the sheriff's department was done with the scene."

"They are. He wanted to show us a ring that was found with Demetra's remains."

Lonny circled around the hood of the truck. "A ring? How come?"

"They're trying to figure out if it belonged to Demetra or possibly her killer," Hope said.

He retrieved two bags of groceries from the passenger's seat and nudged the door shut. "Did you recognize it?"

"No. I'm pretty sure it didn't belong to Demetra, so maybe it's a clue that will lead the sheriff to the murderer."

"Is it unique enough for that?" Lonny asked as he joined us by my car.

I answered while Hope peeked into one of the grocery bags in her husband's arms. "Probably. It was a gold ring with a small ruby, inscribed with the word 'always.'"

The color drained from Lonny's face.

"Does that sound familiar?" I asked.

"No," he said quickly. "Not at all."

"You'd better get the ice cream in the freezer before it melts," his wife said, still inspecting the contents of the grocery bags. "Did you remember the hot dogs?"

Lonny shifted the bags in his arms and kept his eyes away from mine. "I did. They're in the bottom of the bag. I'll get everything inside now. It was good to see you, Marley." He headed for the house with long strides.

"You too," I called after him.

I said goodbye to Hope and waved to Brett one last time before getting in my car and setting off for home. As I followed the winding driveway toward the road, I couldn't stop thinking about Lonny's reaction. Despite what he'd said, I was convinced he at least knew *something* about the ring.

Chapter 16

My visit with Hope left me with several new questions swirling around in my head—questions about Lonny, the ring, and Quaid Hendrix. As I busied myself with opening The Flip Side for business the next morning, my thoughts hovered around the gardener turned food blogger. The party in the woods had taken place not far from what was now the Wildwood Inn, and I wondered how Chloe and her friends had come and gone from the party spot. Was there a road or trail leading into the woods? Or, had they cut across the mansion's property?

That was something I could ask Chloe. If Demetra had passed by the Victorian on her way home that night, it was possible she'd run into Quaid. And if that had happened, it wasn't inconceivable that the situation could have taken a nasty turn. Maybe Quaid had made a pass at Demetra and she'd brushed him off. It wasn't difficult to imagine him losing his temper, especially if his ego had taken a hit.

But what about Lonny? He'd lied about recognizing the description of the ring—I was sure of that—so what did that mean? He seemed like such a nice guy, and I didn't want to believe he could have had anything to do with Demetra's death, but he was hiding something. I wanted to find out about his connection to the ring, but I wasn't sure how to go about that. Hope hadn't noticed his reaction, and I felt certain she'd told the truth to Deputy Devereaux when she'd said she didn't recognize the piece of jewelry, so I wasn't sure I could get any answers from her. Besides, I wasn't keen on going to her with an accusation that her husband had lied to us.

When the first customers of the day arrived, I tried my best to push thoughts of Lonny and Quaid to the side. I set a plate of Boston cream crêpes in front of a young woman with her nose buried in a fantasy novel and spent a moment chatting with another diner. A short time later, the front door opened and Sienna entered the pancake house. She waved at me, and I crossed the dining area to meet her.

"What brings you by?" I asked.

"I had a bit of time to kill before school so I thought I'd drop in and see if you have a suspect list yet."

"For Demetra's murder?"

"Of course."

"She died long before I moved to town," I reminded her.

"So? Last winter you solved a murder that was way older than this one."

That was true, though I'd had help from Lisa's neighbor. And of course I did have some suspects in mind, but I wasn't bursting to share my thoughts on the matter with the seventeen-year-old. A few months earlier she'd developed a sudden interest in amateur sleuthing, something that had worried me from the start. She'd narrowly missed a run-in with a murderer not long after that, so now I was even more hesitant about stoking her enthusiasm for unofficially investigating crimes.

Sienna must have guessed my thoughts. "Come on, Marley," she pleaded. "I'm just curious. I'm not going to do any snooping."

"Do you promise?" I asked.

"Cross my heart," she said, tracing an X over her chest with her finger.

I was still hesitant, but I'd never been good at resisting when she turned the full force of her pleading brown eyes on me.

I glanced around the pancake house. All of the half dozen early diners were in the midst of eating, and Leigh was making the rounds with the coffeepot, offering refills. Nothing needed my immediate attention.

"Have you had breakfast?" I asked Sienna.

"Just an apple."

"Come on, then."

I didn't miss the smile that lit up Sienna's face as I turned toward the kitchen.

"Hi, guys," she said to Tommy and Ivan as the door swung shut behind us.

"Shouldn't you be at school?" Ivan asked.

"Not yet," Sienna said. "I stopped by to find out what Marley knows about the murder case."

Ivan directed his dark gaze at me.

I held up my hands in surrender. "I'm not encouraging her to get involved." At least, I hoped I wasn't. "She hasn't had much of a breakfast," I said, hoping to distract him.

Fortunately, it seemed to work. Some of the steel disappeared from his eyes, and I could have sworn that he almost smiled as he set to work making a crêpe.

"Are you making what I think you're making?" Sienna asked him, her face hopeful.

Ivan replied with a grunt. I interpreted it as an affirmative response, and so did Sienna.

"Yum," she said, pulling a stool up to the counter and perching on it. She turned her attention to me while the crêpe cooked under Ivan's watchful eye. "So, who are your suspects?"

I started with Tyrone, telling her what I'd learned about him from various sources.

"Ex-boyfriend with a temper." Sienna nodded. "He definitely belongs at the top of the list."

Ivan slid the crêpe onto a plate and added a generous glob of custard to it. Then he folded it and drizzled chocolate sauce over the top before pushing the plate across the counter to Sienna. I fetched a knife and fork for her before pulling up a stool of my own.

Sienna sighed with happiness when she put the first bite into her mouth. "Best. Crêpes. Ever."

Again, I was certain I caught the barest hint of a smile on Ivan's face before he turned away to check on some frying bacon. As gruff as he was, the burly chef had a big heart and a definite soft spot for my youngest employee.

I couldn't stop a smile from spreading across my face as I watched Sienna digging into her breakfast. I loved spending time at The Flip Side with my staff. The pancake house was cozy and charming on its own, but the people were the heart of the place. I couldn't have asked for a better group to work with.

I got my smile under control before anyone noticed me looking goofy. Luckily, Tommy and Ivan were busy preparing orders and Sienna was fully engrossed in her breakfast, savoring every bite.

The Boston cream crêpes were a recent addition to the menu. We had several standard items we offered year-round, but I liked to mix things up a bit by having a few special dishes on the menu for a limited time. Some, like the pumpkin pie crêpes—my personal favorite—were seasonal, while others depended on the results of Ivan's latest experiments.

As soon as Sienna had tried the Boston cream crêpes for the first time, she'd been hooked. I couldn't blame her. I'd indulged in my fair share over the past month. The chocolate sauce and custard made for a heavenly combination.

"Do you have any other suspects?" Sienna asked once she'd had a few more bites.

"Demetra's best friend, Chrissy Mazurek. Apparently they were quite competitive with each other, despite being besties. I think there might have been some jealousy at play."

"Jealousy is a good motive for murder," Sienna said before going in for another bite.

"And then there's Quaid Hendrix."

Ivan's sharp gaze cut my way.

"The judge who got sick last weekend?" Sienna asked.

"That's him," I confirmed.

"What does he have to do with the girl who got killed?" Tommy asked from across the kitchen.

From the way Ivan opened and then shut his mouth, I guessed that he'd been about to voice the same question.

I explained that Quaid had lived in the cottage near the woods where the party had taken place all those years ago. "And he has a reputation for being a sleaze," I added.

"But you don't know for sure that he knew the victim?" Sienna asked.

"No," I admitted. "So maybe he's not the strongest suspect."

"I think you're right to keep an eye on him, though," Tommy said as he unloaded the dishwasher. "On the first day of the cooking competition I saw one of the sheriff's deputies walking along the street. Quaid saw him too and ducked out of sight."

"Are you sure he was trying to avoid the deputy?" I asked.

"Pretty sure."

"Interesting." I mulled over that new information.

The discovery of Demetra's remains might have made Quaid uneasy. Maybe he was afraid the authorities would turn their attention on him, if they hadn't already.

Had he been questioned ten years ago when Demetra was reported missing?

That was another question I couldn't answer.

"You should steer clear of Tyrone *and* Quaid," Ivan warned as he delivered two plates of pancakes and bacon to the pass-through window.

Leigh appeared on the other side of the window, swooping in to fetch the plates before disappearing from sight.

"I'm not going to argue with you there," I said to Ivan. "I've heard too much about Tyrone's temper, and Quaid certainly isn't someone I want to go near if I can help it."

I couldn't bring myself to mention my suspicions about Lonny. Fortunately, Sienna didn't press me for any further suspects.

"Is Quaid going to be judging the finals?" Sienna asked. "Or will you?"

"Quaid will be," I said. "Apparently he recovered quickly from whatever made him sick."

"Oh." Sienna looked disappointed.

"Why do you ask?"

"Ellie was hoping you'd be judging again. Quaid can be mean, and he kind of scares her."

"I'm sure it will be okay," I said. "She got through the first round with him as a judge."

"That's true." Sienna set her knife and fork on her empty plate and slid off her stool with obvious reluctance. "I guess I should go to school now."

"You should," Ivan agreed.

I walked her out and stayed at the front of the restaurant to help Leigh with the customers.

Around midmorning I was jotting down an order for churro waffles and banoffee crêpes—featuring toffee made from dulce de leche, bananas, and whipped cream. As I made a note that both dishes were to have a side of crispy bacon, the front door opened and another customer entered the pancake house. I turned for the kitchen and nearly stopped in my tracks when I saw the newcomer standing by the door, scanning the dining area for a free table.

Somehow I managed to continue on my way to the pass-through window, smiling at the man as I went and telling him to choose whichever free table he wanted. He headed for a small two-seater by the window.

My heart thumped away in my chest like I'd run a mile. Now that I had a chance to get a better look at him, I saw that the man really did resemble the photos of my long-dead father. My eyes hadn't played tricks on me after all.

I grabbed the coffeepot and headed for the man's table. "Good morning," I said with a smile. "How are you today?"

"Good, thanks." His response was somewhat curt, though not quite unfriendly. He glanced at me for a second before returning his attention to the menu he had in front of him.

"Would you like some coffee to start? Or something else to drink?"

"Coffee's good."

"Are you from out of town?" I asked as I filled a mug.

"Mm." His gaze was still fixed on the menu. "Just here for a few days."

"Whereabouts are you from?"

He hesitated briefly before replying. "Back east."

"I'm Marley McKinney, the owner of The Flip Side." I waited, hoping he'd introduce himself.

His gaze flicked my way before returning to the menu once again. "Joe." The name came out as little more than a mumble.

I was hanging on his every word, even as few as they were, but I knew I needed to stop grilling him before I crossed the line from friendly to nosy, if I hadn't already.

"Are you ready to order, or do you need a few more minutes?"

"Bacon cheddar waffles and sausages."

"Coming right up."

On my way to the kitchen, I gathered up some dirty plates from a table where four diners had enjoyed crêpes and coffee before heading out. I tried to contain my disappointment, but I wasn't very successful. The most recent arrival to the pancake house clearly wasn't interested in making conversation, and I hadn't managed to learn much about him. I had a feeling that was intentional. Most people were quite happy to share their name and say where they were from when they came to Wildwood Cove for a visit, but Joe's answers had been vague and reluctant. I wasn't even sure if I believed he'd given me his real name. Maybe he was just a private person, but maybe he had another reason for keeping information about himself under wraps.

Like what? I asked myself. *Because he's your father and faked his death decades ago and doesn't want anyone finding out who he really is?*

Okay, when I thought about it like that, it did seem ridiculous.

But could we be related in some other way? My dad was an only child, but maybe this man was a cousin of his.

Unlikely, but not impossible.

On a whim, I grabbed my phone and surreptitiously snapped a photo of the man, just in case it would come in handy later. Maybe with a picture to compare with the ones of my dad, I'd feel more comfortable talking to Brett about Joe.

I didn't try questioning the man further when I delivered his meal to him, but I couldn't stop myself from glancing his way every so often. He didn't spend long over his breakfast, and when he got up and headed for the counter to pay, I made sure I was the one there to meet him.

"How was everything?" I asked him as he dug his wallet out of his pocket.

"Good, thanks."

I had to smother a flicker of disappointment when he handed over cash to pay for his meal. If he'd used a credit card, I at least could have found out his surname and confirmed his first name. I didn't let my disappointment show.

"I hope you enjoy the rest of your time in Wildwood Cove."

He acknowledged that with a nod and was out the door seconds later. I stared after him, frustrated that I'd learned next to nothing about the mystery man—and even more frustrated that I couldn't get him out of my mind.

Chapter 17

After I'd finished work for the day and had gone for a run with Bentley, I set to work making a batch of lentil curry. Once I had all the ingredients in the pot and the curry was simmering away, I gave in to the temptation that had been gnawing away at me all afternoon. I retrieved the photo album I'd had out the other day and settled on the couch with it. Unfortunately, comparing the photos of my dad with the one I'd taken of Joe didn't help to settle my mind.

Nothing had changed since the last time I'd looked through the album. The picture I'd taken with my phone wasn't of great quality, but when I studied it, Joe—if that was really his name—still resembled my father and I hadn't managed to rid myself of the suspicion that there could be a family connection.

When I'd gone through the entire album again, I set it on the coffee table and grabbed my laptop. I didn't know a whole lot about my dad's side of the family. His parents hadn't approved of his relationship with my mom. They'd wanted him to marry a Catholic girl, and my mom wasn't religious. Then my mom ended up pregnant with me before she and my dad were married, and that had only displeased my paternal grandparents all the more.

After my dad died they'd wanted even less to do with my mom than they had when he was alive. They met me once, shortly after I was born, but then they moved across the country and my mom never saw them again. She'd sent them Christmas cards each year, and they did the same in return, but that was the extent of their relationship.

I knew my dad was an only child, but I didn't know much else about his family, other than the fact that his grandparents had immigrated to this country from Ireland.

Now I was hoping I could find out more about his family tree. *Our* family tree.

I signed up for a free trial on a genealogy website and spent some time poking around, getting up now and then to check on the curry. I managed to track down my dad and his parents on the site, and I followed the branches out from there. A short time later, I shifted my laptop to the coffee table, frustration buzzing through me.

Getting up from the couch, I checked the time and gave the curry another stir. Brett would probably be home soon. While I waited, I wandered out onto the back porch, leaving the French doors open behind me. Bentley took advantage of the freedom, rushing down the porch steps and bounding across the yard and back before busying himself with a serious sniffing study of all the logs at the top of the beach.

Flapjack was more sedate about emerging from the house. He padded out through the open doors and stopped for a languid stretch. Then he jumped up onto the porch railing and wandered along it until he reached the spot where I was leaning against it. He bumped his furry cheek against my arm and sat down. I ran a hand over his fur, and his eyes closed to mere slits as he purred with happiness.

"I know it's silly, Jack, but I wish I could find a connection between Joe and my dad. I was thinking he could be a cousin, but from what I can tell, my dad only had female cousins."

Flapjack gave his tail a swish and turned his head to look out over the beach. Below us, Bentley found a suitable spot to lift his leg and then came trotting back up to the porch to flop at my feet.

"I'm wasting my time thinking about this, aren't I? I'm not even sure why I'm so hung up on it."

Flapjack looked my way and then slowly closed his eyes as his tail swished again. I buried my face in his fur, his purr rumbling in my ear. Bentley whined, jealous of the attention I was giving the tabby.

I could have called my mom and told her about Joe, but I didn't want to dredge up the past for her. She'd recently married her new husband, Grant, and I didn't want to spoil her happiness.

"How about some dinner?" I said to the animals, deciding to focus on something else, at least for a while.

Bentley jumped up and ran into the house ahead of me. I left the doors open, and Flapjack came inside when he heard the spoon clink against his dinner dish. A moment later he was tucking into his food in the laundry room while Bentley dug into his dinner in the kitchen. Brett arrived home a minute or two later, and I hoped his presence would distract me from all the thoughts crowding my mind.

After we'd finished our dinner of lentil curry, Brett cleaned up the kitchen while I fetched fabric samples from my tote bag and sat down at the table to study them.

"What are those for?" Brett asked as he loaded the dirty dishes into the dishwasher.

"The settee and chairs in the living room. I was hoping we could get them reupholstered before long."

"Seeing anything that catches your eye?" he asked a few minutes later.

By then I'd flipped through all the samples. "I've narrowed it down to three that I like."

Brett finished wiping down the counter and crossed the kitchen to join me by the table. I set out my top choices for him to see. There was a damask fabric in pale and dark gray that I thought was classy and sophisticated, a shiny teal one with a pattern of curlicues in a darker shade of teal, and a bold one with a geometric design in black and white.

"Which one do you like?" I asked as he looked over my shoulder at the samples.

"All of them."

"Really?"

"Sure."

"That's not very helpful."

He pulled his phone from his pocket and dropped into an armchair. "You like all three of them too."

"Which is why I was hoping you'd help me narrow it down."

He tapped at his phone. "Close your eyes and point at one."

The frustration that had hounded me earlier crept its way back under my skin. I shoved the fabric samples off to the side and left the table.

"What are you doing?" I asked Brett as I dropped down on the couch.

"Checking my email." He glanced up from his phone. After a couple more taps at the screen, he set the device down on the coffee table. "Want to tell me what's on your mind?"

I slouched back against the couch cushions. "Fabric samples."

"Aside from that. You're not usually so easily frustrated."

My gaze drifted to the closed photo album I'd left on the coffee table. I was about to tell him about Joe when the doorbell rang.

Bentley had been snoozing on the family room rug, but he was on his feet in a split second and charging toward the front door, barking as he went. Brett followed after him, and I pushed myself up off the couch to trail behind them. By the time I reached the foyer, Brett had already opened the door and let his sister in.

"We've already eaten if you're hoping for free food," he said.

Chloe glared at him. "I'm not here to mooch."

"Why else would you be here?"

Chloe punched him in the arm, and my frustration drained away as a smile tugged at my mouth.

"Be nice," I told Brett before turning my attention to Chloe. "What's up?"

"I'm lonely." She made a face. "Does that sound pathetic?"

"Of course not," I replied.

"Yes," Brett said at the same time.

This time I swatted his arm. "Stop being such a—"

"Big brother?" Chloe interrupted. "He can't. It's an incurable condition."

I tucked my arm through hers and led her toward the back of the house before Brett had a chance to come up with a retort.

"How come you're lonely?" I asked.

"I can't stop thinking about Demetra, and doing that on my own makes me feel sad and blah."

"Have you heard any news about the case?"

"Not today. Have you?"

"No. But I did learn something the other day." I headed for the fridge. "Do you want something to drink?"

Chloe peeked over my shoulder at the fridge's contents. "Sweet tea, please."

I grabbed the jug and shut the fridge. "Chrissy didn't recognize the ring."

"How did you find that out?" Brett asked.

"That dress I bought? It's from her store." I poured sweet tea into a glass and handed it to Chloe. I held up the jug and glanced Brett's way, but he shook his head. I poured a glass for myself and returned the iced tea to the fridge. "I overheard her talking about the ring when I came out of the changing room."

"Ooh, a new dress," Chloe said with interest. "Can I see it?"

"Sure." Leaving my glass on the kitchen counter, I found the shopping bag I'd left on a chair and pulled out the green dress.

"Wow." Chloe fingered the fabric. "It's gorgeous. Are you going to wear it to the garden party?"

"That's what I was thinking."

"You definitely should."

"I second that," Brett said.

Smiling, I carefully returned the garment to the bag, making a mental note to hang it up in my closet later. I grabbed my glass of iced tea, and the three of us wandered into the family room.

"Do you want us to talk about anything other than Demetra?" I asked.

"I don't mind talking about her." Chloe sank into the armchair Brett had occupied earlier. "I just don't like thinking about her death over and over when I'm by myself." She tucked her legs beneath her. "So, Chrissy didn't recognize the ring."

"Nope." I sat down on the couch.

"So it probably wasn't Demetra's." Brett sat next to me and rested an arm along the back of the couch.

"That sounds most likely to me." Chloe took a sip of her iced tea. "Maybe it belonged to her killer?"

"That's a theory most people seem to be gravitating toward," I said.

"It's a woman's ring. So the murderer is a woman?"

"Could be."

Lonny's reaction to hearing about the ring replayed in my head. I was hesitant to bring his name into the discussion. I liked him and Hope, and I didn't want to believe that he could have harmed Demetra. But I couldn't ignore what I'd seen on his face.

"How did you and the others get to and from the party that night?" I asked Chloe. "Did you cut across the inn's property or go another way?"

"Most of us went in by the road."

"There's a narrow dirt road that follows the river through the woods," Brett explained. "It dead-ends not far from where we found Demetra's skeleton."

"And you left the same way?" I directed the question at Chloe.

"I didn't, but I'm sure lots of people did. I didn't want to walk through the woods by myself so I cut across the inn's land. I knew Hope's aunt wouldn't mind. It was still creepy walking alone in the dark, but not as bad as going through the forest. I followed the driveway down to the road and kept walking from there."

"You should have called for a ride," Brett said.

"I was upset. I didn't want to talk to anybody at the time."

"It was after dark, and there was a killer wandering around. Walking by yourself wasn't smart."

"I didn't know there was a killer!" Chloe glared at her brother. "And this was all ten years ago. Why are you being a jerk?"

Brett opened his mouth to respond, but I beat him to it.

"He doesn't like to think about you being in danger." I nudged him in the chest. "Right?"

He didn't come out and admit it, but he also didn't deny it, and the tension in his jaw and shoulders eased slightly.

Chloe's shoulders dropped too, and the annoyance faded from her expression. "To be honest, I don't like to think about what might have happened if I'd gone through the woods. Maybe Demetra's murder was targeted, but maybe it wasn't." She stared down into the remains of her iced tea. "Anyway, I made it home safely."

"Did you see anything along the way?" I asked. "Was there anyone else out and about, or did you hear any noises?"

"I don't think so. I remember it being a pretty lonely walk." She was about to take a sip of her drink when she stopped. "There were lights on in Hope's house. I remember that. Light was spilling out the windows, and it helped me to see where I was going."

"But you didn't see anyone?" I asked, wondering if Quaid could have been lurking about that night.

"No."

"What about at the gardener's cottage?"

Chloe drummed her fingers against the side of her glass as she thought about that. "The lights were on there too, I think. It's hard to say for sure, though. It was such a long time ago. But I didn't see anyone, I remember that much for certain."

"Was Quaid the gardener back then?" Brett asked.

"He was," I replied.

Chloe made a face. "I can't stand that guy. Do you think he could be the killer?"

"I think it's a possibility," I said.

"But what about the ring?" Brett asked.

I shrugged. "Maybe he'd bought it for a woman in his life and hadn't given it to her yet? I don't know, but he's definitely a suspect in my mind."

"I walked right past his cottage that night. If he is the killer..." Chloe shuddered.

Brett frowned at that thought.

"What about Lonny?" I decided not to skirt the issue any longer.

Brett's gaze shifted from his sister to me. "What about him?"

"Was he at the party that night?"

"No," Chloe said. "He was invited, even though he wasn't part of our graduating class, but he had to work early the next morning. He and Hope had been in town earlier, so they picked me up and Lonny drove us into the woods and dropped us off."

So he was in the vicinity of the party at one point that night.

My heart sank. No matter how much I liked him and his wife, it seemed liked Lonny deserved a place on my list of suspects.

Chapter 18

"Do you know where Lonny went after he dropped you off in the woods?" I asked, hoping I could find an easy way to eliminate him from my pool of suspects.

"Home. He wanted to go to bed because he had to be up early."

"Are you sure he went home?"

A crease appeared across Chloe's forehead. "That's where he said he was going. Why?" Her eyes widened. "No way! You can't be thinking Lonny is the killer."

"I don't want him to be."

"Why would you even suspect him?" Brett asked. "Did he know Demetra at all?" He directed that last question at his sister.

"He knew who she was," Chloe replied, "but I don't know if they ever had anything to do with each other."

They both looked to me, so I told them about Lonny's reaction to hearing about the ring.

"Are you sure that's what he was reacting to?" Chloe asked. "Maybe it was something else. Maybe he wasn't feeling well."

"I could be mistaken," I said, although I didn't really believe that I was.

Chloe had a tight grip on her empty glass. "You must be. Lonny wouldn't hurt anyone. And why would he recognize the ring, anyway? It's a woman's ring."

"It was for Hope," Brett said.

Chloe and I looked at him.

"Didn't they get married pretty soon after you and Hope graduated?" he asked Chloe.

"About a year later," she confirmed.

"So he was carrying the ring around, planning to propose to her, waiting for the right moment." He shrugged when Chloe and I didn't say anything. "It's possible."

"It is," I agreed.

"But he didn't propose to her until around Christmastime," Chloe said.

I remembered what Hope had told me the day before. "New Year's Eve."

"Because he lost the ring," Brett said. "He probably had to save up to buy another one."

It made sense, unfortunately.

Chloe shook her head. "No. I don't want to believe it."

I didn't either and said as much.

Brett shifted his arm from the back of the couch to rest across my shoulders. "What about a motive?"

Chloe perked up. "Exactly. He hasn't got one." She sent an apprehensive glance my way. "Right?"

"I don't know of any."

She visibly relaxed. "I'm sure it wasn't Lonny."

"I hope you're right." I decided to shift the conversation slightly. "When I was at Chrissy's store and overheard her talking about the ring, Amy Strudwick was there too."

"Is she the photographer?" Brett asked.

Chloe drained the last of her iced tea. "Yep. She has a studio in Port Townsend now."

"Was Amy at the party?" I asked.

"No. And she never had much to do with Demetra. She hung out with the artsy people like the Olafson twins, and I don't think Demetra was very nice to her in middle school. Not that Demetra was nice to anyone, but there were a few people she picked on in particular, me and Amy being among them." She pressed her lips together. "Although…"

"Although?" I prodded.

Chloe took a second before responding. "Amy did help out Demetra with her modeling portfolio senior year. Demetra wanted some pictures to take with her when she went to New York, and Amy was already a good photographer back then. It surprised me at the time that Amy was willing to help her out, but I guess Demetra must have paid her. Amy's family didn't have much money and she wanted to go to a photography school, so I guess getting paid might have made it worthwhile to her."

I thought over that information, but I still couldn't move any pieces together in the puzzle of Demetra's murder.

Brett squeezed my shoulder. "I can see the gears moving in your head."

"It's not doing much good," I said.

Chloe got up from her seat. "I know what you mean. I've been over it a thousand times in my mind, but I don't seem to get any closer to figuring it out. It doesn't help that it happened so long ago. The only reason I remember anything is because we were questioned about it a few weeks after the party."

"Hopefully Ray and his deputies know more than we do," Brett said.

"That's probably the case." I got up and took Chloe's glass into the kitchen with my own, setting them in the sink.

Chloe paused by the kitchen table. "What are these fabric samples for?"

I told her about my plans for the furniture in the front living room. "These are my top three favorites." I spread out the gray, teal, and black-and-white ones.

"They're all gorgeous," Chloe said. "But I'd go with either the gray or the teal. They're more welcoming than the black and white. I think that one's a little too modern."

Brett joined us by the table. "How can fabric be welcoming?"

Chloe rolled her eyes. Brett grinned and headed for the fridge.

"I think you're right." I moved the black-and-white sample off to the side. "Thanks. That narrows it down, at least."

Chloe was ready to head out, so I walked with her to the foyer while Brett popped open a can of soda in the kitchen. Bentley trotted along the hall with us, and when we reached the foyer Chloe crouched down to give him some attention. His tail wagged with pure happiness, and he gave her a sloppy kiss on the cheek.

She laughed and wiped her face with her sleeve as she straightened up. "No Flapjack?" she asked me.

"I think he's asleep upstairs somewhere."

"Give him a kiss from me?"

"I will."

Brett had joined us in the foyer by then. He walked Chloe out to her car while Bentley trotted across the dark yard to sniff at the bushes near the fence. I waved to Chloe and retreated to the back of the house. When Brett returned, I was standing by the kitchen table, staring at the teal and gray fabric samples again.

He stopped behind me and wrapped his arms around my waist. "Still can't decide?"

"Nope."

He tapped the teal one. "This one. It's more you."

"But is it more *us*?"

"Definitely."

I smiled. "Okay. Teal it is." I leaned back and relaxed against him.

"Want to tell me what was on your mind earlier?" he asked.

I rested my hands over his, hesitant to share. "It's silly."

"But it was bothering you."

"It was," I agreed, "but I don't even know why. It doesn't make sense."

He kissed the top of my head. "Maybe I can help you make sense of it."

I stepped out of his arms and took his hand, tugging him toward the couch. "Okay. You'll probably think I'm crazy, but there's this man...."

"Should I be worried?" he asked when I trailed off.

He sounded more amused than anything, but I stopped and put my hands to his face anyway. "As if."

That got a grin out of him.

I sank down onto the couch and picked up the photo album from the coffee table. "I'll show you."

He sat down next to me as I flipped open the album and pointed to a portrait of my father. "That's my dad."

"Okay."

I grabbed my phone from the coffee table and brought up the picture I'd taken at the pancake house that morning. "And I've seen this man in town a couple of times now."

Brett took the phone out of my hand and studied the picture. "Okay... I'm not seeing the connection."

"You don't think they look alike?"

Brett cast a sidelong glance my way before returning his attention to the photos. He studied one, then the other. "I guess if you ignore the age difference, they look fairly similar." He turned his eyes to me. "Hold on. Are you saying they're the same person? Because didn't your dad die before you were born?"

"He did."

I could feel his eyes on me during the beat of silence that followed.

"Are you trying to tell me you think your dad is back from the dead?"

I couldn't blame him for sounding so incredulous.

"No," I said. "Well, okay, part of me did wonder at first if it was possible that my dad was still alive, but I know that's crazy. My mom wasn't there with him when he died, but she went to his funeral and saw his body. Besides, why would he or anyone else have faked his death, right?"

"It might be a plausible scenario if we were living in a soap opera."

"I know. It's unrealistic. I can accept that now. But I can't ignore the fact that there's a definite resemblance. And I can't help but wonder if this Joe guy is related to me in some way."

Brett studied the photos again. "An uncle, maybe?"

"My dad was an only child, and I can't find anyone on my family tree that fits."

Brett shut the album and set it on the coffee table along with my phone. "Then it's just a coincidence that he looks like your dad." He rested an arm across my shoulders. "It happens sometimes. People who are completely unrelated look like they could be siblings."

"I know." I let out a heavy sigh and leaned against him.

"But you want him to be a relative."

I shouldn't have been surprised that he could read me like that. "It's silly, but in a way I do."

"Why? You don't know anything about him."

I had to think about my answer for a moment. "It doesn't have anything to do with *him*, exactly. I guess I just..." I had to take another second to sort out my thoughts. "I don't have much family left. Aside from some really distant relatives I've never met, it's just me and my mom now. I guess part of me wishes I had more family. And I wish everyone I loved who's already gone could meet you, could see how happy you make me."

Brett put two fingers to my chin and turned my head so he could kiss me. "I wish I could have met them too. And I know you've lost a lot of loved ones, but I don't want you to feel like you're short on family. I want you to feel like my family is yours too."

"Really?" I blinked back tears.

"Really." He pulled me closer and rested his chin on the top of my head.

"I'm well on my way to that," I said. "Chloe is one of my closest friends, and your parents are great." I glanced over at the photo album. "I'm not sure I can stop thinking about this Joe guy, though."

"If you want to know for sure if he's related to you, then why don't you ask him if that's a possibility? Or at least get his full name."

"That's another thing. He was reluctant to share any information about himself. I'm not even convinced that Joe is his real name. I don't think he really wanted to talk to me at all."

"Ah," Brett said.

I tipped my head back to look at him. "What?"

"You think he's hiding something."

"That's the feeling I got."

"And little did he know that by holding back on you he'd make you want to know about him all the more."

I didn't have to see his face to know he was smiling.

"I can't help that I'm curious by nature."

I felt more than heard his short rumble of laughter. "No, you can't. Curiosity. That's *your* incurable condition."

I smiled. "I can't argue with that diagnosis."

Brett got up and pulled me to my feet. "That man doesn't know what he's in for. But why don't we forget about him for tonight?"

"I can try, but I'm not sure if I'll be able to shut my mind off."

He tugged me closer and gave me a kiss that almost sent me floating away.

"Did that help?" he asked once the kiss was over, a grin tugging at one corner of his mouth.

"Mmm." I slipped my arms around him. "Only a little. I might need more of that kind of help."

His grin widened. "That's definitely not a problem."

Chapter 19

While I didn't exactly forget about the mysterious man Joe, I did manage to push thoughts of him to the back of my mind for the next couple of days. He hadn't returned to the pancake house, and I hadn't run into him around town. One of the few things he'd told me was that he was only in Wildwood Cove for a short time, so I knew there was a good chance he was already long gone. While it bugged me that I'd likely never know anything more about him, there wasn't anything I could do about it, so I tried to focus on other things.

That wasn't too difficult, considering that Demetra's murder remained unsolved. I wasn't keen on questioning Quaid since I couldn't stand the guy and didn't want to get him mad at me if he was indeed capable of murder. But I was also hesitant to approach Lonny in an attempt to get more information out of him. I wasn't entirely sure if that was because I liked him and didn't want to upset him or if I was worried I'd find out something I'd rather not know.

By the time I finished work on Friday afternoon, I hadn't taken any further steps to add new names to my suspect list or to strike off any of the current ones. I was frustrated with myself for that lack of progress, so I knew I needed to come up with some sort of plan to move forward. Based on the lack of news flying around town over the past couple of days, it seemed like the official investigation hadn't moved forward either. Hopefully that wasn't really true, but in case it was, I wanted more than ever to dig around and see if I could find out anything helpful.

With Bentley and Flapjack out in the yard with me, I headed for the detached workshop and fetched a spade that had come with the property when I'd inherited it. After arriving home, I'd changed into my oldest pair of jeans and my green "Raise a little kale!" graphic tee. Appropriate gardening wear, I thought. I'd been waiting months for a chance to start my own garden in the raised beds my cousin Jimmy had constructed out front of the house. Now that we were enjoying some pleasant spring weather, I could finally get to work. Maybe gardening would clear my head.

I decided to start by turning the soil, so I climbed up on the edge of the first raised bed and balanced there while I drove the spade into the dirt. It didn't go in as easily as I expected, giving my arms a jolt. I stepped up on the edge of the blade and used my body weight to sink it deeper into the soil. That got it all the way in, so I hopped off the spade and turned the clump of dirt. I did that a few more times and then stopped for a rest.

I'd never been super strong, but I also wasn't a complete weakling, so I hadn't expected the job to be so difficult. The spade seemed to be the problem more than the dirt. It was a heavy, cumbersome tool. I left it stuck in the soil and returned to the workshop, searching every corner for a smaller, lighter spade. I was already pretty sure there wasn't one, but I checked just in case I'd missed something all the previous times I'd been in the small building. Unfortunately, another spade hadn't magically appeared for me to find, so I was stuck working with the one I already had.

I wandered back out into the yard and wrestled with the spade for a few more minutes before I needed another rest. At this rate it was going to take me all spring to get the four beds ready for planting. And my mind hadn't exactly cleared during my struggles.

As I brushed my hair out of my face, getting ready to attack the soil once more, I heard someone call my name. When I turned around, I saw Sienna and Patricia at the top of the beach, heading my way. Without a shred of reluctance, I abandoned the spade and hopped down from the edge of the raised bed.

"It's a nice day for gardening," Patricia commented when they drew closer.

"That's for sure," I said. "I'm not getting anywhere very fast, though."

"At least you've started. I need to get busy on my hanging baskets. Normally I'd have them all done by now, but those weeks of rain set me back."

"That's probably true for everyone," I said. "I need to get some hanging baskets for The Flip Side, but I'll probably buy them at a nursery. My hands will be full enough with this garden."

"What are you going to plant?" Sienna asked.

"Tomatoes, carrots, beans, maybe some squash."

She looked at my T-shirt. "And kale?"

"Definitely kale," I said with a smile.

"If only I could get Sienna to eat kale," Patricia said.

Her daughter made a face. "Not a chance."

"She's not a big fan of leafy greens," Patricia explained.

"You prefer Boston cream crêpes, right?" I said to the teen.

"Always and forever."

Bentley appeared from around the side of the house, racing over to see our visitors.

"What brings the two of you by?" I asked as Sienna knelt down to give Bentley's fur a good rub.

"We're heading into town for some pizza," Patricia said. "We've got several guests arriving tomorrow, so I figured it would be good to enjoy some downtime tonight."

"Sounds like a good plan." My thoughts returned to Joe the mystery man. "Did you have any guests at the B&B earlier this week?"

"A retired couple from Utah. They left yesterday. We've got quite a few bookings for the weeks ahead, though. The low season is winding down."

"I'm looking forward to the tourist season," I said. "It's definitely good for business."

"That it is," Patricia agreed.

Sienna got to her feet and brushed off her jeans. "Want to come out for pizza with us?"

I rested a hand on Bentley's head as he sat down by my feet. "Thanks, but maybe another time. I'm waiting for Brett to get home. Although, pizza sounds good, so who knows, maybe we'll see you there later."

"We'll keep an eye out for you," Patricia said. "Enjoy your gardening."

"I'll try," I said, eyeing the spade.

Patricia and Sienna returned to the beach and headed in the direction of town. Bentley tried to follow after them, so I whistled to him and he came running back. I threw a tennis ball for him, not overly eager to get back to fighting with the spade.

I knew from Patricia's answer to my question about the B&B that the mystery man hadn't stayed there during his visit to Wildwood Cove. The Wildwood Inn wasn't open for business yet, but there was another bed-and-breakfast in town—away from the water—and there was a motel beyond the marina and across the river. The man struck me more as a motel kind of guy than a B&B guest, but of course I couldn't say for sure.

Let it go, I advised myself. *Forget about him.*

I grabbed the spade and got back to work. By the time I had half the soil in one of the beds turned, my arms ached and I was more than ready to give up. Brett's work van turned into the driveway, so I abandoned the spade and held on to Bentley's collar so he wouldn't run out in front of the vehicle.

Once Brett had parked, I let go of Bentley and he charged across the yard. He was there, wiggling with happiness, when Brett climbed out of the van. Brett laughed and crouched down to shower the dog with attention.

"Hey, buddy. It's nice to be greeted so enthusiastically."

"I might not move as fast as Bentley," I said as I approached Brett, "but I'm no less enthusiastic to see you."

As soon as Bentley gave me a chance, I moved in to give Brett a kiss. It lasted until Bentley whined and nosed his way between us, his tail still wagging furiously.

"I should come home several times a day if this is the welcome I get," Brett said, giving Bentley a pat on the head.

"I don't think either of us would complain if you did that," I said with a smile.

Brett put an arm around my waist and pulled me close to his side, his gaze sweeping across the yard and coming to rest on the spade stuck into the soil. "I see you started working on the garden."

I leaned into him. "Yes, but it's slow going. The spade weighs a ton. I've hardly made any progress, and my arms are already aching."

He ran a hand up and down my arm. "I've got a smaller one in my van that you can use. And I'll help you out this weekend. We should get some manure or compost mixed into the soil."

Flapjack had been snoozing in a sunny patch on the front porch, but then he got up and lazily made his way over to us. Brett scooped him up off the ground, and the tabby snuggled against his chest, purring.

"He probably wants his dinner," I said.

"Is that it?" Brett asked the cat.

Flapjack bumped his head against Brett's chin, still purring.

I gave the tabby a scratch on the head. "I think that's a yes." My stomach grumbled. "And I feel the same."

"Me too," Brett said.

We made our way around the house to the back door, Flapjack still in Brett's arms and Bentley dashing ahead of us to take the lead.

"Patricia and Sienna stopped by a while ago," I said when we reached the back porch. "They were on their way to get pizza."

"The perfect Friday night dinner," Brett said.

"My thought exactly. Want to go to Pete's?"

Pete's was the only pizzeria in Wildwood Cove.

"Definitely. I just need to get cleaned up first."

"Same."

While Brett headed upstairs for a quick shower, I fed the animals and then changed out of my gardening clothes. We drove into town in Brett's truck and found a parking spot near the pizzeria. It was Friday night, so I wasn't surprised that the restaurant was packed. The patrons ranged from families with young kids to groups of teenagers, with a few older couples as well. All the booths and tables were occupied, but as Brett and I waited, Patricia and Sienna left their booth and came over to chat with us on their way out of the pizza parlor. By the time they left a minute or two later, one of the servers had cleaned the booth and waved us over.

I settled onto one of the red vinyl benches and didn't bother to look at the menu. Neither did Brett. I ordered a mini vegetarian pizza and ginger ale, while Brett ordered a pepperoni one and Pepsi. Our waitress hurried off to the kitchen with our order, her dark brown ponytail swinging.

"Lonny and Hope are here," Brett said, tipping his head toward a booth on the other side of the restaurant.

I swiveled in my seat to get a look. The inn owners couldn't see us easily from where they were sitting, so I didn't bother waving. They had drinks but no food in front of them, so I figured they probably hadn't arrived too long before us.

"Maybe we'll get a chance to talk to them later," I said.

I didn't mention that I wanted to question Lonny about the ring. I wasn't sure Brett would like that idea, especially since Lonny was one of his clients.

The waitress arrived with our drinks, and we shifted our conversation to Brett's work at the Wildwood Inn and other topics. Before long, our pizzas arrived, piping hot and delicious. I ate until I was full and then sat back and relaxed while Brett finished the rest of my pizza, having already polished off his own.

After we'd paid for our meals, we headed out of the pizzeria. The booth Lonny and Hope had occupied was now vacant, a server busy gathering up the dirty dishes. I worried we'd missed our chance to talk to the couple, but once we got outside I was relieved to see them on the sidewalk, heading for Lonny's truck.

"Hope!" I called out to get their attention.

When she turned and saw me and Brett, she smiled and waved. Lonny had been about to circle around his truck to the driver's side, but he backtracked to stand next to his wife.

"Were you at Pete's?" Hope asked when Brett and I reached them.

"Along with about half of Wildwood Cove," Brett said with a grin.

Hope smiled in return. "It was packed in there, wasn't it? It usually is on a Friday night."

"Have you heard any more news about the investigation?" I asked.

She and Lonny shook their heads.

"Have you?" Hope asked.

"No," I replied. "But I was hoping to ask you something, Lonny."

His eyebrows pulled together in confusion. "About the investigation? I don't really know much about it."

"But you know *something*," I said. I plowed ahead before I could have second thoughts. "You know about the ring that was found with Demetra's skeleton. You know who it belongs to."

Chapter 20

The color drained from Lonny's face for the second time that week. "I don't know what you're talking about." The fear in his eyes said otherwise.

Hope was the one looking confused now. "How could he know anything about the ring? He's never even seen it."

I could feel Brett's gaze on me, but I didn't look his way. I was afraid I might see disapproval on his face.

"Maybe not recently," I said. "But he recognized the description of it."

"How is that even possible?" Hope was clearly on the verge of getting annoyed. "It was a woman's ring." She took Lonny's left hand in her own and held it up so we could see his gold wedding band. "And this is the only ring Lonny's ever worn. Right, Lonny?"

He nodded, but didn't say anything. His face was still pale, and his expression resembled that of a deer caught in headlights.

Hope's confusion returned as she studied her husband's face. "Lonny?" She no longer sounded so sure of herself.

Lonny cleared his throat. He slipped his hand out of Hope's and ran it over his hair.

I finally glanced Brett's way. He was watching Lonny, his expression puzzled but also concerned.

"What is it, Lonny?" Brett asked. "What do you know?"

Lonny shook his head as we all watched him. "I didn't hurt Demetra. I swear."

"Of course you didn't," Hope said with conviction. Her confidence appeared to slip and her voice wavered when she added, "What's going on?"

Lonny rubbed the back of his neck and looked around as if to make sure no one else was within earshot. Aside from three teenagers hanging out at the far end of the street, no one else was out on the sidewalk with us.

"The ring that was found with Demetra," he said finally, "it sounds like my grandmother's ring."

"I don't understand," Hope said. "How could Demetra have ended up with your grandmother's ring?"

I felt sorry for her. She looked so confused. Maybe even a bit lost and scared.

"I don't know for sure," her husband replied. "But I think she must have stolen it."

Hope's confusion remained in place. "From your parents' house?"

Lonny shook his head again. "From me." He took Hope's hand. "After you graduated, I wanted to propose. My mom gave me my grandma's ring to give to you. I carried it around for days, waiting for the right moment to pop the question. And then one day it was…gone."

"But you didn't propose until New Year's Eve."

I could tell Hope was having trouble processing everything. She held tightly to Lonny's hand, her eyes dazed.

"That's because I lost the ring. Or at least I thought I'd lost it. I had to save some money before I could buy a new one. I thought my mom would kill me, since it was a family heirloom. But she didn't get mad like I thought she would. She said my grandma's marriage wasn't exactly a happy one, so maybe it was best that I wasn't giving you her wedding ring."

Brett spoke for the first time in several minutes. "Are you sure it was Demetra who stole it? Maybe it was the killer instead."

"Maybe…" Lonny didn't sound convinced.

Hope seemed to be overcoming her shock. "It wouldn't have been out of character for Demetra to steal it. Those of us who knew her suspected her of stealing other things over the years. Cash, costume jewelry, even candy of all things."

"But did she have an opportunity to steal it?" I asked.

Hope looked to her husband. "You were hardly ever around her."

"Hardly ever," he agreed. "But there was that one time."

"What time?" I pressed.

"I was leaving your place one night," he said to Hope. "Our place now. Demetra asked for a ride home. It was after dark, so I wasn't about to say no and leave her to walk alone."

"What was she doing there?" Hope asked.

"She'd come from the gardener's cottage and caught up to me in the driveway as I was getting into my truck."

"The gardener's cottage?" Hope echoed with confusion. "Why would she have been there?"

"I'd seen her there before," Lonny said. "I'm pretty sure she had a thing going on with the gardener."

"As in Quaid Hendrix?" I asked.

"I think that was his name."

Hope nodded. "Quaid was living there at the time." She addressed her husband again. "You never said anything about that before."

"I figured it wasn't any of my business. She was eighteen by then."

"But if their fling was going on for more than a few days before the party, she had a boyfriend at the time," Hope pointed out. "Tyrone."

Lonny shrugged. "I didn't know if they were still together or not. And, like I said, I figured it wasn't any of my business."

"But if Quaid knew Demetra," I said, "and they were involved romantically... Sheriff Georgeson should know that."

Lonny looked uncomfortable, but he didn't have a chance to say anything in response.

"How come you never mentioned giving Demetra a ride?" Hope asked.

Lonny shifted his weight. "I didn't want to upset you."

"Why would I have been upset?"

"Because Demetra...uh...she sort of came on to me."

Hope let out a sigh. "Of course she did."

"I didn't reciprocate," Lonny said quickly. "I shut her down right away."

Hope put a hand on his arm. "I wasn't thinking any differently, not for a second. But I'm surprised Demetra didn't tell me about it, with some embellishment about how you were into it. That was her style."

"Maybe she didn't get around to it before she died," Brett said. "If that was right around the time of the party."

We all looked at Lonny.

"I don't remember exactly when it was, but it was somewhere around that time."

"So you had the ring on you when you gave her a ride?" I checked.

"Probably? Like I said, I can't remember exactly when I gave her a ride, but it was a warm night so there's a good chance it was after Hope and Demetra's graduation." He glanced at Hope. "She was...ah...kind of all over me at one point, so it's definitely possible that she took the ring out of my pocket."

Hope didn't look pleased, but she kept quiet.

"And I'm not positive," Lonny continued, "but it could have been that night that I realized it was gone. I know I was really confused at the time because my pocket was pretty deep. I never expected the ring to fall out."

We all went quiet for a moment, taking time to absorb everything Lonny had said.

I was the first to break the silence. "You need to tell all of this to Sheriff Georgeson."

Lonny shook his head. "No way."

Hope came to his defense. "He'll think Lonny's the killer."

"It'll look worse if you don't tell him and he figures it out on his own," I said.

"She's right," Brett said.

"He won't figure it out." There wasn't much confidence behind Lonny's words.

"Can you be sure about that?" I asked.

Lonny glanced at Hope. Her face showed the same fear as his.

She gripped her husband's hand. "But if he arrests Lonny…"

"He won't do that without evidence," Brett said.

"Isn't the ring enough evidence?"

"If you tell him what you told us… I don't think so."

Hope shook her head. "We can't risk it."

Lonny rubbed the back of his neck. "Maybe they're right."

"What?" Hope stared at him, aghast. "You could get thrown in jail!"

"Even if that happens, it'll only be until they find the real killer."

"They won't be *looking* for the real killer if they've got you locked up for the crime."

"But Brett and Marley are right. It'll look worse for me if I don't come clean."

Hope was on the verge of tears. "Please, Lonny. I won't be able to handle it if you're arrested."

Lonny took both her hands in his. Some of the fear had left his expression, resigned determination having moved in to replace it. "Trust me, okay? Everything will be all right."

A tear rolled down Hope's cheek, but she didn't protest any further.

"I'll tell the sheriff," Lonny said to me and Brett. "Tomorrow morning."

Brett took my hand and gave it a gentle squeeze. I returned the pressure, agreeing with his unspoken sentiment that it was time to leave the couple alone.

We said our goodbyes, and Brett and I didn't speak again until we were sitting in his truck, our seat belts on.

"Do you think Lonny will be arrested?" I asked.

"I hope not." He caught the worried glance I shot his way. "I doubt it, but I won't be surprised if Ray asks him a lot of questions."

I leaned back in my seat. "I hope we didn't give him bad advice."

"We didn't." Brett started up the truck. "It really will be far worse for him if he keeps quiet and Ray manages to connect him to the ring. And he will connect the dots, because we can't keep this information from him."

I knew all of that was true, but I still felt uneasy.

I stayed quiet as Brett pulled the truck out into the street. I watched out the passenger window as we passed by darkened storefronts in the center of town. We were about to turn onto Wildwood Road when I caught sight of two men on the corner of Main Street, standing beneath a streetlamp.

Tyrone was one of the men and the other…

I sat up straighter when I recognized him. "Look! It's him!"

Brett stopped at the corner and ducked to look around me out the side window. "Tyrone?"

"The other guy." I hurried to unbuckle my seat belt. "The one who looks like my dad."

"Marley!"

I heard Brett say my name, but I was already clambering out of the truck.

By the time I jumped up on the curb, Tyrone was striding off down Wildwood Road and the other man was heading up Main Street. I ran after him.

"Excuse me!"

He stopped and turned around, wariness registering on his face, visible even in the semidarkness.

I stopped in front of him. "Sorry to bother you. We met at the pancake house."

"I remember. What can I do for you?" His words were etched with the same wariness as his face.

"My name's Marley McKinney. I know this might sound crazy, but you look so much like my late father that I was wondering if we could possibly be related?"

A single second passed with him just staring at me, but then he started to turn away. "We're not."

"How can you be sure?" By the time I got the question out, he was already several feet away.

He glanced back over his shoulder. "I know my family tree. We aren't related. Sorry, but I don't have time to talk now."

I watched him hurry off along the street with long strides, as if he couldn't put distance between us fast enough. Footsteps sounded on the sidewalk behind me, and Brett jogged up to my side.

"What happened?" he asked as we watched the man disappear around a corner. "Did you talk to him?"

"Sort of. He clearly wasn't interested in talking to me, but he said we aren't related."

Brett put an arm around my shoulders. "I'm sorry. That was the most likely outcome, though."

"It was." I allowed Brett to guide me back down the street toward Wildwood Road, where he'd hastily parked the truck.

He glanced my way. "What is it? I can see the gears working in your head."

"There's something going on with that man."

We slowed to a stop as we reached the truck.

"But what kind of something?"

"That's the question," I said. "But he arrived in town recently, he's cagey, and now he's been talking to Tyrone." I glanced over my shoulder at the now-deserted street. "And that makes me wonder if he has some kind of connection to Demetra's murder."

Chapter 21

When I woke up the next morning, I had a plan to find out more about Joe. But as eager as I was to put my plan into action, I wouldn't be able to do anything about it until after work. And I didn't have to leave for work for nearly an hour, so I made the most of my time by snuggling up to Brett's side.

His eyes opened slowly, and he smiled sleepily when he saw me looking at him. "Morning."

I returned his smile. "Morning."

Spring might have arrived, but at this early hour, before the sun had risen, the bedroom was a tad chilly. I didn't mind, since it gave me an excuse to snuggle even closer to Brett, not that I needed an excuse.

"Let me guess," he said, running a hand over my messy curls. "You're thinking about your mystery man."

"Guilty as charged." I raised myself up on one elbow. "But I've got a plan."

"Of course you do."

I chose to ignore the amusement behind his words. "Tyrone was talking to him, so I'll ask Tyrone what he knows about the man."

The sleepiness disappeared from Brett's eyes. "Tyrone, the guy known for his temper? I don't like that idea, Marley."

"I won't go alone. If you're not free at the time, I'll ask Ivan to go with me."

"He'll be judging the amateur chef competition this afternoon."

I slapped a hand to my forehead. "I forgot all about that." I thought for a second. "Okay, so either I'll talk to Tyrone after you're done working or I'll have to leave it for another day." I wasn't too keen on the latter idea, but I shared Brett's concerns about Tyrone's temper. If I had to wait so I could have someone with me when I talked to him, that's what I'd do.

Flapjack jumped up onto the foot of the bed and padded his way up the covers to sit on Brett's chest.

"Morning, Jack," I greeted the tabby, running a hand over his fur.

He responded with a loud meow. Bentley heard the sound and jumped up from his spot across the room, trotting over to the side of the bed. He put his front paws on the mattress and nudged his nose against Brett's arm, whining.

"I think our alarm clocks are trying to tell us something," Brett said as he gave Bentley a pat on the head.

Reluctantly, I threw back the covers and wiggled my way to the edge of the bed. "Do you think Lonny will really talk to Ray about the ring?" I asked, wincing as my bare feet touched the cool floorboards.

"If he doesn't, I'll have to." Brett dislodged Flapjack from his chest so he could sit up. "I can't keep that information from Ray, but I'd really rather it come from Lonny. I'm working at Mrs. Rideout's property this morning, but I'll be up at the inn this afternoon."

"And you'll ask Lonny if he's talked to Ray?"

"I will."

With that assurance, I headed for the shower and got my day under way.

* * * *

While working at the pancake house, I kept an eye out for Tyrone and Joe, in case either man happened to make an appearance at the restaurant. Neither of them did, however, so I had to stick to my original plan of talking to Tyrone some other time. Since Ivan had to show up for his judging duties by three o'clock, he didn't stick around The Flip Side as long as usual after it closed for the day, but Tommy was still there when I finished cleaning up the dining room.

"Getting ready to head out?" I asked as I entered the kitchen and took in the sight of the clean and tidy work surfaces.

Tommy took off his apron. "Yep. You?"

"As soon as I grab my bag from the office."

Tommy was planning to watch some of the cooking competition, so we ended up walking over there together. By the time we arrived at the grocery store's parking lot where the competition tent was once again set up, a small crowd had already gathered and spectators dotted the bleachers. I noticed someone waving at me from the seats and realized it was Lisa. I was about to head her way when I saw Quaid talking with Coach Hannigan near the tent.

I still didn't know what to make of the conversation I'd partially overheard between the coach and his mystery companion down by the beach. I'd probably never know what it was about, though, and I was more interested in Quaid at the moment.

"Save a seat for me?" I requested of Tommy.

He assured me that he would, and I continued past the bleachers to approach Quaid.

Whatever the food blogger and former baseball coach had been talking about, their conversation drew to a close and the coach walked away. I intercepted Quaid before he could step beneath the tent's canopy, where Ivan and Marielle stood talking with Patricia.

"I'm glad to see you're feeling better, Mr. Hendrix," I said, trying my best to sound sincere.

He stopped midstride and looked at me as if he'd never seen me before. "Do I know you?"

"I'm Marley McKinney. I own The Flip Side pancake house here in Wildwood Cove, and I stepped in last week when you weren't able to judge the competition."

He stared down at me. "Good thing I'm back this week. At least one judge will know what they're doing. Though I'll probably get sick again, considering the crap I'll likely get fed. I shudder to think who you people let through to the final round."

His attitude rendered me momentarily speechless.

He brushed past me, jostling my arm. That seemed to loosen my tongue.

"Has the sheriff talked to you about Demetra Kozani yet?"

Quaid stopped short and turned around slowly. His dark gaze zeroed in on me, not the least bit friendly.

"Why would he do that?"

I didn't think I imagined the subtle note of wariness beneath his cold words.

"You knew her, didn't you? I understand Sheriff Georgeson is talking to pretty much anyone who knew her."

"Since I *didn't* know her, there's no reason for the sheriff to talk to me."

His words were meant to dismiss me, but I got his attention back with my next words.

"But weren't the two of you in a relationship? She was seen visiting the cottage where you used to live."

He stepped closer, towering over me. "You're mistaken," he said, his voice all ice and steel. "And if you don't want me telling the world that your little pancake house has a rat infestation, you'd better keep your unfounded accusations to yourself."

With one last glare down his nose at me, he strode away, not looking back.

I stared after him, barely able to keep my mouth from hanging open.

Someone gave my arm a gentle nudge. "Marley? What's going on?"

I realized Lisa was standing next to me. "I was talking to Quaid about Demetra."

"Did I hear him threatening you? Something about spreading rumors about rats at the pancake house?"

To my relief, she lowered her voice and whispered that last part.

"You heard right," I confirmed. "That was after he denied knowing Demetra. But Lonny Barron saw her visiting Quaid's cottage on more than one occasion."

"Lies and threats. Sounds like a suspect to me."

"And me," I agreed.

We both watched Quaid as he pulled out a chair at the judges' table and dropped into it. A second later, he focused all his attention on his smartphone. The other judges and several of the contestants had gathered around the refreshments table. Hope wasn't among them, I noticed.

"I'm going to talk to Ivan for a second," Lisa said. "I'm hoping he'll come over to my place for dinner tonight."

She headed around the tent, and I figured I might as well join Tommy up on the bleachers. I was only halfway there when I caught sight of Hope crossing the street, heading for the parking lot. I called out her name, and it took her a moment to spot me by the foot of the bleachers. As I walked over to meet her, I noticed a crease across her forehead that wasn't usually there. Her typical smile didn't make an appearance when I greeted her, and she had anxiety written all over her face.

"Are you okay?" I asked, concerned.

Tears glistened in her eyes, and she blinked rapidly to keep them at bay. "Not really. Lonny went to Port Angeles to talk to the sheriff earlier, and he's still there."

"Being questioned?"

Hope nodded and rummaged through her purse until she came up with a tissue.

"But he hasn't been arrested, has he?"

"No," she said, to my relief. "And when Lonny called, he said he wasn't being detained or anything, but the sheriff wanted him to give a statement. I didn't want him to do that without a lawyer, but he said everything would be fine."

She dabbed at her eyes as a couple of tears tried to escape.

"He's probably right," I said, wishing for that to be the truth.

She crumpled the tissue in her hand. "I can't relax until I know he's on his way home. I don't even know if I'll bother competing."

"But you worked hard to make it to the finals."

"None of that matters if Lonny's in trouble."

"Maybe it will help pass the time," I said.

"I suppose."

"The teens haven't started to compete yet, so you still have time to decide. Why don't you sit down and see what happens over the next while?"

She agreed to that plan and followed me over to the bleachers, where I found Lisa sitting next to Tommy. I sat down on Lisa's right, with Hope on my other side. I was about to introduce her to Lisa, but it turned out they already knew each other. Hope had met Tommy before too, since she'd hired him to take some photos of the Wildwood Inn to use on the website she and Lonny had set up. Tommy did photography as a sideline, and I'd seen enough of his photos to know he had talent. Patricia Murray would have asked him to take pictures at the competition except for the fact that Amy had been filling that role for years already, so she was asked first.

Hope's phone buzzed, and when she checked her text messages, she put a hand over her heart. "Thank God."

"What is it?" I asked.

"Lonny's on his way home."

"That's great news."

"It is." She bit her lower lip as she tapped out a response and sent it. "He thinks he's still under suspicion, but the sheriff didn't arrest him."

"So do you think you'll compete now?"

Hope tucked her phone into her purse. "I think so. I might actually be able to concentrate now." She drummed her fingers against her leg. "But word will probably get out that Lonny's connected to the ring found with Demetra's remains. What if that affects business at the inn when we open? If we don't have guests during the tourist season, our business will go belly up before we've even had a chance to establish it."

"Try not to worry about that," I said. "The inn doesn't open for another couple of weeks. Maybe the case will be wrapped up before then."

"It would be a relief if it were."

Below us, it appeared as though the competition was getting ready to start. All three judges were seated at their table, and three of the four teen finalists were at their cooking stations. I'd only just figured out that it was Ellie Shaw who was missing when Sienna came running around the outside of the tent. She went straight to her mom and spoke to her quickly as she pointed beyond the tent.

Patricia's gaze snapped toward the bleachers, skimming over the spectators before coming to rest on a spot to our left.

"Judith!" she called out as she briskly approached the bleachers.

Ellie's mother got up from her seat and made her way down toward Patricia.

"I'm afraid Ellie's fallen ill," Patricia said.

"Where is she?" Mrs. Shaw asked with alarm.

"She threw up in some bushes," Sienna said. "I'll take you to her."

Sienna led the way across the parking lot, Mrs. Shaw hurrying after her.

Looking concerned, Patricia had a word with Bruce Hannigan.

The coach nodded and approached the microphone. "Ladies and gentlemen, we'll have a short delay here, but hopefully we'll get the competition under way before long. Thank you for your patience."

Conversations sparked around us, and a few people got up to stretch their legs.

"I hope Ellie's okay," I said.

"Maybe it's just nerves," Lisa suggested.

I was about to say I hoped that was the case when a woman sitting on the lowest level of the bleachers jumped up and ran for a large metal garbage can located several feet away. She made it just in time before vomiting. I recognized her as one of the finalists from the adult division of the competition. If I remembered right from the day she registered, her name was Cynthia. A man I assumed was her husband rushed to her side. She vomited again, and then he put an arm around her and hurried her away.

"Another one?" Tommy said. "That must be some bug going around."

I spotted Mrs. Shaw walking as quickly as she could in her high heels, heading for Patricia. I climbed down from the bleachers, intending to ask how Ellie was doing, but Patricia beat me to it.

"How is Ellie, Judith?"

"She's too sick to compete. I have to take her home." Her words were clipped. "This is absolutely disgraceful, and I'll have you know that I plan to take it up with the organizing committee."

"What's disgraceful?" I asked.

Anger practically sparked from the woman's eyes. "That this was allowed to happen." She swept her gaze over the tent and the bleachers before announcing to the world at large, "Someone is sabotaging this competition!"

Chapter 22

A murmur ran through the crowd of spectators. Patricia put an arm around Mrs. Shaw's shoulders and guided her around the tent and out of sight.

"It can't be true," Hope said as I returned to my seat. "Can it?"

"Why would anybody sabotage an amateur cooking competition?" Tommy asked. "Isn't it just for fun?"

"There is a cash prize," I said.

"And some of the contestants are really competitive," Hope added. "Although, I thought the most competitive person of all was Ellie's mom, and she's not even a contestant."

"Maybe her mom's behind the sabotage," Lisa suggested. "She could have been trying to improve her daughter's chances of winning."

"But Ellie's sick," Hope pointed out.

"Maybe Mrs. Shaw didn't mean for that to happen." Lisa nudged my arm. "What do you think, Marley?"

I spotted Patricia returning to the tent without Mrs. Shaw. "I think I want to find out what's going on."

Even though I'd just come back to my seat, I squeezed past Hope and jumped down from the bleachers. Patricia was in the midst of talking to the remaining three teen finalists, her clipboard in hand, but as soon as she turned away from them, I moved in to speak with her.

"Do you think there's any truth to what Mrs. Shaw said?" I asked.

"I hope not, but…"

"I knew there was something suspicious about how I got sick!" Quaid interrupted, looming behind my right shoulder. "The sheriff should be called in!"

Patricia winced. "Don't you think that would be an overreaction?"

"How many more people have to get sick before you do something to stop it?" Quaid demanded. "If I get sick again, I'll have to think about suing."

He stormed off, returning to the judges' table.

Patricia pinched the bridge of her nose.

"What can I do to help?" I asked.

"I don't know. We're already behind schedule. If I call the sheriff in, we might have to cancel the rest of the event."

I thought things over quickly. "Each time someone has fallen ill, it hasn't been during the actual competition, but beforehand. So a problem with the cooking stations shouldn't be the cause. Why don't you go ahead and get things under way? I'll call Ray Georgeson on his direct line and tell him what's happened. He can decide whether it's something he should be looking into."

Patricia's features relaxed with relief. "Thank you, Marley. That sounds like a good plan." She gave my arm a grateful squeeze and hurried over to talk with Bruce Hannigan.

As I wandered away in search of a quiet spot to make my phone call, I heard Coach Hannigan announce the start of the teen competition. Ray didn't pick up, so I left a voice message, briefly outlining the problem and asking him to get in touch with me or Patricia.

When I hung up I noticed Sienna crossing the parking lot. I waved to her, and she altered her path to meet up with me.

"Did Ellie and her mom head home?" I asked.

"Yes. Luckily Mrs. Shaw had her car here, and they only live a short drive away." She frowned. "Poor Ellie. I feel terrible for her. She's so sick, *and* she's missing the competition. She might have won the whole thing."

"It's too bad," I agreed. "But hopefully she'll recover quickly. Maybe she can enter the competition again next year."

"I'm sure her mom will want her to." She scuffed the sole of one sneaker against the pavement. "Mrs. Shaw thinks someone made Ellie sick on purpose."

"I heard."

"Is it true?"

"I don't know, but the circumstances are suspicious. I left a message with the sheriff so he can decide if he needs to investigate."

"But it doesn't really make sense," Sienna said. "I heard that one of the adults is sick too. If one of the competitors wanted to increase their chances of winning, why would someone from the teen division *and* someone from the adult division get sick? I get making a judge sick. Quaid is a jerk, and Ellie said he was meaner to some than others. So with him out of the way last week, some contestants would have had a better chance of making the finals."

"That part does make sense," I agreed. "Maybe this time the plan was to get rid of a competitor or two from one of the divisions. Ellie—or Cynthia, for that matter—could have been an unintended victim."

"So who was the target and what made them sick?"

Behind us, I could hear the competition going on. Dishes clattered against countertops and cooking food sizzled while Bruce Hannigan provided some commentary. I tuned out all that noise and thought things over.

"Quaid drank coffee before he got sick, so I think the most likely scenario is that the saboteur slipped something into the coffee or tea at the refreshments table. Except no one else got sick last week, so it must have been only Quaid's drink that was tampered with."

"That makes sense."

"Was Ellie over there before she got sick?"

"Yes. I was with her. She was nervous so I was trying to keep her distracted by talking about other things."

"And did she drink anything?"

"She had some tea." Sienna's eyes widened. "But she only drank half of it because she didn't like it."

"Did she say why she didn't like it?" I asked.

Sienna shrugged. "She just said it tasted weird."

I tucked that bit of information away in my mind. "Who else was nearby at the time?"

"That blond lady who's competing in the adult division. Is that Cynthia? The woman who got sick?"

"Yes," I said. "Anyone else?"

"Ellie's mom. And that other woman who's competing, the one who always wears her hair in a bun."

"Dorothy."

"Yeah, her. And her husband. Oh, Coach Hannigan too. I think that's all."

That made for more suspects than I would have liked, but maybe we could eliminate some of them.

"Did Cynthia have anything to drink?"

"I didn't actually *see* her drinking, but she poured a drink. Two, actually." Sienna thought for a second. "No, three."

"Who did she give them to?"

"I know she gave one to Ellie. I think she kept one for herself, and the other one was for the man she's competing against. I think his name is Mikey."

"Dd anyone have an opportunity to slip something into the drinks?"

"I don't know. I was mostly only paying attention to Ellie." Sienna's gaze wandered over my shoulder toward the tent.

I guessed what she was thinking. "Do you want to go and cheer on Logan?"

"I do," she said with a relieved smile. "You don't mind?"

"Of course not. But let me know if you think of someone who might have had a chance to tamper with the drinks."

"I will for sure." The enthusiastic light in her eyes was one I'd seen before when she'd helped me out with an unofficial investigation. "See you in a bit."

She hurried off toward the tent and was soon clapping and cheering for Logan. I found my way back to my seat and settled in to watch the rest of the competition. Hope had left the bleachers while I was gone, but Lisa and Tommy filled me in on what I'd missed.

The teen finalists had been given three surprise, mandatory foods—cauliflower, mango, and pistachios—to use in their dishes, plus access to an array of other ingredients. They had thirty minutes to whip up a main dish and a dessert that would—hopefully—wow the judges. I watched, impressed, as the teens chopped, whisked, and cooked at lightning speed. All three of them appeared stressed, but not to the point of panicking.

Soon the clock ran down, and Coach Hannigan blew his whistle. It was time for the teens to face the judges. As with the previous rounds, the judges kept their comments to themselves while they sampled the dishes, making notes on their clipboards after each taste. Once the three competitors had returned to their cooking stations, the judges handed their score sheets over to Patricia. She checked over the results, jotted something down on her clipboard, and handed a slip of paper to Bruce Hannigan.

"Ladies and gentlemen," Coach Hannigan said into the microphone. "I'm pleased to announce the winner of our teen division and the recipient of the five-thousand-dollar prize." He glanced down at the paper Patricia had given him. "And the winner is...Logan Teeves!"

A roar of cheers and applause rose up from the crowd of spectators. As I clapped along with everyone else, I noticed that Logan seemed a bit stunned. He had a dazed look on his face as he came forward to shake Bruce's hand and receive his check. Seconds later he was surrounded by family and friends. His dad clapped him on the back, and Sienna gave him a hug. Some of the shock must have worn off by then, because he was finally smiling.

As soon as the celebration wore down, the adult competition got under way. Cynthia had withdrawn after falling ill, leaving only Hope, Dorothy, and Mikey to compete for the top prize. The format for the adult division was the same as for the teen division, but the surprise ingredients were different. This time the contestants were given collard greens, walnuts, and white chocolate to work with.

The whistle sounded, and the amateur chefs got busy.

"I'm rooting for Hope," Tommy said, his eyes on what was going on in the tent.

"Me too," I agreed.

I spotted Lonny slipping into a free seat on the bleachers. I was glad he'd made it in time to watch his wife compete—and that he was still a free man.

Dorothy Kerwin's husband wasn't sitting down to watch, I noticed. He was pacing off to the side of the bleachers, looking far more nervous than his wife. After a few minutes, Coach Hannigan approached him and clapped a hand to his back. The coach spoke to him, and I got the sense they knew each other well. Eventually, Willard nodded before taking a seat to watch the rest of the competition.

The time seemed to fly by, and soon Hope, Dorothy, and Mikey were lined up in front of the table. Again, the judges gave away no clue as to which dishes they preferred. When Coach Hannigan approached the microphone to announce the winner, I crossed my fingers, wanting him to say Hope's name.

"Before I announce the winner of our adult division," Bruce said into the microphone, "I'd first like to thank the organizing committee, the competition's sponsors, the volunteers, and the town of Wildwood Cove for graciously hosting this event."

The audience applauded, but the clapping died out quickly. Everyone was eager to hear what he would say next.

"And now, without further ado, the winner of the adult division is... Mikey Soldado!"

Grinning from ear to ear, Mikey shook Bruce's hand and accepted his prize with obvious excitement. I wondered if Hope was disappointed, but I soon saw that wasn't the case. She had all her attention focused on Lonny. With her apron still on, she ran out from the tent to meet him at the base of the bleachers. She threw her arms around him, and he held her close, the two of them apparently oblivious to the people around them celebrating Mikey's victory.

Now that the competition was over, the crowd slowly dispersed, the bleachers emptying. I tried to spot Sienna in the crowd but couldn't see her anywhere. I figured there was a good chance she'd gone off to celebrate with Logan. I was planning to head home and was about to say goodbye to Tommy and Lisa when I caught sight of a familiar face near the tent.

Chrissy Mazurek was chatting with Mikey Soldado.

She batted her eyelashes and put a hand to Mikey's arm as she laughed at something he said. I figured she wouldn't appreciate it if I interrupted her flirting, but luckily for me three young men swooped in to congratulate Mikey, and Chrissy was unintentionally ousted from the small but excited crowd.

I made my move before she had a chance to leave.

"Chrissy!" I called out.

She spun around, and when she saw me the curiosity on her face quickly morphed into resignation. No doubt she had me pegged as a busybody after all the questions I'd asked at her store, but I didn't let that deter me.

"Do you know where I can find Tyrone Phillips?" I asked.

Her eyes narrowed with suspicion. "Why are you looking for Tyrone?"

"I need to ask him a question about…a mutual acquaintance." That was pretty much the truth.

She regarded me in silence for a couple of seconds before impatience replaced her suspicion. "He's staying with his mother." She hiked her purse strap up on her shoulder and took two steps away from me. "Mrs. Phillips lives on Saratoga Street. A white house with a purple door."

I thanked her, but she'd already turned away and didn't look back. We certainly weren't going to be friends anytime soon. At least I had the information I needed.

I was eager to get on my way to Saratoga Street. I knew which house Chrissy was talking about. It was only a block away from the house Brett owned on the corner of Saratoga Street and Sea Breeze Drive, where Chloe lived. But as much as I wanted to get over there right away, I remembered my promise to Brett.

Most of the spectators and competitors had left the parking lot. That made it easy to spot Ivan and Lisa chatting with Marielle near the tent. At least, Lisa and Marielle were chatting. Ivan simply stood there, holding Lisa's hand. I recalled that Lisa was hoping to have dinner with Ivan, so I didn't want to pull him away from her to act as my bodyguard. Fortunately, I spotted Tommy across the parking lot. He was on his skateboard, starting to coast away.

I broke into a run and chased after him. "Tommy!"

He glanced over his shoulder, and when he saw me he hopped off his skateboard and flipped it up so he could grab it with one hand.

"Do you have a few minutes?" I asked when I caught up to him.

"Sure. What's up?"

"I want to try talking to Tyrone Phillips, to see if I can get some information out of him, but I don't want to approach him alone."

"Tyrone, as in the ex-jock with a temper?"

"That's him."

"Then not going alone is a good idea. Where to?"

I told him our destination, and we set off along the sidewalk. It only took five minutes to reach the white house with the front door painted in what I though was a pretty shade of light purple. It was a cute house—small, but well cared for. The flower beds on either side of the front steps were practically bursting with color from the blooming plants.

When I knocked on the front door, I listened carefully for approaching footsteps, wondering if it would be Tyrone or his mother who would answer the door. I heard a couple of heavy footfalls, and then the door jerked open. Tyrone stood there, filling the doorway with his tall frame, his hair messy and his clothes rumpled, as if he'd been sleeping in them.

"Yeah?" he said without any warmth.

His attitude and his reputation had me intimidated, but I tried not to let it show.

"Hi, Tyrone. Chloe Collins introduced us the other day."

"If you're selling something, I don't want any," Tyrone cut in before I could say anything more.

"We're not selling anything," I rushed to assure him. "I'm trying to find someone, and I was hoping you could help. Last night you were talking to a man on the corner of Main Street and Wildwood Road. He's maybe in his late fifties, with brown hair going a bit gray."

Tyrone scratched his head, messing up his hair even more. He scrunched his forehead, as if listening to me was taking great effort. When he dropped his hand from his hair, he nodded.

"You mean the PI?"

Chapter 23

"PI?" I echoed. "As in private investigator?"

The look Tyrone shot me said "duh" loud and clear. "What else?"

"What's he doing in Wildwood Cove?" I asked.

"Demetra's mom hired him." Tyrone squinted at me. "If you don't know that, why are you looking for him?"

"I need to ask him something," I said quickly. "Do you know where I can find him?"

"He's staying at Demetra's mom's place." A phone rang somewhere inside the house, and Tyrone turned his head toward the sound.

"Where's that?" I asked.

"Hyacinth Road."

"What's the PI's name?"

"Jake Fellmen." He started shutting the door. "I gotta go."

The door slammed before I could say anything more. I stood there staring at it for a second before Tommy and I descended the front steps.

"So there's a private investigator looking into the case," Tommy said. "I guess that's a good thing. The more people working on it, the more chance there is of it getting solved."

"That's probably true," I said, hoping the PI didn't intend to obstruct the sheriff's investigation in any way.

"Plus, you're working on it too."

"Sort of," I said. "I haven't done much."

"You tracked down the PI."

"Yes, but to be honest, that was to satisfy my own curiosity. I didn't know for sure if he had anything to do with Demetra's case."

As we walked slowly along Wildwood Road, I filled Tommy in on the fact that Jake Fellmen looked like my late father and how I'd wondered if he could be related to me. "He was vague when I asked him where he was from, and he told me his name was Joe. I thought at the time he might have been lying, and it turns out I was right."

"So you want to know why he didn't want to give you any straight answers," Tommy said, amusement in his eyes.

"I can't help being curious."

"Hey, I'm not saying it's a bad thing. Your curiosity has helped solve murders before."

"I don't know that it'll help this time," I said.

We came to a stop on the corner of Wildwood Road and Main Street.

"You're not going looking for the PI right now, are you?" Tommy asked.

"No, I'm heading home for dinner. Thanks for coming with me to see Tyrone."

"No problem." Tommy set his skateboard on the ground and rested one foot on it. "I'll see you in the morning."

"See you."

He pushed off and went sailing along the sidewalk, heading south along Main Street. I continued on along Wildwood Road, arriving home a short while later. Brett was already there, and as soon as I turned into the long driveway, I saw him working on one of the raised beds, turning the soil with far more ease than I had done.

Bentley charged along the driveway to greet me, bringing a tennis ball with him. I gave the dog a quick pat and then threw the ball for him.

I greeted Brett next, leaning into him as I surveyed his work. Two of the raised beds were now ready for planting, and he was partway through the third. I could see he'd mixed some compost into the soil.

"Thank you for this. You must have been at it for a while."

"Not too long." He sank the spade into the soil and left it there as he put an arm around me. "How was the cooking competition?"

I thought about how to answer that question and settled on saying, "Eventful."

Brett eyed me. "What does that mean?"

"I'll tell you about it over dinner."

I found Flapjack snoozing on the front porch and gave him a quick cuddle before we headed indoors. We fed the animals and put together a quick dinner for ourselves. As we got everything ready and settled at the kitchen table, I told Brett about the results of the competition and how

Ellie and Cynthia had suddenly fallen ill, the same way Quaid had the weekend before.

"Ellie's mom believes someone was trying to sabotage the competition, and I'm thinking she could be right, but I'm not sure yet who might be behind it."

Brett grinned. "I'm sure you'll figure it out."

"Because I'm nosy?"

"I prefer curious and persistent."

I smiled. "So do I. But that's not the only interesting thing that happened today." I told him about my visit to Tyrone—first assuring him that I hadn't gone alone—and the fact that "Joe" was really Jake Fellmen, a private investigator.

"And let me guess," Brett said once I'd finished the story. "You want to go talk to him."

"You know me well," I said, spearing some pasta salad with my fork. "Care to join me for an evening stroll to Hyacinth Road?"

* * * *

The sun was on its way down when we set out for our walk, but there was still some warmth to the evening air and the light breeze was scented with the saltiness of the ocean and the sweetness of spring blooms. Before leaving the house I'd texted Chloe, and she'd told me that Mrs. Kozani's house was third from the corner of Hyacinth Road and Pacific Street. It didn't take long for me and Brett to reach the white-and-blue bungalow, but I didn't follow the path to the front door right away, instead remaining on the sidewalk while I took in the sight of the property.

The paint on the house was peeling in places, and the windows showed no signs of life behind the glass. The grass was in need of cutting, though it wasn't overly long or wild. Mrs. Kozani must have hired someone to look after the property in her absence. Still, the house seemed to radiate sadness. Maybe that was my imagination working on overdrive, influenced by the knowledge that Mrs. Kozani had lost her only child far too young.

"Ready?" Brett asked after we'd been standing there for a moment.

By way of response, I started along the pathway, holding his hand. We climbed the three steps to the small front porch, and I rapped on the door, wondering if the PI would be there. I heard movement from within, and a second later Jake Fellmen opened the door.

His expression didn't give too much away, but I thought I caught a glimpse of surprise in his dark gray eyes that quickly shifted to wariness.

"Yes?" he said, not giving any indication that we'd met before.

"I was hoping we could chat for a minute," I said.

"About what?"

"Why you lied to me, for starters."

He frowned at me. "Listen, we're not related, okay? Whatever you said your last name is, I don't have any of those on my family tree."

"McKinney," I reminded him. "But you told me your name is Joe. I know that's not true. It's Jake Fellmen, and you're a private investigator."

"Who told you that?"

"Tyrone Phillips."

The PI swore under his breath and rubbed a hand across his eyes. "I knew that guy wouldn't keep his mouth shut."

"Then why did you tell him you're a PI?" Brett asked.

"I didn't. My client did."

"Mrs. Kozani?" I asked. "She's the one who hired you, right?"

"I'm not sure why you're here if you already know all this." Impatience gave his words a rough edge.

"I was curious about why you gave me a false name. Why not be up front about who you are and why you're in Wildwood Cove?"

"Because this is a small town, and I didn't want my investigation to be the source of gossip. But Mrs. Kozani talked to Tyrone Phillips on the phone and told him she'd hired me."

"Why would Mrs. Kozani talk to Tyrone? Isn't he a suspect? I would have thought she'd want nothing to do with him."

"Mrs. Kozani believes Tyrone's innocent."

"Do *you* think he's innocent?"

"And why would I share that with you?"

"I guess you've got no reason to," I conceded.

"Exactly. And plenty of reasons not to."

He stepped back and made a move to shut the door.

"Are you sure we aren't related?" I blurted out before he could get it closed. "Even distantly?"

He let out a heavy sigh and pressed a fist to his forehead for a second. "I'm positive. And even if we were, what would it matter? I've already got plenty of cousins and other relatives causing me headaches."

"*I* don't," I said. I reached into the pocket of my jeans for the photograph I'd tucked away before leaving home. "This is a picture of my dad a few months before he died about thirty-five years ago." I handed Fellmen the photo. "Can you at least see why I wondered if we could be related?"

The PI studied the picture. "I guess there's some resemblance," he admitted, not without reluctance. "But it's not like I'm his doppelgänger." He handed the photo back to me.

"I guess not." I looked from the picture to the PI. Now that I was able to make a close comparison, I could see that Fellmen's nose was a bit different from my dad's, his forehead higher.

"Look," Fellmen said, his voice losing some of its edge, "I'm sorry if you're short on family, but I've done some genealogy work, and there are no McKinneys in my family. Not even back several generations. I'm in Wildwood Cove to do a job, to figure out who killed Mrs. Kozani's daughter. I'd like to get on with that job without any distractions."

"Fair enough," I said. I couldn't keep myself from asking one more question. "Are you making any progress?"

"That's something I'll only discuss with my client."

That was fair too, although I wasn't without disappointment.

Fellmen turned his head sharply. He swore and lunged out of sight. I took the opportunity to slip inside the house, Brett following. The small living room to the right of the door opened onto an outdated kitchen with yellow countertops and brown cupboards.

"Everything okay?" I asked.

The PI jerked a pot off the stove. The water in the pot had started boiling over, but it didn't look like there was too much of a mess. An unopened box of Kraft Mac & Cheese sat on the counter next to the stove.

"No big deal." Fellmen turned down the heat and returned the pot to the element. "I'm just getting myself some dinner."

While he tore open the box of Kraft Mac & Cheese and dumped the pasta into the boiling water, I glanced around the kitchen. There were dirty dishes in the sink and half a pot of coffee on the counter. On a small table near the window, Fellmen had left papers scattered across the top of a closed laptop.

I shifted closer to the table and took a look at the top paper. It appeared to be a list of potential suspects. Chloe's name jumped out at me. At first I was dismayed, but then I saw that Fellmen had added a note next to her name, stating that she had an alibi for the time when Demetra was likely killed. I was in the midst of scanning through the other names on the list when Fellmen grabbed the papers and stuffed them inside a file folder.

"I've told you everything I can tell you," he said. "It might not be fine cuisine, but I'd like to eat my dinner in peace."

Brett put an arm around me and gave my shoulder a gentle squeeze. I knew he was encouraging me to leave, and I couldn't think of a reason to stay any longer. If Fellmen wasn't going to tell us anything more, there was nothing left to be gained from sticking around and pestering him.

"Thank you for your time," I said. "And good luck with your investigation."

Fellmen acknowledged that with a brief nod and followed us to the door. He shut it behind us, almost catching my heels in the process.

Brett and I didn't speak until we were back on the sidewalk, holding hands and heading for home.

"Did you get what you were hoping to out of that visit?" he asked.

"I think so. I would have liked it if he'd shared more about his investigation, of course, but I'm not surprised he didn't. And I can accept that he's not related to me now. It's just a coincidence that he resembles my dad."

Brett gave my hand a squeeze. "And you're okay with that?"

"I am." As I answered, I realized that was the truth. "But I think maybe it was a good thing for me to wonder for a while."

"What do you mean?"

"Fellmen said he was sorry that I'm short on family. And when I first started trying to find out if he was related to me, that's how I felt. But after talking with you the other day and having time to let everything percolate in my mind, I know that's not the case. There are people I miss, and I might not have any siblings or close cousins or living grandparents, but I've got my mom and Grant, I've got you, I've got your family, and Lisa, and everyone at The Flip Side. That doesn't make me short on family. That makes me lucky."

Brett halted at the end of Hyacinth Road and pulled me in close for a kiss. "That's a good way to look at it."

I smiled and laced my fingers through his again as we resumed walking. "I also got something else out of that visit."

"What's that?" Brett asked as we crossed a quiet street.

"Another reason to suspect Demetra's best friend of killing her."

Chapter 24

I asked Chloe if we could meet up to chat, and she agreed to come by The Flip Side the next day. Since I told her I wanted to know more about Chrissy Mazurek, she said she'd see if Hope would be willing to come to the pancake house with her. She explained that Hope had spent more time with Chrissy and Demetra than she had during their school days, so it was possible the inn owner would have more insights to share.

Chloe showed up at The Flip Side in the early afternoon, just as the lunch rush was petering out.

"Thanks for coming," I said when I stopped to greet her on my way to the kitchen with a stack of dirty dishes. "Is Hope coming?"

"She should be here any minute."

As if Chloe's words had summoned the other woman, the front door opened and Hope stepped into the pancake house. She glanced around and then smiled when she saw me and Chloe.

"We can go in the office or sit in a quiet corner out here," I said, my arms starting to protest against my heavy load of dishes. "I'll be right back."

I hurried into the kitchen and returned to the dining room a moment later, free of dirty dishes. With both Leigh and Sienna working that day, I didn't need to worry about taking some time to chat with friends, especially since closing time was approaching and the pancake house was quickly emptying out.

Chloe and Hope had claimed a table in the far corner, well away from any other remaining diners. Before sitting down to join them, I took their orders for food and drink. I relayed their requests to the kitchen and returned with sodas for Chloe and Hope and a glass of sweet tea for myself.

"Chloe tells me you have some questions about Chrissy," Hope said once I'd settled into a chair. "Do you really think she could be the one who killed Demetra?"

Hope had kept her voice quiet, and I did the same.

"It's possible."

"You said you found some new information that made you more suspicious of her," Chloe prompted, referring to the text message conversation we'd had the night before.

I took a sip of sweet tea. "First of all, I discovered that Demetra's mom hired a private investigator, Jake Fellmen."

"Why?" Chloe asked with surprise. "Ray and his deputies have hardly had a chance to solve the case."

"Mrs. Kozani probably didn't mean it as a slight against your uncle," Hope said. "She's waited a decade to find out what happened to her daughter. She probably wants as many people on the case as possible so she can finally get some answers."

"I guess I can understand that," Chloe conceded. "So did you learn anything from this private investigator? I'm assuming you've talked to him."

"I spoke to him last night. He wasn't willing to share much with me, but I did manage a quick glance at some notes he had lying around."

I told them about the list of names I'd seen, some with notations next to them.

"A list of suspects?" Hope asked.

"That or witnesses he wanted to interview."

"Was my name on the list?" Chloe asked with apprehension.

"It was, but he'd noted that you have an alibi."

"Good," she said with relief.

"I take it Fellmen hasn't approached you."

Chloe shook her head. "Not yet, anyway."

We both looked to Hope.

"He hasn't talked to me either."

"He's spoken to Tyrone," I said. "Not that it did him much good. The notes next to Tyrone's name said 'temper, confrontational, unforthcoming.'"

"That sounds like Tyrone, all right," Hope said. "He *can* be a nice guy sometimes, but he's always had a major chip on his shoulder."

"But was he unforthcoming because he's got something to hide or because he's just being a jerk?" Chloe asked.

"That's the question," I said.

"One I can't answer."

"Neither can I," Hope said.

"What I'm hoping you *can* tell me about is Chrissy." I paused as Leigh arrived at our table with meals for all three of us.

"Afternoon, ladies," she greeted before setting the plates on the table.

She brought marzipan pancakes for Chloe, mocha mascarpone crêpes for Hope, and banoffee crêpes for me. My crêpes were topped with whipped cream and shaved chocolate, and the mere sight of them made my mouth water in anticipation.

We all thanked Leigh before she headed off to accept payment from a couple ready to leave the pancake house. Chloe and Hope dug into their food, and I did the same, savoring the delicious blend of dulce de leche, banana, and cream.

"So what is it you want to know about Chrissy?" Hope asked once we'd all had a chance to sample our meals.

"I already knew she and Demetra were more like frenemies than besties, at least some of the time. But according to Fellmen's notes there was a more specific rivalry going on between them. Something to do with Demetra wanting to become a model. Unfortunately, the notes were sparse, and I didn't have more than a few seconds to read them."

"I definitely remember Demetra going on about how she planned to become a supermodel," Chloe said as she speared a piece of pancake with her fork. "But I don't know if that bugged Chrissy any more than the rest of us."

"I think it did," Hope said.

"How come?" I asked.

"Chrissy wanted to be a model too. I remember her saying so way back when we were about twelve. The summer before senior year, she stayed with her aunt in Seattle and did a bit of modeling. Shopping mall fashion shows, that sort of thing. She boasted about it when she was back here in town, and then suddenly Demetra decided *she* was going to be a model. But she made it clear she'd be far above modeling at a mall."

"I can see how that might have rubbed Chrissy the wrong way," I said.

"They both always wanted to be the best. That's what caused most of the friction between them over the years. At first it just annoyed Chrissy, I think, but then Amy helped Demetra come up with a portfolio. That really ticked Chrissy off, probably because Demetra was actually taking steps to prove she could be a better model than her."

"So suddenly it wasn't just talk."

"Exactly." Hope took a bite of her crêpes and sighed happily. "These are amazing, by the way."

I smiled. "I'm glad you like them."

Chloe cut into her last pancake. "So you think the whole modeling rivalry could have ended up getting deadly?"

"It's something I'd like to look into," I said. "Do you know if Chrissy left the party before or after Demetra?"

"They were both still there when I left," Chloe replied, "but I think I remember hearing that Chrissy left first."

I looked to Hope, but she was staring off into space, worry lines creasing her forehead.

"Hope?" I prodded. "Are you okay?"

She snapped out of her daze. "Sorry. I'm just worried about Lonny. What were you saying?"

I repeated my question about Chrissy.

"I think she left before Demetra did, but not by too long."

I considered that. "So she could have waited in the woods until she had a chance to catch Demetra alone."

"She definitely could have," Hope agreed. "Should we be talking to Sheriff Georgeson about this?"

"We don't really have much to tell him beyond what he likely already knows," I said. "I think we need more information before we go to him."

"So you're going to talk to Chrissy?" Chloe guessed. "You're good at getting information out of people."

"I'm not so sure I would be this time. I've already asked her some questions, and she didn't much like me being nosy."

"Maybe she'd be more willing to talk to me and Chloe," Hope suggested.

I smiled. "That's exactly what I was going to say."

* * * *

Chloe and Hope hung around and helped me out as I closed up the pancake house and tidied up the dining room. When that was done, we walked into the heart of town, our destination Chrissy's boutique. I was concerned that the mere sight of me might be enough to make Chrissy clam up, but if she was willing to talk to Hope and Chloe, I wanted to be there to hear what she had to say, so I followed them into the shop.

Chrissy was busy ringing up purchases for a well-dressed, middle-aged woman when we arrived. Hope and Chloe waved to their former classmate, and Chrissy acknowledged them with a quick smile before turning her attention back to her customer. I quietly slipped among the racks of clothing, putting some distance between myself and the sales counter, while Hope and Chloe remained near the displays closest to the door.

When the middle-aged woman left the shop a few minutes later, Hope struck up a conversation with Chrissy.

"How are you doing with everything these days, Chrissy? This can't be an easy time for you."

I flipped through the skirts and tops hanging on the rack in front of me, pretending to be interested in them while surreptitiously watching what was happening at the front of the store.

"It's really not," Chrissy said. "Everyone's gossiping and casting Demetra in a bad light. I wish the case would get solved so all the speculation can get put to rest. So Demetra can be put to rest too."

"I'm sorry it's been so rough for you," Chloe said. "Getting questioned about everything that happened so long ago hasn't been easy for me, and I wasn't close to Demetra like you were. And now it's not just the sheriff's department asking questions. There's a private investigator, too."

Chrissy nodded and picked a yellow silk blouse up off the sales counter. "I understand why Mrs. Kozani hired the PI, but I don't know how helpful he's going to be. He came in here yesterday and grilled me. I felt like he was trying to pin the crime on me." She had a frown on her face as she came out from behind the counter, slipping the blouse onto a hanger.

"But why would he suspect you?" Hope said, managing to sound surprised. "You were Demetra's best friend."

"Sure, but everyone knows we fought sometimes." She hung the blouse on a rack fixed to the back wall. "And we weren't really getting along at the time she disappeared."

"Because of the modeling thing?" Chloe asked. When Chrissy shot a sharp glance her way, she added apologetically, "I've heard some of the gossip that's going around."

Fortunately, she didn't reveal that I was the source of that particular gossip. Or, information, as I preferred to call it.

"It's such a load of crap," Chrissy said with vehemence. She straightened out a display of handbags with more force than necessary. "Like I would have killed my best friend over something so ridiculous!"

She dropped her chin, and her shoulders shook. It took a second for the three of us to realize she was crying. We all hurried her way. I couldn't bring myself to stay lurking in the background when she was in tears.

Hope put an arm around her. "I'm so sorry you're going through this, Chrissy."

"We all are," I said, and Chloe murmured her agreement.

CRÊPE EXPECTATIONS 149

Chrissy wiped at her tears. "It was so *stupid*. If we both wanted to model, we could have. There was no point in fighting about it. But we did. And we didn't have a chance to patch things up before she disappeared."

She broke down into full-out sobs.

Hope kept her arm around her, and Chloe patted her back. I grabbed a box of tissues that was sitting on the sales counter and brought it over to Chrissy. She pulled a tissue from the box, giving me a tremulous smile of thanks. It took a couple of minutes and another two tissues to get her crying under control.

"I'm sorry," she said in a shaky voice as she dabbed the last of her tears off her cheeks. "It's been so difficult. Ten years later and I still have the same regrets. And I still miss her. I couldn't bear to pursue modeling after she was gone. We fought from time to time and we were competitive with each other, but Demetra was my best friend and I loved her. It hurts to know some people suspect me of killing her. I never would have. *Never!*"

Fresh tears rolled down her cheeks. She grabbed another tissue from the box I held and wiped them away quickly. She sniffled and closed her eyes briefly.

"I'm so sorry," she said again. "I didn't mean to break down like this."

"You have nothing to apologize for," Hope assured her, giving her a hug.

"Is there anything we can do for you, Chrissy?" I asked, feeling terrible that my quest for information had triggered her meltdown.

"No, I'll be okay." She moved behind the sales counter and produced a small compact from somewhere out of sight, checking her makeup in the small mirror. She must have been wearing waterproof mascara because her tears hadn't made it run. "Work is what's helping me cope."

She snapped the compact shut and squared her shoulders, as if ready to bravely face an onslaught of customers.

"Then we should leave you to it," Hope said.

Chloe held up a brightly colored top. "I'd love to buy this before we go."

That seemed to cheer Chrissy up, if only slightly. She rang up the purchase, and when we left the store she even managed a small smile and a wave.

"So, what do you think?" Chloe asked once we were walking along the street, leaving the boutique behind us.

"I don't know her as well as you two do, of course," I said, "but I thought she was genuinely upset. I might be wrong, but I don't think she's the killer."

"I don't think so either," Chloe said with confidence. "I feel so bad for her."

We both focused on Hope, who'd remained quiet since we left the boutique.

"What are your thoughts?" Chloe asked her.

"I guess I believe her," Hope said after a moment.

"You don't sound too sure," I said.

She gave her head a curt shake, as if trying to jolt herself out of a daze. "You two are probably right. I think I'm just disappointed that we're no closer to finding the killer."

I thought I knew the true source of her disappointment. "I'm sure Lonny's situation will get sorted out soon. I doubt he's the only suspect on the sheriff's radar. Everything will be okay in the end."

Hope forced a smile. "You're right," she said, her voice more certain this time. "Everything will be okay."

Chapter 25

I'd hoped to spend Monday with Brett, but he left home shortly after breakfast to get some work done. He usually took Sundays and Mondays off each week, but he'd been spending so much time at the Wildwood Inn lately that he needed an extra day to catch up on work for his other clients. I worried that he was working too hard and would wear himself out, but the Wildwood Inn project would slow down once the garden party was over, and he'd assured me he was considering hiring someone to help him in the near future, at least on a part-time basis.

For now, though, he was doing everything himself, and that meant I didn't get to enjoy his company on my day off. I lazed around during the morning, reading a book on the couch between loads of laundry, and I took care of some housework after lunch, but by midafternoon I'd grown restless. Bentley had too, so I decided we could both use some exercise. He wholeheartedly supported that idea, if his excited barks and wagging tail were anything to go by.

With Bentley on his leash and trotting at my side, I jogged along Wildwood Road, heading away from town, until we reached the eastern end of the cove. Slowing to a walk, we left the road and followed the narrow path between two private properties until we reached the beach. I unhooked Bentley's leash, and he charged across a wet sandbar to the water's edge.

I followed more slowly, pausing to remove my shoes and socks before leaving the soft dry sand. My bare feet sank into the wet sand as I headed for the water, leaving a trail of footprints behind me. The sun shone brightly from a gorgeous blue sky, and the beautifully fresh breeze had enough of a cool touch to feel good against my warm skin.

When I caught up to Bentley, I paused and let the waves break over my feet. I winced at the cold bite of the water. It definitely wasn't quite as pleasant as the breeze. Bentley didn't seem to mind, but I retreated to the higher ground of the sandbar so my feet wouldn't go numb. It would be several weeks yet before the ocean would be warm enough for swimming without getting uncomfortably cold. In the meantime, though, I could still make the most of the nice weather by enjoying strolls on the beach.

We slowly made our way back up the beach at an angle, aiming for home. When we reached dry sand at the high-water mark, I spotted two familiar figures approaching the beach from the Driftwood Bed-and-Breakfast. Bentley saw them too. He didn't know Ellie Shaw, but he knew and loved Sienna and raced across the sand to greet her.

"Hi, Bentley." Sienna dropped to her knees to give him a hug and to accept kisses in return.

Ellie patted his head, smoothing back his curly fur. "You're so cute."

Bentley gave them a big doggie grin, lapping up the attention.

"Just home from school?" I asked as I approached the girls.

"Yes." Sienna got to her feet, brushing sand from her jeans. "Freedom, finally."

I smiled at that. "How are you feeling, Ellie?"

"Much better, thanks. I didn't feel sick for too long."

"I'm glad to hear it. I'm sorry you missed out on the last round of competition."

"Me too, but it's okay."

"Except that someone might have *made* you sick," Sienna said to her friend.

"That's what my mom thinks."

"And Marley thinks it could be true. Right, Marley?"

"I do," I agreed. "Any idea who might have been behind it, Ellie?"

The teen shook her head and tugged at her braid. "I can't believe anyone would do that."

"That's because you're nice," Sienna told her. "Not everyone is."

"Unfortunately, that's true," I said.

"Ellie remembers more about what was happening at the refreshments table than I do," Sienna said. "I was going to text you about it, but now Ellie can tell you herself."

I wasn't surprised that Sienna had pursued the matter on her own. Sometimes her enthusiasm for amateur sleuthing worried me, but this time it seemed harmless.

Sienna gave her friend a gentle nudge with her elbow. "Tell Marley what you told me."

Ellie tugged on her braid again. "I didn't see anyone putting anything in the drinks, but there were several people hanging around the table. I went over there to get some tea, and Sienna came with me. Cynthia was already there—she was competing in the adult division."

I nodded. "She got sick too."

"She'd made herself a cup of tea and was going to get some coffee for Mikey Soldado," Ellie continued. "But when I got there she made tea for me instead. Then while it was steeping she poured a cup of coffee for Mikey."

"Were you watching the mugs the whole time?" I asked.

"No," Ellie replied. "I was talking to Cynthia and Sienna. Oh, and then that photographer lady came by and took a picture of us."

"So there was a distraction," I said. "Maybe someone slipped something into the mugs while you were all focused on the photographer."

Ellie shrugged. "Maybe."

I glanced at Sienna, but she shrugged too. "I forgot all about the photographer. Ellie's memory is better than mine."

"And you thought the tea tasted strange?" I said to Ellie.

"Yes, so I didn't finish it. I thought maybe it was some weird herbal stuff."

"Who else was near the table at that time?" I asked.

Ellie thought for a moment. "That older woman who was in the competition."

"Dorothy Kerwin," I supplied.

"And her husband," Sienna added.

"Right," Ellie said. "My mom wasn't far away. She was talking to that coach guy. The MC."

"Coach Hannigan," I said. That all matched what Sienna had told me on the weekend. "Do you remember anything else?" I directed the question at both girls, but they shook their heads.

"So who do you think did it?" Sienna asked me.

"I really don't know. It seems like there were several people who had the opportunity to slip something into the drinks. And a motive. Apart from Coach Hannigan, anyway. I don't know why he'd care who won the competition."

"Then how do we figure out who's guilty?"

"I'm not sure yet," I admitted. "But I'll think it over."

Sienna gave Bentley another pat. "We're on our way to Logan's place. Text me if you figure it out?"

"I will," I said.

They headed up the beach to Logan's house, next door to my own. Before leaving the beach myself, I turned around and gazed out at the ocean, taking a moment to soak in the beautiful view that never got old. I spotted a heron perched on one of the rocks at Myler's Point, and closer to me a group of four kids ran across the sand to the water's edge, their happy shouts and laughter ringing out through the spring air.

I was about to turn around when I paused, catching sight of a woman perched on a log, snapping a photo of the ocean view with her phone. An idea took shape in my head and by the time I reached home, I knew how I might be able to find out who had sabotaged the amateur chef competition.

Chapter 26

I had to wait until the next day to visit Amy Strudwick's photography studio in Port Townsend. By the time I'd looked up her website, her studio was about to close, and I wouldn't have had time to drive there before she shut her door to the public. Since Amy had been snapping pictures during the amateur chef competition and even when the contestants were milling about waiting for the cooking to get under way, I was hoping she might have caught the saboteur in action in one of her photographs.

After I'd had breakfast, I checked my phone and found a series of text messages from Patricia. Ray had seized the tea and coffee urns as well as the mugs used at the cooking competition. He was having all of those items tested for substances that might have caused the bouts of vomiting, but it would be a few days before the results would be in. That meant there was still no proof someone had slipped something into the coffee and tea, but that seemed to be the most likely scenario, and my gut told me that was what had happened.

No matter what the results of the tests would turn out to be, they wouldn't necessarily narrow the field of suspects, so I still wanted to carry out my plan to visit Amy at her studio. I didn't set out for Port Townsend as early as I would have liked, though. I first had to pick up some groceries and a few other things in Wildwood Cove, and I took Bentley for a walk on the beach. But by late morning I was on the road, and soon after I was pulling into a parking spot in picturesque Port Townsend.

It was another beautiful spring day, with sunlight streaming down, birds singing in the trees, and a gentle breeze that smelled of the ocean. I parked in the first free space I found, even though it was a few minutes' walk from Amy's studio. I hadn't visited Port Townsend for several weeks, and I wanted the chance to stroll around and enjoy the weather and the sights.

Leaving my car behind, I set off along the street, passing several shops and the Crab and Gull, a restaurant I'd seen many times but had never eaten at. I'd heard it was good, and I made a mental note to suggest to Brett that we have dinner there sometime.

I turned a corner and followed the street that ran along the side of the restaurant. As I drew close to the back of the building, angry voices floated toward me on the breeze. I couldn't hear the words spoken, but it sounded like two men were arguing.

At the rear of the building was a small parking lot, and when it came in sight I stopped in my tracks. Quaid was standing in the middle of the lot, his expression thunderous as he yelled at Jake Fellmen.

Now that I was closer, I could hear what they were saying, and none of it was friendly.

Quaid called Fellmen a string of unflattering names before jabbing a finger in his chest and saying, "If you keep poking your nose into my business, you'll be sorry."

Fellmen appeared completely unfazed, despite the fact that Quaid was taller and bulkier than him. "Sounds like you've got something to hide."

Quaid swore. "I don't have anything to hide. I just don't like you sticking your nose into my business."

I took a few steps toward the two men. "If you don't have anything to hide, how come you were dodging one of the sheriff's deputies at the amateur chef competition?"

A flicker of surprise passed over Fellmen's face when he saw me, but he quickly schooled his features back into a neutral expression. Quaid wasn't nearly so controlled. His stormy expression grew even stormier, and he practically snarled at me.

"What are *you* doing here?"

"Just passing by," I said.

Quaid took a step toward me. "Like hell—"

Fellmen put out an arm to stop him. "Leave the lady alone."

Quaid smacked Fellmen's arm away. "Keep your hands off me." He glared at me and Fellmen. "What is this? Are the two of you trying to set me up?"

"She and I don't even know each other," Fellmen fibbed. "But how about you answer her question?"

"I didn't want the deputy harassing me like the two of you are now. So I had a fling with that girl before she died. So what? She was eighteen at the time. I didn't have anything to do with her death. But I knew her, and I lived near the woods. So the cops are probably going to try to pin the crime on me."

"Has the sheriff talked to you since the remains were found?" I asked.

"They called me in to Port Angeles this morning to grill me."

He'd probably been as charming to Ray and his deputies as he was being to me and Fellmen.

"And I told them what I'll tell you now so you'll get off my back," he continued. "If you want to know who killed Demetra Kozani, talk to that boyfriend of hers."

"Tyrone Phillips?" I said.

"That's him. He came by my place the night of that party. Late. He was drunk. He knew I had a thing going on with Demetra. She'd dumped him by then, but he still thought she was his girl. He ranted at me about leaving her alone. Even tried to take a swing at me. He was so drunk he missed."

"Then what happened?" Fellmen asked.

"I told him to get lost. Last I saw he was stumbling off into the woods."

"And did you see Demetra that night?"

"No. She told me she might come by after the party, but she never showed. And I never heard from her again." Quaid yanked open the driver's door of a black sports car. "Don't bother me again or I'll have you charged with harassment."

With that threat hanging in the air, he climbed into the car and slammed the door. The engine roared to life, and he tore out of the parking lot, disappearing down the street within seconds.

Fellmen fixed his gaze on me. "You seem to be showing up everywhere."

"Small towns," I said with a shrug. "I really was just passing by."

He continued to watch me steadily. "Guys like Quaid Hendrix and Tyrone Phillips can be dangerous, you know."

Annoyance prickled over my skin, but I tried to keep it out of my voice. "I'm aware of that."

"I'd advise you to leave the investigating to the professionals. You're better off flipping pancakes."

He strode past me without another word.

I spun around to watch him go, biting my tongue to keep myself from yelling something at his retreating back. I'd had that same lecture several times before from Ray, but he'd never been so condescending about it.

"I don't flip the flipping pancakes," I muttered. "And the guy who does? He's ten times the man you'll ever be."

I stormed off, realizing I was actually glad the private investigator wasn't related to me.

* * * *

Instead of resuming my path to Amy's photography studio, I made a detour to spend some time down by the water. I needed to soak in the soothing effect of the ocean view after my encounter with Jake and Quaid.

As I strolled along the waterfront, I focused on the warmth of the sun on my face and the cries of the seagulls as they circled overhead. My irritation ebbed away, and my shoulders relaxed. There was no point in letting the private investigator get under my skin. And despite not liking his parting words, my encounter with him and Quaid had left me with some new information.

If Tyrone had confronted Quaid on the night of the party and was angry enough to try to punch him, could he have then directed that anger at Demetra? When he stumbled back into the woods after leaving Quaid's cottage, maybe he'd run into his ex-girlfriend as she was leaving the party.

I didn't know if I should believe Quaid when he said he hadn't seen Demetra that night, but if his story about Tyrone was true, that confirmed for me that the former baseball star deserved a spot at the top of my suspect list. Confronting Tyrone likely wouldn't get me anywhere, even if I had someone with me to ensure my safety, but hopefully I wouldn't have to worry about getting information out of him.

Quaid said he'd told the authorities about Tyrone's visit to his cottage on the night of the party. I figured Tyrone had already been questioned by the sheriff's department when he arrived in Wildwood Cove, and this new information would probably result in him getting grilled again.

Maybe this time Tyrone would crack under the pressure and confess to killing Demetra.

If he *had* killed her.

Deciding not to worry about the murder case for the time being, I turned my back on the water and headed for my original destination. I'd come to Port Townsend with the hope of identifying the person who'd sabotaged the amateur chef competition, so that was what I'd focus on. All thoughts of murder and condescending private investigators could wait.

It took me under five minutes to reach the street where Amy's studio was located. Before going inside, I stopped outside the large window to check out the photographs displayed there. They were primarily portraits, some shot in studio and others outdoors. I was admiring a photograph of a young couple and their golden retriever, taken down by the water's edge, when I glanced through the narrow space between two portraits and into the studio.

I forgot all about the photos on display. The interior of the studio was dimly lit compared to the sunny outdoors, but I could see enough to tell that the place was a mess. I opened the front door and stepped over the threshold. Even in the couple of seconds it took for my eyes to adjust to the change in lighting, I knew something was terribly wrong.

It looked like a hurricane had swept through the small reception area I'd entered. The gray-carpeted floor was strewn with photographs, papers, brochures, pens, and a jumble of other office supplies. A desk sat off to my right, all of its drawers open, the contents spewing out. A chair had been overturned, and a vase of flowers lay on its side on the floor, the carpet wet where the water had spilled out.

A chill ran through my body.

"Amy?" I called out. "Is anybody here?"

I thought I detected a quiet moan from somewhere deeper in the building.

Although apprehensive that the person who'd made the mess might still be lurking somewhere inside, I couldn't ignore the sound I'd heard. I picked my way across the messy floor and through an open doorway that led to a hallway. At the far end of the hall was a metal door with an "exit" sign above it. To my right was a shadowy storage room with a tripod lying on the floor. To my left was a large studio space, stretching toward the back of the building.

I took only a cursory glance at the layout because I was too focused on what was ahead of me.

In the middle of the narrow hallway was Amy Strudwick, facedown on the gray carpet, her short, curly hair matted with blood.

Chapter 27

"Amy!"

I hurried to her side and dropped to my knees. When I rested a hand on her shoulder, she moaned, making the same sound I'd heard moments earlier.

She turned her head to the side, moaning again as she did so. Her eyes fluttered open, and I exhaled with relief.

"You'll be okay," I said calmly, even though I didn't know for sure if that was the case. "I'll call for help."

As I called 911, Amy struggled to focus her eyes on me.

"Who are you?" she asked, her voice thick and groggy.

"My name's Marley McKinney," I told her before speaking to the dispatcher who'd answered my call.

Amy shifted on the floor. I put a hand to her shoulder again. "Try not to move too much."

She ignored me and slowly rolled onto her back with a groan. She touched her hand to the back of her head, and her eyes widened when she saw the blood on her fingers.

"It looks like there was a break-in or something," I told the dispatcher once I'd answered some questions. "But there's no sign of anyone else here now."

Amy pushed herself into a sitting position and leaned her back against the wall. She closed her eyes for a moment while I continued to talk with the dispatcher, and when she opened them again, her gaze wasn't quite so hazy.

"You look familiar," she said, her voice stronger now.

I held my phone away from my ear for a second. "I filled in as a judge one day at the amateur chef competition in Wildwood Cove."

"Right." She nodded as she spoke, but then grimaced, as if the motion had pained her.

A siren sounded in the distance, quickly growing louder. I told the dispatcher that help had arrived and ended the call.

"Sit tight," I advised Amy. "I'm going to show the paramedics in."

I hurried into the reception area as a patrol car from the Jefferson County Sheriff's Office pulled up to the curb. I waved to catch the deputy's attention as he climbed out of the driver's seat. Another siren continued to blare, and a second later an ambulance turned the corner and came to a stop in the middle of the street.

"Deputy Henry," the driver of the patrol car introduced himself as he stepped into the studio. "I understand someone was injured during a break and enter."

"I don't know if it was really a break-in," I said, "but someone trashed the place. It's the owner of the studio who's injured."

By then the paramedics had followed the deputy into the reception area. I pointed them in Amy's direction, hanging back since space in the hallway was limited. Amy was still sitting on the floor with her back to the wall. The paramedics crouched down to speak with her, and she indicated the wound on the back of her head.

Deputy Henry hovered next to the paramedics for a minute, listening to what Amy was saying, but then he disappeared first into the studio area and then into the storage room. When he emerged from the storage room, he headed my way. I backed up a few steps so he could join me in the reception area.

"Are you a friend of Ms. Strudwick's?" the deputy asked me.

"No," I said. "I came to talk to her about some photographs she took at an amateur chef competition in Wildwood Cove recently."

"And the front door was unlocked when you arrived?"

"Yes. I walked right in, but I knew something was wrong right away because of the mess."

The deputy's gaze swept over the disarray around us. "Did you hear or see anyone when you arrived?"

"Just Amy. I called out to see if anyone was around. She didn't answer, but I heard a moan so I went into the hallway and saw her on the floor. She was facedown and barely conscious."

"Did she say anything about what happened?"

"No. She asked who I was but that's it."

Deputy Henry produced a notebook and pen. "Could I please have your name and contact information?"

I provided him with those details, and he wrote them down. As he was putting away his notebook, he paused, as if listening to a voice in his earpiece.

Outside the window, another sheriff's department cruiser arrived on the scene.

"Would you mind coming outside with me?"

I followed the deputy out onto the sidewalk. He exchanged a few words with his newly arrived colleague, a woman with short blond hair. Then he returned to where I stood waiting.

"Did you touch anything aside from the front door?" he asked me.

I thought back over my movements. "No."

"And was there anyone else on the street when you arrived?"

Again, I took a second to think before responding. "I don't remember seeing anyone. I think a couple of cars went by on that street." I pointed to the perpendicular road at the end of the block. "But I don't remember anyone on foot."

"I'd like you to stay here for the moment."

"Of course," I said.

The two deputies entered the studio, wearing gloves, while I waited out on the sidewalk. I tried to peer between the photos displayed in the window without being too obvious about it, but all I could see were the backs of the two deputies as they stood inside the door, surveying the reception area.

For the first time since I'd found Amy, I had a chance to settle my thoughts and think about what had happened.

Why would someone trash a photography studio?

The obvious answer was to steal expensive equipment. But then why tear apart the reception area? I'd only caught a quick glimpse of the actual studio space, but it had appeared to have been untouched. Aside from the tripod on the floor, the same was true of the storage room, as far as I could tell. But if Amy had interrupted the burglar, maybe he or she simply hadn't had a chance to search beyond the reception room.

That still didn't make much sense, though. I'd noticed a laptop sitting on the reception desk. Why wouldn't the thief have grabbed that? And why target the place during business hours? Sure, that saved the burglar from actually having to break in, but it seemed awfully risky. Much of the front window was blocked by the display of photographs, but anyone—like me—could have walked in off the street at any moment.

Forgetting about the timing for the moment, I considered another angle. What if the person who tore apart the reception room wasn't looking for photography equipment to be able to sell? What if that person had come to the studio for the same reason as I had?

Maybe the saboteur had realized that Amy might have caught him or her on camera. The person could have come to the studio with the intention of destroying any such evidence.

The front door to the studio opened, and I set my thoughts aside temporarily. The paramedics wheeled Amy out on a stretcher, Deputy Henry following close behind.

"Hold on a second," Amy said, rubbing her forehead. "I remember something."

The paramedics brought the stretcher to a stop, and Deputy Henry moved to Amy's side.

"What's that?" the deputy asked.

"I saw who hit me. Just a glimpse before it happened."

"Was it a man or a woman?"

"A man," Amy said.

"Do you think you could describe him for me?" Deputy Henry asked.

"I can do better than that." Amy clasped her hands tightly, her knuckles turning white. "I can tell you his name. He's a former classmate of mine—Tyrone Phillips."

Chapter 28

The paramedics whisked Amy off to the hospital soon after she'd mentioned Tyrone's name. When Deputy Henry had asked if Tyrone had any reason to tear her studio apart, she'd seemed reluctant to say that he could have been after equipment to sell for some quick cash. Tyrone was staying in Wildwood Cove with his mom, so why he would come to Port Townsend to commit a burglary, I didn't know. Unless it was to put some distance between himself and the crime. And maybe he'd specifically targeted Amy's studio since he knew she was a photographer and would have valuable equipment.

But if Tyrone was the person who'd hit Amy, then my theory about the saboteur looking for incriminating photos likely wasn't correct. After all, what interest would Tyrone have in the outcome of the amateur chef competition?

None that I could think of.

Still, I decided I should tell Deputy Henry about the competition and the reason why I'd come to the studio. He made a few notes as I filled him in, and he seemed to take me seriously. By the time he'd asked me a couple of questions about the sabotage, the ambulance had left the scene. Deputy Henry told me I didn't need to hang around any longer, so I set off along the street.

Fortunately, it seemed like Amy would be okay. Not so fortunate was the fact that I'd be leaving Port Townsend with more questions than answers. That was frustrating, to say the least, considering that I'd made the trip with the hope of solving one of the two cases that had recently plagued Wildwood Cove.

When I reached my car, I paused with one hand on the driver's door. My stomach gave a loud grumble, and I realized I was hungry, too hungry to want to wait until I got home to eat lunch. I'd passed a fish-and-chips shop while walking around the town earlier, and I decided to head back that way. Maybe getting some food in my stomach would help me sort out my jumbled thoughts.

Doubtful, but it was worth a shot.

I'd made it halfway to the fish-and-chips restaurant when I stopped short in the middle of the sidewalk. The white cube van Brett used for work was parked across the street, unmistakable thanks to the name of his business written in large letters on the side of the vehicle.

If his van was in Port Townsend, then Brett was too. Somewhere.

I was about to set off in search of him when I spotted him walking toward his van on the opposite side of the street. I called his name and waved. He stopped in his tracks when he saw me, but then he smiled and waved back.

I waited for a couple of cars to pass by and then crossed the street. When I reached Brett's van, he had the passenger door open and was setting a couple of bags on the seat.

He shut the door when I reached him.

"I thought you'd be back in Wildwood Cove by now," he said.

"I thought I would be too. But I didn't start out as early as I thought, and things didn't quite go as planned. I didn't expect to find you here."

"I came to pick up a few things before heading off to my next job."

I raised myself up on tiptoes to peer through the passenger window at the bags holding his purchases.

"Hey." Brett took my hand and tugged me closer to him.

"Hey, what?" I asked, but I barely got the words out before his lips touched mine.

He kissed me in that way of his that always left me feeling like I was floating in the air, like he'd stolen all the air out of my lungs.

"Um, wow," I managed to say when he rested his forehead against mine. "What was that for?"

"Does there have to be a reason?"

"No," I said, so quickly that Brett grinned. "That's definitely not required."

He kissed me again, and it was with great reluctance that I pulled back a moment later.

"We're on a public street," I reminded him.

"Unfortunately," Brett said with a grin.

I took half a step back but held his hands in mine. "Do you have to head back to work now?"

"Not right away. I could take another half hour."

"Good," I said with a smile.

"Why?" he asked with the lopsided grin that always made my stomach flip-flop. "You want to make out in the van?"

I poked him in the shoulder. "I was thinking about lunch."

"I must not have kissed you well enough if you're able to think about anything."

"You're welcome to try again later," I said. "When we're home."

His grin widened. "I'll take you up on that."

"For now, how about some fish-and-chips?"

"I'll take you up on that too."

* * * *

We ate our fish-and-chips outdoors, claiming a small table and two chairs in the sunshine. I had to keep my hoodie on to stay warm with the breeze coming off the ocean, but it was still a nice day for eating outside.

A seagull perched nearby and eyed our lunch but fortunately kept its distance. Eventually it gave up on us and went in search of another food source. While I enjoyed my battered cod and munched on fries, I told Brett about my visit to Amy's studio.

"Is she going to be all right?" Brett asked when I described how Amy had been hit on the head.

"I hope so. She was really groggy when I found her, but she seemed wide awake by the time she was put in the ambulance."

I filled Brett in on what Amy said about her attacker, and my theory about the saboteur.

"But if Tyrone was the one who trashed the studio and hit Amy, the saboteur must not have been involved, right?"

"That's what I'm thinking," I agreed. "I don't know why Tyrone would sabotage the competition."

Brett eyed me, a French fry halfway to his mouth. "Please don't tell me you're going to confront Tyrone."

"Of course not. I'll leave that to the cops."

Brett relaxed and resumed eating.

"I don't really know what I'm going to do next," I said after enjoying a big bite of fish. "Amy still could have photos of the saboteur in action, but with her in the hospital I don't know when I'll get a chance to look at them."

"I think you should tell Ray and let him deal with it."

"I guess you're right," I admitted. "I mentioned my theory to the deputy who responded to the situation at the studio, but I'll tell Ray too."

Since Port Townsend was in a different county than Wildwood Cove, there were two different sheriff's offices. I figured they probably shared information, but contacting Ray directly might speed things up.

"Hopefully he won't think I'm snooping too much by giving him the information."

Brett squeezed my hand. "At least you're not tangling with a murderer this time. Well," he revised, "not at the moment."

"Oh, speaking of which…"

"I take my words back," Brett said with a shake of his head, but I could tell he was fighting a smile.

I recounted my conversation with Quaid and Fellmen.

Any hint of a smile disappeared from Brett's face. "I don't like Quaid, and I really don't like you being around him."

"I wasn't alone with him."

"I'm not sure I like that private investigator much more."

"He's not as bad as Quaid, but I wouldn't say he's my favorite person." I finished off the last of my fish. "I hope Ray knows more than I do, because I feel like there's a whole lot of suspects in the murder case and not much in the way of concrete clues."

"I don't think it'll be an easy case for anyone to solve now that ten years have passed since Demetra died, but Ray probably does know more than he's letting on."

I pushed my remaining fries toward Brett. He'd already polished off his lunch, and I didn't have room in my stomach for anything more.

"I'll call Ray later."

"Good idea." Brett got to work on demolishing the last of the fries. "Then what will you do?"

I shrugged. "Relax?"

He laughed.

"What?" I asked. "I know how to relax."

"When there's a mystery to be solved?"

I crumpled up our food wrappers. "Don't you need to get back to work?" I was pretending to be miffed, but he wasn't buying it.

"I do," he said as we got up from the table and tossed our garbage in a trashcan. He took my hand. "But first I'm going to walk you to your car."

* * * *

The unexpected chance to have lunch with Brett left a smile on my face as I drove along the highway toward home. Not even thoughts about Demetra's murder or the attack on Amy managed to dampen my spirits. I was so content that I didn't spare much thought to those unsolved mysteries until I neared the turnoff for Wildwood Cove.

Two sheriff's department cruisers driving on the opposite side of the highway reached the turnoff ahead of me, catching my attention before they disappeared onto the quieter road. When I left the highway and rounded a bend, I spotted the two cars up ahead of me. I couldn't help but wonder why two patrol cars were heading toward town. They didn't have their lights or sirens activated, but clearly more than one officer was required for some reason.

I was nearing home when I glanced at my rearview mirror and spotted a third patrol car behind me on Wildwood Road. I turned into my driveway, and a few seconds later the third car drove by. Coming to a quick decision, I turned my car around. If Ray was in one of the cruisers, he wouldn't be pleased to know I'd decided to follow them to their destination, but my curiosity pushed me to keep the three patrol cars in sight.

After passing by Main Street, the cruisers turned off Wildwood Road and into a quiet residential neighborhood. When I saw them pull to a stop on Saratoga Street, I steered my car over to the curb and parked, deciding it would be a good idea to stay back. I didn't want to get in the way of whatever might happen next.

Four officers emerged from the three vehicles. I recognized Ray easily, but I didn't get a good look at the deputies with him. Staying in my car, I watched as Ray approached the front of Tyrone's mother's house with one deputy by his side. The two other deputies circled around toward the back of the house.

Maybe they were about to arrest Tyrone. For the murder, or for trashing Amy's studio and assaulting her?

My hands gripped the steering wheel as Ray knocked on the front door. He didn't get an immediate response.

Movement off to the side redirected my attention. I leaned forward for a better look out my windshield. Someone was creeping along the roof of the house.

It was Tyrone, I realized a second later. He carefully made his way along the overhang at the side of the house.

I gasped when he jumped from the roof and grabbed a thick tree branch several feet away. I thought for sure he'd fall, but he made the jump easily.

He'd probably done it dozens of times as a teenager sneaking out of the house.

I glanced toward the front porch. Ray knocked on the door again, but still no one answered. I wondered if I should somehow alert him to the fact that Tyrone was now shimmying down the tree at the side of the house. He reached a lower branch and then swung down and let go, landing easily on the grass.

He glanced toward the front of the house, but the sheriff and deputies still had no idea he was there. I opened the car door as Tyrone vaulted over the fence and disappeared into the neighbor's yard. A deputy came around the corner from the back of the house and broke into a run. He must have seen Tyrone before he got out of sight.

I settled back into my seat and shut the car door, deciding to stay put. Two deputies climbed up over the fence to give chase. They must have alerted Ray by radio, because he and the third deputy ran back toward the cruisers. Two of the patrol cars roared off seconds later, leaving me wondering if they were in pursuit of a burglar or a killer.

Chapter 29

I sat in my car for another ten minutes, waiting to see if anyone would return. No one did. A woman walked by my car, pushing a baby in a stroller and casting a curious but wary glance my way. I decided I should probably leave before someone reported me for suspicious loitering.

As I drove home, I kept my eyes peeled for any sign of Tyrone or the deputies, but I didn't see them anywhere. I had a sinking feeling that Tyrone had managed to get away. Where he would go, I didn't know, but maybe he'd somehow manage to catch a ride back to Seattle without getting caught.

When I got home, I tried to relax on the back porch with a book, Bentley napping near my feet. But it turned out Brett was right—I was too caught up in the two unsolved mysteries to shut my mind off and enjoy some downtime. I gave it a good effort, but after reading the same page four times, I had to admit defeat.

Setting the book aside, I got up and moved over to the railing where Flapjack was enjoying the afternoon sun, his front paws tucked under him, his orange tail twitching occasionally when a bird flew by. I gave him a scratch on the head, and he rewarded me with a purr.

"I wonder which crime Ray was trying to arrest Tyrone for. Killing Demetra? Assaulting Amy? If he *was* trying to arrest him. But since he showed up with three deputies, you'd think that would be why."

Flapjack closed his eyes to mere slits, and I could have sworn there was a contented smile on his furry face.

"I know," I said to him. "Human problems are of no consequence to you, right?"

Flapjack twitched his tail, but that probably had more to do with the chickadee that fluttered past than anything I'd said.

My curiosity was making me restless, so I grabbed my phone and sent a text message to Chloe, thinking she might hear rumors about Tyrone since she knew more people who knew him. I couldn't expect a response right away, though. She'd still be busy with her students for another hour or so.

As I set my phone aside, Bentley woke up from his nap and stretched before sitting at my feet, gazing up at me expectantly.

"Want to get some exercise?" I asked.

I interpreted the enthusiastic wagging of his tail as a yes.

"I think that's a good idea."

I took Bentley for a short run, returning home along the beach as we often did. The fresh air and exercise helped make me feel less restless, but my head was still filled with racing thoughts. Bentley seemed content, however. He took a long drink of water from his bowl in the kitchen and then flopped down on his bed in the family room, ready for another snooze.

After a quick shower, I checked my phone, my hopes rising when I saw that Chloe had responded to my text message.

Let me see what I can find out, her response read.

She'd sent another text since then.

Hope hasn't heard anything. I'll call Ray and see what he'll tell me.

I hoped her uncle would be more forthcoming with her than he would with me. She had what was probably a more legitimate interest in Demetra's case than I did. She also wasn't in the habit of annoying him by sticking her nose in every murder investigation that came across his desk.

After calling her uncle, Chloe phoned me.

"I talked to Ray," she said after we'd exchanged greetings. "He wants to question Tyrone again about his movements on the night of the party."

I wondered if that was because of the information Quaid had recently provided.

"But the arrest warrant is for assaulting Amy," Chloe went on. "I had no idea that had even happened!"

"It was only a few hours ago," I said.

"That's what Ray said. So of course I didn't know, since I've been working. But still, I was shocked. I mean, it's no secret that Tyrone has anger issues, but *Amy*?"

"She thinks she interrupted him while he was robbing her studio. Does that sound possible to you?"

"Maybe? I guess it could be true. I don't think Tyrone has a criminal record, but it's not like his past is squeaky clean either. And who knows what he's been up to since he dropped out of college? He's mostly been living in Seattle since then."

"Do you know if Ray and his deputies ever did arrest Tyrone?"

"They didn't. Tyrone gave them the slip, and they haven't been able to find him. Ray talked to Coach Hannigan, thinking Tyrone might have turned to him for help, but he hasn't heard from him. If we know anything we're supposed to tell Ray right away. He didn't beat around the bush about that."

"*Do* you know anything? Do you have any idea where he might have gone?"

"I figure he probably hightailed it back to Seattle. Ray said his truck's still at his mom's place, but he could have hitchhiked. Ray said the Jefferson County sheriff has some people watching the ferries, but maybe Tyrone managed to slip past them."

"Or he's still in Wildwood Cove," I said. "Does he have any close friends here anymore? Anyone he might turn to for help, aside from Coach Hannigan?"

"Um, hold on one second." Chloe's voice grew more distant as she talked to someone at her end.

I poured myself a glass of sweet tea while I waited, downing half the glass in two gulps. Carrying the rest of my drink with me, I wandered out onto the back porch. Flapjack was now snoozing on the windowsill in the kitchen, but Bentley followed me outside to flop down in the sunshine.

As I leaned against the railing, Chloe came back on the line.

"Sorry about that. I'm on my way out of the school and had to talk to a colleague for a second. I don't think Tyrone's all that close to anyone in Wildwood Cove anymore, except his mom, of course." I heard the beep of a car lock from Chloe's end of the line and a second later a car door shut. "Aside from Coach Hannigan and Mrs. Phillips, I'd say Chrissy is probably the person who knows Tyrone best. Do you want to meet me at her shop? She might not have anything to tell us, but we can always ask."

I was already heading inside to grab my car keys. "I'll definitely meet you there."

* * * *

Chrissy wasn't exactly happy to see us.

"I don't want to talk about Demetra anymore," she said before we could even say hello to her.

A frown had appeared on her face as soon as she saw us coming into the store, and she wouldn't make eye contact with us.

"It's too difficult and I don't want to cry. I can't be scaring my customers away."

Aside from the three of us, the store was empty at the moment, but the shop wasn't due to close for another half hour, and even as she spoke to us, two women stopped outside the front window to admire a sleek satin dress displayed on a mannequin.

"We don't want to upset you," Chloe told her. "We just want to know if you have any idea where Tyrone might be hiding."

Chrissy set down the skirt she was about to clip to a hanger. "Hiding? Why is he hiding?" Her eyes widened. "Are the cops going to arrest him for killing Demetra?"

"Not for that, no," I said. "Not yet, anyway."

Chloe quickly told her what had happened to Amy earlier in the day.

"Why would Tyrone rob Amy's studio in the middle of the day?" Chrissy asked once Chloe had finished. "He's no genius, but I don't think he's *that* stupid."

"We don't know for sure what his motive was," I said. "We just want to find him. He took off when the sheriff went to his mom's place, and he hasn't been seen since."

The bell above the boutique's door jingled. The three of us turned as one to see who was there. Jake Fellmen stepped into the shop, his discerning gaze quickly taking in the sight of us gathered by the sales counter.

"You again," Chrissy said with a distinct lack of enthusiasm. "How many more times do I have to answer the same questions?" She didn't give Fellmen a chance to respond, instead addressing me and Chloe again. "I haven't seen Tyrone. And I haven't heard from him either. He's more likely to go to Coach Hannigan for help than me."

"Coach Hannigan hasn't heard from him," Chloe said.

"Then I guess the sheriff will have to hunt him down."

"He hasn't had any luck with that so far," Fellmen said.

No one spared him anything more than the briefest glance.

"You can't think of anywhere he might have gone?" I pressed.

Chrissy slapped the skirt and hanger down onto the counter. I thought she was about to lose her temper with me, but then her expression shifted from exasperated to thoughtful.

"There was a place we used to hang out sometimes," she said. "An old abandoned cabin."

"The one by the river?" Chloe asked.

"Yes. It must really be a wreck by now, but that's the only place I can think of."

The bell jingled again, and this time a young woman with a toddler in tow entered the boutique.

"I really need to get back to work," Chrissy practically hissed at us, keeping her voice low.

I said a hurried thank-you to her and left the shop with Chloe. Fellmen followed us out onto the sidewalk.

"This is Jake Fellmen, the private investigator Demetra's mom hired," I told Chloe.

"Are you looking for Tyrone too?" she asked him.

"I am. I want to question him about some information I got from Quaid Hendrix this morning. I'm sure the sheriff wants to talk to him about it too. But I hear Tyrone's got himself into even more trouble, in Port Townsend this time."

"So it seems," I said.

"I should call Ray." Chloe dug through her purse and pulled out her phone.

"The sheriff's her uncle," I explained for Fellmen's benefit.

Chloe tried calling Ray, but she soon shook her head. "He's not picking up. Should I call back and leave a message? Should we call 911?"

"I'll scout out the cabin and see if Tyrone's there," Fellmen said. "No point in calling in an emergency if that's not his hideout."

"You won't be able to find it," Chloe said. "It's not on any road or trail."

"Then show me the way."

Chloe and I shared an uneasy glance.

"I'm pretty sure my uncle would want us to leave it to him to check," she said to the PI.

Fellmen took a step backward. "Fine. You keep trying to reach him. If you're not willing to give me directions, I'll ask someone else."

He turned his back on us and strode away.

Chloe stared after him. "What the heck?"

"I think he only cares about his own investigation, not the official one," I said.

"If Tyrone is at the cabin and he spots that guy looking around, he'll bolt." Chloe tried Ray's number again. "I'm leaving a message."

She did so, letting her uncle know what Chrissy had said about the old cabin.

"What do you think we should do now?" she asked me after she'd hung up.

I had my focus on a spot down the street. Fellmen had disappeared into Wildwood Cove's general store moments before, and he'd just reappeared on the sidewalk. He jogged across the street and got into a gray sedan.

"I think," I said, already heading for my own car, "that we should head for the cabin."

Chapter 30

"Are you sure about this?" Chloe asked as she slid into the passenger seat of my car.

"No," I admitted. "But if Fellmen scares off Tyrone, maybe we can keep an eye on him and see where he goes."

"I don't know." Chloe had a death grip on her phone. "Maybe we really should call 911."

"I think you're right." I could see Fellmen's car up ahead of us, heading toward the river. I followed after him. "We'll wait on the road. When Ray or his deputies show up, we can point them toward the cabin. Maybe Tyrone isn't there, but better safe than sorry."

"I agree."

While Chloe talked to the emergency dispatcher, I left the paved road for a dirt one. I'd jogged along this route a few times, but I'd never followed the road too far into the woods.

Within minutes we were farther along the road than I'd ever been before. The river was on our right, both it and the road curving eastward. I wasn't entirely sure where we were, but I figured we were still a mile or two away from the Wildwood Inn.

"We're almost as close as we can get by car," Chloe said to me after ending her call.

We rounded a bend and saw Fellmen's gray sedan up ahead. He hadn't had much of a head start on us, but he was nowhere in sight, his car unoccupied. I pulled up behind the sedan and parked.

"Do you think Fellmen will be able to find the cabin?" I asked.

"Depends on the directions he got. There are a few landmarks to go by—this big stump being the first." She pointed at a four-foot-high stump at the side of the road. "But I haven't been to the cabin in years, so who knows how much things have overgrown?"

I lowered the windows to let in the evening breeze and to make it easier for us to hear any sounds of someone approaching.

"It could be another ten minutes before Ray or one of his deputies shows up," Chloe said.

She sounded uneasy, and I couldn't blame her. If Tyrone was nearby and he really was guilty of attacking Amy—and possibly killing Demetra too—there was no telling what he'd do if he felt trapped or cornered.

"How long will it take Fellmen to get to the cabin if he finds it easily?" I asked.

"Maybe five minutes if he's going at an average pace."

I drummed my fingers against the steering wheel, watching the woods on the other side of the narrow road. Nothing other than the occasional bird moved between the trees, and all I could hear was the rushing of the nearby river and the tap-tap-tap of my fingers against the steering wheel. I glanced in the rearview mirror, hoping to see a sheriff's department cruiser approaching, but the road was deserted behind us.

"He's probably not there," Chloe said, not sounding too certain. "He probably skipped town and went back to Seattle, right?"

I detected another sound aside from the roar of the river. Someone was crashing through the forest's undergrowth.

I sat up straighter. "Maybe not."

The crashing grew louder, and I caught sight of a flash of movement among the trees.

"It's Tyrone!" Chloe said, opening the passenger door.

We both jumped out of the car as Tyrone broke through the tree line. He careened to a stop, staring at us with wide, wild eyes.

"What are you doing here?" he asked in a panicked voice. His eyes darted left and right. "Did you bring the cops?"

"Tyrone," Chloe said, "hiding isn't going to help you."

He ran a hand through his messy hair, practically bursting with agitated energy. "They want to lock me away for something I didn't do. I didn't hurt Demetra!"

"What about Amy Strudwick?" I asked.

"Amy?" Confusion replaced some of the panic in his eyes. "What does Amy have to do with anything?"

"The sheriff wants to talk to you about Demetra's case, but he wants to arrest you for assaulting Amy."

"Assaulting..." He shook his head, looking dazed. "I didn't touch Amy!" Understanding dawned on his face. "He's behind it, isn't he? He's behind *all* of it."

"Who is?" Chloe asked.

"Coach Hannigan, of course!"

Chloe and I glanced at each other with surprise.

Someone moved through the undergrowth in the forest behind Tyrone. He whirled around. Fellmen wasn't yet in sight, but the sound of his approach grew louder.

The panic returned to Tyrone's eyes as he focused on us again. He reached into the pocket of his jeans and whipped out a knife before I had a chance to realize what he was doing.

Chloe and I took a step back as he brandished the blade. I bumped into my car, unable to move any farther away from him.

"Toss me your keys," he ordered me.

"What?" I was so focused on the sharp blade of the knife that I could hardly process what he'd said.

"Your keys!"

I hesitated until he advanced on me with the knife. I threw the keys, and he snatched them out of the air with his free hand.

"Out of my way!"

Chloe grabbed my arm and pulled me away from the car.

"Running will only make things worse, Tyrone," she said, her voice shaking.

He slid into the driver's seat and slammed the door. I glanced toward the forest. Fellmen was running toward us, but he still had a ways to go before he reached the road.

"I'm not going down for what he's done," Tyrone said through the open window as he started the engine.

"Why do you think Coach Hannigan is behind this?" I asked over the sound of the car's engine.

But Tyrone didn't answer. He just reversed my car like a shot, dirt from the road spraying out from beneath the tires. Chloe and I hurried out of the way as he zoomed forward and back in a wild three-point turn. When he had the car faced away from us, he stepped on the gas and raced off along the road.

Fellmen burst through the tree line. "You let him get away?"

"He had a knife!" Chloe glared at him. "What were we supposed to do?"

Fellmen was already climbing into his car.

Chloe glanced at me, and I nodded. I ran around the hood of the sedan and jumped into the passenger seat while Chloe got into the back.

"I thought you were just going to see if he was at the cabin, not send him running," I said as Fellmen maneuvered his car around, barely more controlled than Tyrone had been.

"He was outside. Saw me coming."

We bounced along the dirt road. As we zoomed out of the woods and onto the paved street, Fellmen screeched to a stop and swore.

My car was nowhere in sight.

"He's going to see Coach Hannigan," I told Fellmen.

"Where does he live?" the PI asked.

"Green Hill Road," Chloe replied. She opened the back door. "I'll wait here until someone shows up from the sheriff's office. Then I'll send them your way."

Before I could question whether it was a good idea to leave Chloe by herself, she slammed the door and Fellmen stepped on the gas.

I told him how to get to Green Hill Road while I pulled out my phone, trying to find an exact address for the former baseball coach. When I found Bruce Hannigan's house number online, I knew we were only minutes away. What I didn't know was what we'd find once we got there.

Chapter 31

I gripped the edge of my seat as Fellmen tore along the street.

"Does he think Hannigan's going to help him get out of the mess he's in?" the PI asked.

"Actually, he seems to believe Coach Hannigan's behind everything."

"Everything as in Demetra Kozani's death and...?"

"And the attack on Amy. I really don't think Tyrone's responsible for that. He seemed genuinely surprised to hear about the assault."

"But why would he think Hannigan would try to rob a photographer's studio?"

"I didn't get a chance to tell him about the studio getting trashed," I said. "He seems to think the attack on Amy is related to Demetra's death. At least, that's what I got out of those few seconds of talking to him."

Fellmen's jaw was tense and his eyebrows were drawn together as he kept his eyes focused on the road ahead of us. "Even if Hannigan killed Demetra, what would Amy have to do with that?"

"I don't know," I said. "Did you have the coach pegged as a suspect?"

Fellmen didn't reply, but the frown on his face was answer enough.

I tightened my grip on my seat as Fellmen barely slowed before turning onto Green Hill Road. "Why would Hannigan kill Demetra?" I asked. "Something to do with Tyrone being his star player?"

"Maybe he thought Demetra was too much of a distraction for Tyrone."

"Still, killing her? That would be kind of extreme."

"Tyrone was the best player Hannigan ever coached. If Tyrone had gone on to be a star in the major leagues, that could have given Hannigan's career a boost. Or at least his reputation. For some people, that's enough to drive them to murder."

"Okay," I said, thinking things over. "But even if that's the case, how does Amy fit into things?"

"Maybe she knew something."

"All these years and she never said anything?" A thought struck me. "Her photographs. I wanted to ask her if she had any pictures of the cooking competition's saboteur in action. What if ten years ago she caught something on camera that would cast suspicion on Coach Hannigan?" I shook my head, disappointment smothering my momentary burst of excitement. "No. If he suspected that, why would he wait until now to do something about it?"

Fellmen finally slowed the car before turning into a long driveway. I could see my blue hatchback parked up a hill, near a one-story gray home that was surrounded by a couple of acres of land. Fellmen headed for the house.

"Maybe we're about to find out," he said.

* * * *

Fellmen didn't go straight to the front door. Instead he approached a large window from the side and peeked through it. Tyrone might have heard us driving up to the house, but I figured it was a good idea not to go bursting in there without an idea of what was happening.

When Fellmen pulled back from the window, frowning, I took his place, sneaking a glance into the house. My heart almost stopped when I saw the scene inside, lit by a lamp and the glow from a large flat-screen television mounted on the wall.

Coach Hannigan stood with his back to the television, his hands raised in the air as if in surrender. Tyrone stood three or four feet away from him, holding the same knife he'd pulled on me and Chloe.

"Stay out here," Fellmen said in a low voice.

He quietly opened the front door and slipped inside.

I ducked down to stay out of sight and crept beneath the window until I reached the corner of the house. Fellmen had left the front door open behind him, and I didn't want anyone hearing the call I was about to make.

When the emergency dispatcher answered, I quickly filled her in on what was happening, stressing that Tyrone had a knife and believed he was confronting Demetra Kozani's killer. The dispatcher wanted me to stay on the line, and I assured her that I would.

When I heard a yell from inside the house, I peeked through the window again. Tyrone now knew Fellmen was there. The PI had his back to me, and Tyrone was trying to cover him and Coach Hannigan with his knife. I ducked down again and hurried toward the front door, my phone in my hand at my side, still connected to the dispatcher.

I paused for a moment, whispering into the phone that Tyrone was now threatening two men with his knife. Then I crept closer to the open door, staying out of sight but listening to what was unfolding inside.

"I swear I never hurt Demetra, Tyrone," Hannigan said. It sounded like he was trying to keep his voice calm, but a thread of tension still ran through his words.

"You thought she was bad for me, for my career," Tyrone said. His voice wavered, and I suspected he was crying.

"But she broke up with you and was going off to New York City. You would have forgotten about her once you got off to college. I had no reason to kill her."

"He's telling the truth, Tyrone," Fellmen said.

"What do you know?" Tyrone yelled. "He killed Demetra and then he tried to kill Amy to keep her quiet."

"Amy Strudwick?" Hannigan sounded as baffled as Tyrone had when I'd brought up her name earlier. "The photographer? Someone tried to kill her?"

"You did!"

"It wasn't me," Hannigan said. "None of it was me. Why would I kill either one of them?"

"You know why!"

I chanced a glance through the front door in time to see Fellmen lunge at Tyrone as he moved closer to Hannigan. The PI tackled Tyrone, and they crashed to the floor together. Hannigan dove into the mix as the other two men struggled on the floor.

A second later, the coach straightened up, Tyrone's knife in his hand. He backed off as Fellmen climbed to his feet, hauling Tyrone up with him, holding the younger man's hands behind his back.

I spun around at the sound of tires crunching on gravel. Relief rushed through me at the sight of the two sheriff's department cruisers coming up the driveway. I ended my call with the dispatcher and ran over to meet Ray as he climbed out of his patrol car.

"Coach Hannigan and Jake Fellmen got the knife away from Tyrone," I said.

"The private investigator?" Deputy Rutowski asked as he climbed out of the second cruiser.

"Yes."

Ray was already drawing his gun. "Marley, stay here."

I hung back by the vehicles while Ray entered the house, Deputy Rutowski going with him. Dusk had fallen since I'd arrived at Coach Hannigan's house. The lamplight in the living room helped me to see people moving about inside, but I only had a general idea of what was going on. Fortunately, it seemed like the situation was still under control.

A couple of minutes later, Tyrone came out the front door, his hands cuffed behind him, Deputy Rutowski guiding him over to the nearest cruiser.

Ray appeared in the doorway and motioned to me to join him. "We'll need a statement from you, Marley," he said as he returned to the living room with me on his heels. He had a plastic evidence bag in one hand with Tyrone's knife inside.

"No problem," I said.

"Any idea why Tyrone was threatening you?" Ray directed the question at Coach Hannigan.

The former baseball coach was seated in an armchair, looking a bit pale. "He seems to think I killed Demetra and hurt Amy Strudwick somehow." He shook his head. "I don't know how he came up with that idea."

"He was pretty convinced," I said, not sure if I believed Hannigan.

"Maybe so." He got up from the chair. "But I can prove I didn't kill Demetra Kozani."

"How?" Fellmen asked. "That was ten years ago."

"I'll show you." Hannigan led the way into a dining room that appeared to function more as an office than an eating space.

The large table was covered with piles of papers and file folders. A stack of sports magazines took up one chair while a messy heap of newspapers and junk mail occupied another. Hannigan went straight to a gray filing cabinet sitting in one corner. He riffled through the contents of one of the drawers before taking out a file folder.

He pulled some papers from the folder and handed them over to Ray.

"The day before Demetra was last seen alive, I ended up in the hospital with a ruptured appendix," Hannigan explained. "I didn't get home for a week, and even then I wasn't fit enough to go around killing people."

Ray nodded as he finished studying the papers, apparently satisfied.

"What about Amy Strudwick?" I asked.

Ray shot me a look that wasn't difficult to interpret. He wanted me to leave the questions to him.

"What about her?" Hannigan asked. "I still don't know what happened there. Did someone try to kill her? Is she all right?"

"She was hit on the head at her studio this morning," Ray replied. "She has a concussion, but she's expected to make a full recovery."

"I was visiting my sister in Port Angeles this morning," Hannigan said. "Feel free to confirm that with her."

"You weren't a suspect," Ray assured him. "Amy thought Tyrone was the one who assaulted her."

"I don't think he did," I said.

Ray focused his stern gaze on me. "You and I will chat in a minute."

Yikes. I sensed a lecture coming my way.

Ray was quiet for a moment, and I guessed he was listening to someone talking through his earpiece.

His expression grew even more serious.

"I need to leave," he said to all of us. "There's an accident out on the highway. I'll need statements from all three of you. If you could stop by my office tomorrow, I'd appreciate it."

We barely had a chance to indicate our assent before he was out the door. I followed a few seconds behind him, and by the time I got outside, both cruisers were already turning around in the driveway. They set off toward the road a moment later, activating their lights and sirens.

I hoped no one was badly hurt in the accident.

My gaze fell on my blue hatchback, and I jogged toward it, peering in through the open window. I breathed a sigh of relief. Tyrone had left my keys in the ignition.

Fellmen came out of the house, Hannigan following him as far as the doorway.

"Crazy," the coach said, running a hand over his balding head.

"What's your explanation for Tyrone's behavior?" I asked him.

He shrugged. "I don't really have one. Thinking things through was never the kid's forte, at least off the baseball field. I have no idea how he came up with those crazy notions."

I nodded, though a wedge of uneasiness lodged in my chest.

"Do you think he's the killer?" Fellmen asked.

"Nah," Hannigan said. "He's got his issues, but he's no killer."

After the things I'd seen pass across Tyrone's face that evening, I tended to agree with him on that.

"We'll get out of your hair," Fellmen said, heading for his car.

Hannigan raised a hand in acknowledgment and disappeared into his house, shutting the door.

"What do you make of all this?" I asked the PI.

He opened the driver's side door of his car and regarded me over the roof. "I report to Mrs. Kozani, not you."

He didn't give me a chance to say anything in response, getting into his car and starting the engine. That was probably for the best. I didn't have anything pleasant to say to him in that moment.

I didn't like that everything was still up in the air, Demetra's murder still unsolved. Maybe that was the reason I felt so uneasy. Hopefully Ray and his team would soon figure out who killed her.

I got into my car and turned it around, following a few seconds behind Fellmen as he drove down the hill toward the road. I flicked on my headlights. Dusk had slipped into darkness while I was in the house.

At the bottom of the driveway, I slowed to a stop. Something flickered in my right side mirror. My foot still on the brake, I turned in my seat to look over my shoulder.

My eyes hadn't played a trick on me, I realized.

Someone was on Hannigan's property, moving stealthily through the shadows toward the house.

Chapter 32

I made a split-second decision.

Shutting off my car's lights and engine, I pocketed my keys and phone and climbed out of the car, shutting the door as quietly as possible. My feet crunched on the gravel driveway with each step, so I hurried over to the grass so I'd make less noise.

I jogged up the hill, scanning the darkness as I went. I caught sight of another flicker of movement as the shadowy form of the prowler headed around Hannigan's house toward the back.

I picked up my pace and ran straight to the front door, keeping my knock fairly quiet.

Hannigan answered a few seconds later, surprise and a hint of wariness registering on his face when he saw me.

"You've got a prowler," I said without preamble. "Heading around the back of your house."

"Did you get a good look at him?" Hannigan was already heading down the hallway.

I shut the front door behind me and followed him. "No, I just saw a moving shadow."

I put my hand to the pocket of my jeans where my phone was tucked away. "Do you want me to call 911?"

"The sheriff and his deputies are tied up with more important things at the moment," Hannigan said. "I'll turn on the lights out back. That'll probably scare him off."

He flipped a switch on the wall and opened the back door.

"Maybe you shouldn't—"

A baseball bat swung through the air and connected with Hannigan's head with a sickening crack.

I gasped. Hannigan crumpled to the floor, blood running down his face.

"You weren't supposed to be here," Amy said, her gray eyes fixed on me.

Still clutching the baseball bat, now smeared with blood, she stepped over Hannigan's body. I backed up in a rush, bumping into the kitchen wall. Amy raised the bat.

I ducked to the side. The bat connected with the wall. The sound of the impact reverberated in my ears. I didn't take the time to check if it had left a hole. Amy was already drawing back the weapon.

I lunged across the hall and through the nearest door, slamming it shut behind me and turning the lock. It wasn't secure enough to hold Amy off for long, but it might buy me some time.

Backing away from the door, I took in my surroundings. I was in a bathroom with a tiled floor, a tub on my left, a pedestal sink and toilet to my right. A quick glance over my shoulder was enough to tell me I had no way to escape. There was a window, but it was far too small for me to fit through.

The doorknob rattled. My heart beat furiously in my chest as I dug my phone out of my pocket with shaking hands. It took me two tries to unlock it.

The baseball bat smacked against the door. I nearly jumped out of my skin. My phone slipped from my hands and clattered into the sink.

Amy struck the door again, and it rattled on its hinges. I snatched my phone out of the sink as the bat connected with the door once more. My whole body jerked at the loud impact, but this time I kept my phone in my grasp.

"Why are you doing this, Amy?" I yelled through the door as I put a call through to 911.

"Why do you think?" She punctuated her question with another strike at the door.

"You killed Demetra." I still didn't understand everything, but I knew I was right about that.

My heart gave a painful jolt when the bat made impact again.

I heard wood splinter. The door wouldn't hold her back much longer.

"Police," I gasped into the phone when the dispatcher answered. "There's a woman with a baseball bat."

Amy struck again. A small, splintered hole appeared halfway up the door.

Fear sent the pitch of my voice up a notch. "She's got me trapped in a bathroom and she's trying to break down the door! She already attacked a man!"

"What's your location, ma'am?" the dispatcher asked calmly.

I rattled off the address. I barely had all the words out when Amy hit the door yet again.

"Hang up the phone!" she yelled at me from the hallway.

She renewed her attack on the door, striking faster and harder now. The small hole grew bigger with each blow.

Eventually she stopped her onslaught, and I could hear heavy breathing through the door.

"I really don't know why you attacked Coach Hannigan," I said loudly, still gripping my phone but holding it away from my ear. "Did he know you killed Demetra?"

"No, but he wanted me dead. He sent his cousin to kill me, to shut me up for good."

I struggled to process what she was saying, my fear and pounding heart making me want to escape rather than think.

"Tyrone is Coach Hannigan's cousin?"

"Not Tyrone," she said between heavy breaths. "Mr. Kerwin."

"Willard Kerwin?" I asked, confused. "But you accused Tyrone of attacking you."

"I just told the cops that to get back at Tyrone. I knew all along it was Mr. Kerwin. Hannigan must have sent him. Why else would he attack me?"

I could think of a possible reason—if he was the saboteur—but she didn't give me a chance to share it with her.

She'd obviously caught her breath because she struck hard at the door again.

"You were the one who met with Coach Hannigan in the trees by the beach," I said. "Why did he want to silence you?"

My attempt to distract her didn't work. She ignored me and upped the intensity of her attack on the door.

The dispatcher was talking to me, but I dropped my phone onto the edge of the sink and grabbed a metal towel rack, prying it loose from the wall. It was a pathetic weapon in comparison to Amy's bat, but it was all I had to work with.

The bat struck the door again, widening the hole further. Amy pulled back the weapon and peered at me through the splintered gap. Her eyes were flat and emotionless. The sight of them sent a sharp chill through me.

I wrenched the towel rack free from the wall and caught sight of myself in the mirror above the sink. Unlike Amy's eyes, mine were wide with fear.

She struck at the door again.

I looked at the towel rack in my hands.

Maybe I could get a better weapon.

I was about to strike the mirror with the towel rack, hoping to break away a shard, when I heard a strangled cry from the hallway.

Everything went quiet for a second or two, and then I heard a muffled thud.

I stood frozen, listening, my pulse beating like a drum in my ears.

"You all right in there?" a man called out.

My knees went weak with relief. It was Jake Fellmen's voice.

"It's safe to come out now," he said.

My hands still trembling, I unlocked the door and cautiously opened it a crack.

Amy was lying slumped on the hallway floor, her eyes closed. Fellmen stood over her, the baseball bat held loosely at his side. I couldn't tell if Amy was breathing.

I opened the door wider.

"Is she...?" I couldn't bring myself to finish the question.

"Just unconscious," Fellmen assured me. He looked at me over Amy's unmoving body. "Something tells me we've finally got the killer."

Chapter 33

The weather couldn't have been more perfect on the day of the garden party at the Wildwood Inn. The sky was a brilliant shade of blue, and the bright sunshine was pleasantly warm but not too hot. The neatly trimmed lawn and the leafy trees provided a gorgeous green backdrop for the bursts of white, purple, red, pink, and yellow from the flowers Brett had planted and tended.

Everyone seemed in awe of the beautiful house and garden, and I couldn't help but smile with pride every time someone complimented Brett on his work. The turnout for the party was fantastic, with what seemed like half the town showing up to enjoy the spectacular setting and the delicious catered food that was set out on two long tables beneath a white canopy.

I'd become separated from Brett while I was talking with a few of The Flip Side's regular customers, but as I wandered toward the food tables on my own, I spotted him over by the punch bowl. He was talking with his mom and his aunt—Ray's wife—but his gaze kept drifting my way.

He filled glasses with punch for his mom and aunt, and then filled two more and headed toward me.

"Thirsty?" He offered me one of the glasses.

"Thank you." I took a sip of the refreshing drink, enjoying the fruity flavor. As the skirt of my green dress fluttered in the breeze, I realized Brett was grinning at me, his own drink untouched. "What?"

"I can't take my eyes off you. That dress… Have I told you how beautiful you are?"

"Only half a dozen times so far today," I said with a smile. I gave his blue tie a gentle tug. It matched the color of his eyes perfectly, and he wore it with a gray suit. "You're looking pretty darn good yourself, but that's not unusual."

He leaned toward me. I was about to accept his kiss when I heard someone call my name.

I turned to see Hope and Chloe crossing the grass toward us, Chloe carrying a small plate with a piece of cake on it.

"Sorry to interrupt, lovebirds," Chloe said with a smile. "But we've heard several versions of what happened at Coach Hannigan's house, and we want to hear the story from someone who was there."

"We don't want to upset you, though," Hope said quickly. "So if you don't want to talk about it, Marley, we understand."

"It's okay," I assured them. I'd already told the story many times over, first to Ray and his deputies, then to Brett, and then to several people at the pancake house in the days since Amy's arrest.

Brett's hand came to rest at the small of my back as I recounted what had happened from the time Tyrone confronted Bruce Hannigan to the point when Jake Fellmen rendered Amy unconscious with a sleeper hold.

"I was so shocked to hear that Amy's the killer," Hope said.

"Same," Chloe chimed in. "Is it true she did it because she was being blackmailed? I can picture Demetra as a blackmailer, but I never would have guessed that she'd target Amy."

"That was part of it," I said.

Amy had regained consciousness before Ray had hauled her away from Coach Hannigan's house in handcuffs, but she hadn't said anything more at the scene. Jake Fellmen had filled me in on the details a few days later. He'd stopped by The Flip Side before leaving town and had told me what he'd learned from speaking with people at the sheriff's department and Mrs. Kozani. He'd been nicer to me since Amy's arrest, possibly because of the fright I'd experienced.

"When you were in high school, Coach Hannigan paid Amy to tutor Tyrone and help him pass his classes," I explained. "Only it was more like doing his homework and helping him cheat on exams than actual tutoring. Amy needed the money so she could go to photography school, so she did what Hannigan wanted. But Demetra found out somehow. She threatened to spill the beans, so Hannigan had to pay her off and Amy had to help her with her modeling portfolio for free."

"But you said the blackmail was only part of it," Chloe said as she sank her fork into her piece of cake.

I nodded. "After Amy helped her with her portfolio, Demetra started demanding money from her as well as from Coach Hannigan. But the final straw came on the night of the party. Demetra figured out that Amy was in love with Tyrone. When Demetra was leaving the party, she saw Amy in the woods, just arriving. She'd dressed up more than usual, was planning to tell Tyrone about her feelings for him that night. Demetra taunted her."

I paused, not wanting to put the next part into words. It was too awful. Even though I'd had a chance to digest the story since I'd heard it from Fellmen, it was still disturbing.

"Amy snapped," Brett picked up the story. I'd already shared everything I knew with him. "She shoved Demetra hard. Demetra fell and hit her head on a rock. Amy panicked and buried her body and then went home."

Silence fell over our small group. Chloe rested her fork on her plate, leaving the rest of her cake uneaten.

"To think some of us weren't that far away when it happened," Hope said quietly. "And none of us had a clue."

I took a sip of punch, waiting out the wave of sadness washing over me.

"But why would Amy want to kill Coach Hannigan?" Chloe asked after a moment. "I still don't get that part."

"She thought he'd sent his cousin—Willard Kerwin—to attack her at her studio," I said. "Hannigan was worried the murder investigation would prompt Amy to tell someone about the blackmail and the cheating. He'd already warned her that he didn't want his reputation ruined, and she figured he was trying to silence her for good."

"But Amy accused Tyrone of hitting her on the head," Chloe said.

"To distract everyone, and to punish Tyrone," I explained. "According to Tyrone, Amy had confessed her feelings for him later that summer, a couple of weeks after the party. He laughed at her."

"Ouch," Hope said sadly. "Compassion never was his forte."

"Apparently she held a grudge all these years," I said.

"That's just…" Chloe trailed off. "I don't even know what to say." She poked her cake with her fork. "At least Coach Hannigan survived. I hear he'll be out of the hospital soon."

"That's one bit of good news," I said as two women I didn't recognize approached our group.

"Hope, everything's so beautiful!" one of the women said, putting an arm around the party's hostess and ushering her away.

"Thanks for filling us in," Chloe said, giving my arm a squeeze. "I'm so glad you're okay."

"Me too," I said.

I had Fellmen to thank for that. When my car hadn't turned out of the driveway after his, he'd gone back to see what was keeping me. Amy hadn't heard him coming when he'd let himself into Coach Hannigan's house to look for me.

"I'm going to grab myself some of that punch." Chloe hurried off toward the refreshments.

"I'm thinking I need to taste that cake," Brett said. "Do you want some?"

"No, thanks. I'm good with my punch for now."

As Brett jogged off to catch up with his sister, I noticed Sienna heading my way with Ellie Shaw.

"Hi, girls," I said as they reached me.

"I was just telling Ellie the news," Sienna said.

"About Willard Kerwin?" I guessed.

"I can't believe it," Ellie said. "His wife, Dorothy, is so nice. Why did he want to make everyone sick at the competition?"

I'd told Ray what Amy had said about recognizing the intruder at her studio as Willard Kerwin. As soon as the sheriff confronted him, the man broke down and confessed to the assault and to slipping syrup of ipecac into some of the drinks at the cooking competition. He'd gone to Amy's studio to find and destroy any potential photographs of him doctoring people's drinks. He went during business hours because he didn't have the nerve to actually break in. Instead, he waited until Amy went out into the back alley and then quickly set about searching the studio. He hadn't had a chance to get past the reception area before Amy returned, interrupting his search. In a panic, he'd struck her with a tripod before escaping.

"His wife has been through a lot over the past couple of years," I said in answer to Ellie's question. "He wanted her to win the competition so she'd have something to be happy about."

"But now she has more to be *unhappy* about," Sienna said.

Ellie tucked her hair behind her ear as the breeze tried to lift it in front of her face. "That's so sad. Will he go to jail?"

"Hopefully not," I said. "But I don't know for sure. He's never been in any trouble before, so maybe that will weigh in his favor. From what I've heard, he feels terrible about everything. So does Dorothy, even though she didn't know anything about it."

"Maybe I should go visit her," Ellie said. "Or write her a letter. You know, to let her know I'm not mad about getting sick."

I was impressed by her compassion. "That would be nice. I bet she'd like that."

The afternoon was slipping toward evening by then, and the crowd in the garden was slowly thinning. I found Lisa and Ivan near the small waterfall Brett had recently installed by the house. I spent a few minutes talking with them and then went in search of my boyfriend.

"Have you seen Brett?" I asked Chloe when I found her at the punch bowl, refilling her glass.

"Oh," she said, nearly spilling the punch as she ladled it into her glass. "He's gone home."

"Home?" I echoed, confused. "Without me?" We'd both come to the party in his truck.

"He asked me to give you a ride." She grabbed a paper napkin and dabbed at the dribbles of punch running down the outside of her glass.

"Why did he leave without me?" It wasn't like him to do that without saying something to me first.

"You were talking to someone and he didn't want to interrupt."

"But why did he need to take off in such a hurry?" I was still confused.

Chloe shrugged, her gaze sweeping over the selection of desserts on the table. "I guess he had something he needed to do?"

I still didn't understand why he'd done something so out of character, but Chloe didn't seem to have any real answers for me.

"Are you ready to go?" I asked her.

"Oh...maybe soon," she hedged. "Just let me finish my punch and another piece of cake. Have you had any? It's delicious."

She hurried off down to the end of the table where only a few pieces of cake remained. She seemed flustered, which wasn't like her. What was wrong with the siblings, I didn't know, but I decided it wouldn't hurt to try the cake.

It really was delicious—light and fluffy and layered with buttercream. Even so, I was glad when Chloe finally declared that she was ready to head home. I wanted to find out what was so important that Brett had hurried away without a word to me.

By the time Chloe stopped her car in front of my house, it was almost completely dark out. Brett's truck was parked between my hatchback and his work van, so I knew he'd arrived home.

After saying goodbye to Chloe, I let myself in the front door. I expected Bentley to race to the foyer to greet me, but the house was still and quiet.

"Brett?" I called out. "Bentley?"

Silence was the only response.

I locked the front door and made my way to the back of the house. Flapjack was snoozing on the couch, but it appeared as though he and I were the only ones home. Maybe Brett had taken Bentley for an evening walk.

I kicked off my shoes and was about to drop my clutch on the coffee table when I heard my phone chime from inside it. I dug out the device and checked my messages.

Meet me on the beach? Brett had texted.

Why? I wrote back. *What's up?*

His response came almost right away.

I want to show you something.

That piqued my curiosity. Leaving my purse and phone behind, I slipped my feet into flip-flops and went out through the back door.

Right away I noticed a flickering glow of light coming from the beach. As I headed down the porch steps, Bentley bounded out of the shadows, his whole body wiggling with excitement.

"Hey, buddy," I said with a laugh, pausing to give his fur a good rubdown. "What have you done with Brett?"

When I took a step toward the beach, Bentley raced off ahead of me. I took another two steps and paused. Two heart-shaped sparklers with long stems were stuck into the sand, shooting glowing sparks into the darkness.

I took a few more steps until I was standing between the sparklers. Ahead of me, more pairs of fiery hearts marked a pathway down the beach.

My own heart upped its tempo, and something fluttered in my stomach. My legs didn't want to work, but I forced them to. With each step, my feet sank into the soft sand and my heart beat faster. I followed the path of sparklers toward the pulse of the ocean's breaking waves.

Near the water's edge, at the end of the pathway of glowing hearts, Brett stood waiting for me. He still wore his suit and tie from the garden party.

My heart broke into a full-out gallop at the sight of him.

His eyes gleamed with the light from the sparklers, and he smiled at me like he couldn't possibly have been any happier.

I drew to a stop in front of him, my heart ready to fly right out of my chest.

"Hi?" I didn't mean for the word to come out as a question, but my mind had suddenly gone all giddy and off kilter.

Brett laughed and took my hands in his. "Hi."

His eyes burned into mine, his gaze hotter than the sparks lighting up the darkness around us.

I could hardly breathe, could hardly feel my feet in the sand.

I gripped his hands tighter. He returned the pressure and cleared his throat.

"Marley." He released my hands and reached into his pocket as he went down on one knee.

I covered my mouth with my hands, certain that my heart was about to fly off into the night.

"Marley," he said again, opening a small box to reveal a stunning ring set with diamonds and sapphires. "When I first met you nearly twenty years ago, you were the most beautiful girl I'd ever seen." His voice shook slightly, and he took a second to steady himself before continuing.

"I was too shy to tell you that back then, but I'm glad I have the chance to tell you now. I never forgot you over the years, and when you came back into my life, I knew it was meant to be. You're the light of my life, my perfect match. I hope our love story is just beginning, and I want us to live every chapter of it together." He took the ring from the satin cushion. "Will you marry me, Marley?"

I fought to pull air into my lungs as tears welled in my eyes. "Yes," I said, the word coming out as little more than a gasp. I tried again, my voice stronger this time. "Yes! Of course I will."

Relief and happiness lit up his face. He slid the ring onto my finger as my hand trembled.

"Holey buckets," I said through tears. "Brett!"

As soon as he stood up, I threw my arms around him.

"I love you so much," I said.

"I love you too."

He lifted me up off the ground and spun me around.

Bentley barked and rushed over to us, bouncing around as Brett sent me down on my feet, both of us laughing.

He kissed me, and it didn't matter that I couldn't form a coherent thought. I could *feel*, and that was more than enough.

Brett put both his hands to my face and rested his forehead against mine.

"You're shaking," he said, grinning.

"I can't believe it," I said, unable to keep more tears from spilling onto my cheeks. "Is this really happening?"

"It's definitely happening."

He kissed me again, and then I wrapped my arms around him, hugging him and resting my cheek against his chest.

"Together forever?" I whispered.

"Forever," he said.

Recipes

Marzipan Pancakes

 2 tablespoons butter, melted
 1½ cups (~200 g) marzipan or almond paste, cut in small
pieces
 1½ cups all-purpose flour
 1 tablespoon sugar
 2 teaspoons baking powder
 ½ teaspoon baking soda
 1 large egg
 1¾ cups unsweetened almond milk
 1 teaspoon vanilla extract

Melt the butter and set it aside to cool. Cut the marzipan/almond paste into small pieces.

Mix together the flour, sugar, baking powder, and baking soda. In a separate bowl, beat together the egg, almond milk, melted butter, and vanilla. Make a well in the dry ingredients. Add the liquid ingredients to the dry ingredients and mix together. Stir in the marzipan/almond paste.

Ladle the batter into a greased skillet and cook on medium heat until bubbles form on the top and don't disappear. Flip and cook second side until golden brown.

Serve with butter and maple syrup. Serves 4.

Banoffee Crêpes

Crêpes:

> 1 cup all-purpose flour
> 1 tablespoon sugar
> 2 eggs
> 1½ cups milk
> ½ teaspoon vanilla extract
> Butter or oil for greasing pan

Sift flour and sugar into mixing bowl. In separate bowl, whisk together the eggs, milk, and vanilla. Make a well in the dry ingredients. Pour in half the liquid ingredients. Whisk until smooth. Add the remaining liquid ingredients. Whisk until smooth again.

Optional: Refrigerate batter for up to 6 hours.

Heat crêpe pan or small skillet over low heat for several minutes. Grease lightly. Increase to medium heat and leave for 1 to 2 minutes. Pour ¼ cup batter into the pan. Tilt and swirl to coat the pan. Cook until lightly browned. Remove from pan; repeat process. Makes 12 to 16 crêpes.

Filling:

> 2 tins dulce de leche
> 4 large bananas, sliced
> Whipping cream
> Chocolate shavings

Spread some dulce de leche on each crêpe and add several banana slices. Fold the crêpe and top with whipped cream and chocolate shavings.

Boston Cream Crêpes

Crêpes:

Use the same crêpe recipe as for the Banoffee Crêpes.

Custard Filling:

    1½ cups milk
    ¼ cup sugar
    2 eggs, slightly beaten
    ½ teaspoon vanilla extract

Scald the milk in the top of a double boiler. Stir in the sugar. Add a small quantity of the hot liquid to the slightly beaten eggs. Repeat 2 or 3 more times. Then gradually add the eggs to the hot liquid in the double boiler.

Cook, stirring constantly, until the custard is thick enough to coat a metal spoon.

Remove from heat and immediately place the pan in cold water. Continue to stir for 2 minutes to release the steam. Stir in the vanilla. Chill.

Chocolate Sauce:

    ½ cup milk
    1 cup chocolate chips
    1 teaspoon vanilla extract

Heat the milk in the top of a double boiler. Add the chocolate chips and stir until smooth. Remove from heat and stir in the vanilla.

Place a couple of spoonfuls of custard filling on each crêpe. Fold or roll the crêpe and drizzle with chocolate sauce.

Acknowledgments

I'd like to extend my sincere thanks to several people whose hard work and input made this book what it is today. I'm forever grateful to my agent, Jessica Faust, for helping me bring this series to life and to my editor at Kensington Books, Martin Biro, for helping me shape this manuscript into a better book. Thank you to Sarah Blair for always reading my early drafts and cheering me on, and to Jody Holford for providing feedback and being such an enthusiastic Marley and Brett fan. Thanks also to my wonderful friends in the writing community, the Cozy Mystery Crew, and all the readers who have returned for another of Marley's adventures in Wildwood Cove.

If you enjoyed *Crêpe Expectations*, be sure not to miss the previous books in Sarah Fox's Pancake House mystery series, including

Winter has come to Wildwood Cove, and riding in on the chill is Wally Fowler. Although he's been away for years, establishing his reputation as the self-proclaimed Waffle King, the wealthy blowhard has returned to the coastal community to make money, not friends—by pitting his hot and trendy Waffle Kingdom against Marley McKinney's cozy pancake house, The Flip Side. Wally doesn't see anything wrong in a little healthy competition, until he's murdered in his own state-of-the art kitchen.

Marley isn't surprised when the authorities sniff around The Flip Side for a motive, but it's her best friend Lisa who gets grilled, given her sticky history with the victim. When a second murder rocks the town, it makes it harder than ever for Marley to clear Lisa's name. Marley's afraid that she's next in line to die—and the way things are looking, the odds of surviving her investigation could be stacked against her.

A Lyrical Underground e-book on sale now.

Keep reading for a special look!

Chapter 1

My car's headlights cut through the darkness, illuminating the driving rain. The windshield wipers swished back and forth in a rapid rhythm as I carefully navigated my way along the deserted streets of Wildwood Cove. Normally I preferred to walk to work each morning, trekking along the beach so I could listen to the crashing waves and smell the salty air. Lately, however, I'd been making more use of my blue hatchback. Over the past several days the weather had been less than inviting, drizzling with rain if not outright pouring, and chilly enough that the occasional glob of slush splattered against my windshield along with the pelting raindrops.

The rain was supposed to let up in the next day or so, according to the weather forecast, so I hoped it wouldn't be much longer before I could get back to enjoying my early morning walks along the shoreline. For the moment, though, I was grateful for the warmth and shelter of my car.

When I turned into the small parking lot behind The Flip Side pancake house, I pulled up next to the only other car in the lot—a baby blue classic Volkswagen bug belonging to The Flip Side's chef, Ivan Kaminski. He arrived even earlier than I did each morning, as did his assistant, Tommy Park. It was barely six o'clock, but I knew the two of them would have been working for a good while already.

I shut off my car's engine and grabbed my tote bag off the passenger seat, steeling myself for the upcoming dash through the pouring rain to the back door of the pancake house. As soon as I climbed out into the rain, I slammed the car door, ducked my head, and made a beeline for the slim bit of shelter provided by the recessed doorway.

Despite having spent mere seconds exposed to the elements, I had damp hair and droplets of water running down my face. I wiped them away with my sleeve and jiggled my ring of keys until I found the right one. As I put the key into the door, I caught sight of something white from the corner of my eye. A flyer lay plastered against the pavement, waterlogged and with a muddy footprint stamped across it.

I darted out of the shelter of the doorway and peeled the soggy paper off the ground. When I was once again out of the rain, I peered at the flyer, the exterior light above my head providing me with enough illumination to read by.

When I took in the bold black words printed across the saturated paper, my former good mood did a nose-dive. I'd seen the flyer before. I'd seen several them, in fact, plastered all over town on utility poles, signposts, and community notice boards. I'd also received one in the mail. That one had gone straight into the recycling bin. This one I crumpled up in my hand as I unlocked the door, the words "Wally's Waffle Kingdom" disappearing from sight as the paper scrunched up into a soggy ball.

Once inside, I unlocked the door to my office and tossed the scrunched flyer into the wastepaper basket. If I never saw another one, I'd be happy, although I knew the advertisement wasn't the real problem. That was the Waffle Kingdom itself. The Flip Side had become a fixture in the small seaside town of Wildwood Cove, with many faithful customers who returned again and again to enjoy Ivan's scrumptious breakfast creations. There were other restaurants and cafés around town, but none of them specialized in breakfast foods like The Flip Side did.

Up until a couple of weeks ago, I'd never really worried about competition. Then Wally Fowler had moved to town—moved *back* to town actually, since he'd grown up here—and my mind had remained unsettled ever since. I wasn't about to roll over and give up on the pancake house just because of some competition, but I couldn't keep my niggling concern at bay.

If the Waffle Kingdom's fare was as good as the flyer proclaimed ("the best waffles EVER!") it wasn't unrealistic to think that The Flip Side would lose some of its business to the new establishment. In the summertime, when tourists flocked to the small town, that might not be such a problem. There would probably be enough business for both restaurants during those weeks. But during the rest of the year? That could be a definite issue.

I'd been hoping to give each of my three full-time employees a raise in the near future. Now I was keeping that plan to myself, unsure if I'd be able to follow through. I'd have to wait and see what happened once the waffle house opened. As Wally and his flyers had been announcing to the whole town for several days, the grand opening of the Waffle Kingdom would take place next week.

It would take time to know the full extent of the effect on The Flip Side, so I was determined to carry on as usual. I just wished I could get rid of that ever present worry lingering at the back of my mind.

With the wet flyer in the trash and my jacket hung on the coat stand, I ran a hand through my damp curls and made my way into the dining area. I flipped on the lights, and immediately some of the tension that had crept into my shoulders fizzled away. There was something so comforting about the cozy pancake house. Like the beach and the charming town, The Flip Side had easily worked its way into my heart, becoming a second home away from my blue-and-white beachfront Victorian.

Smiling, I glanced out the large front windows, seeing nothing but inky darkness and rivulets of water running down the panes.

Well, almost nothing else.

I walked quickly across the room to the front door, bone-chilling damp air hitting me as soon as I pushed it open. Staying beneath the awning so I wouldn't get soaked, I approached the two white rectangles taped to one of the windows, spaced a couple of feet apart. When I got close enough to recognize them as two more Waffle Kingdom flyers, I let out a growl of annoyance.

Ripping the flyers off the glass, I stormed back into the pancake house. "Of all the nerve!"

Twenty-one-year-old Tommy Park poked his head out the pass-through window to the kitchen. "What's up?" he asked.

I waved the crumpled flyers. "Wally the Waffle King strikes again."

The kitchen door swung open and Ivan appeared. Tommy ducked away from the window and came through the door a second later.

"These were taped to the front window," I said, waving the flyers again.

Ivan grabbed one and glowered at the piece of paper. While an intimidating scowl was the chef's typical expression, this one was far darker than usual.

"He's rubbing your nose in it," he declared, crumpling the flyer as his large hand closed into a fist.

Tommy took the other flyer from me. "Totally not cool."

"It's one thing to open up a waffle house that will compete directly with us," I said, "but it's hitting a new low by plastering the ads all over the front of this place."

"He's trying to get under your skin." Ivan tossed the crumpled flyer toward the wastepaper basket, making a perfect shot.

"But why? Does he really think annoying us will get us to close up shop so all our business goes his way?"

"Not going to happen," Tommy said.

"Definitely not," I agreed. "But why else try to aggravate us?"

"Probably for fun," Ivan said. "Some people enjoy riling others up."

"That's true." I'd learned that firsthand several months back when a bitter and vengeful woman had tried to make my life miserable.

"And I hear Wally Fowler's a slimeball," Tommy said. "I'm not sure anyone in town actually likes him."

Ivan nodded his agreement. "Wildwood Cove would be better off without him."

If enough people believed that, maybe I had nothing to worry about. The townsfolk weren't likely to give the self-proclaimed Waffle King their business if they despised him.

"I guess it's best to ignore him and focus on keeping our customers happy, like we always do," I decided.

"Sounds like a plan." With a flick of his wrist, Tommy sent the second flyer arcing into the trash can.

He returned to the kitchen and Ivan followed after him, his scowl as dark as ever. Was he more worried about the new waffle house than he was letting on? With his bulging muscles, numerous tattoos; and dark, intense eyes, Ivan wasn't one to be easily fazed. But something in his face led me to believe he was taking the potential problem posed by Wally and his waffle house very seriously.

My worries tried to resurface, but I forced them back down, focusing on starting a fire in the stone fireplace to keep myself busy. The Flip Side would be fine, I told myself. It was a well-established restaurant, with a solid and loyal customer base that loved Ivan's cooking and the cozy atmosphere.

Surely it would take more than Wally the Waffle King to destroy what we had here. After all, how much damage could one man cause?

* * * *

About an hour after opening, the pancake house was getting busy. The town was waking up, the residents heading out to brave the weather, some of them ending up at The Flip Side. All of the tables near the cheery, crackling fire had been claimed, the welcoming warmth of the flames drawing in the customers as they escaped the cold and the rain. On my way around the restaurant to offer refills of coffee, I paused to talk with two of The Flip Side's most loyal and reliable customers, Gary and Ed. They were lifelong residents of Wildwood Cove and had been best friends since they were five years old. Now retired, they split most of their time between the pancake house, the local seniors' activity center, and the bowling alley.

"What do you know about this Waffle Kingdom that's opening up next week, Marley?" Ed asked.

"I've heard the self-proclaimed Waffle King grew up here in Wildwood Cove," I said. "But other than that, I really don't know anything more than what's on those flyers he's spread around town."

"A waste of paper, if you ask me," Gary spoke up as he poured maple syrup over his stack of pancakes. "Why would anyone eat there when they could come here? It's not like anyone can compete with Ivan's cooking."

I smiled. "Hopefully you're not the only ones who feel that way."

"We're not," Ed assured me. "And I don't think it'll much matter to people that Wally grew up in Wildwood Cove. He's been away for years, and he wasn't good for much when he was here."

"I've yet to run across a fan of his," I said, topping up the coffee mugs.

Gary chewed on a forkful of pancakes. "Adam Silvester was buddies with Wally back in the day, but I don't know if they stayed in touch. And there's his sister, Vicky, of course. Half-sister, technically. But aside from those two, I'm not sure if anyone's much keen on Wally. People around here have long memories."

I wasn't sure what he meant by that, but I needed to move along and see to other customers.

"I guess we'll have to see what happens when the waffle house opens," I said, happy that I managed to sound unconcerned.

"You'll never find us over there, that's for sure," Ed declared. He lowered his voice. "Unless you want us to go undercover to do some recon."

I couldn't help but smile again. "I doubt that will be necessary, but thank you."

Gary saluted me with his coffee mug. "You can count on us, Marley."

Cheered by their support, I thanked them again and moved on to the next table.

The breakfast rush kept me and Leigh—The Flip Side's full-time waitress—busy for the next hour or so, but I eventually found time to slip into the kitchen and make myself a cup of tea.

"Are you going to the ladies' night at the hardware store tonight, Marley?" Leigh asked as she pushed through the kitchen door, bringing a load of dirty dishes with her.

"I'm planning on it. Are you?"

"No, I'll be looking after the kids. Greg's working at the store tonight."

I took a cautious sip of my hot tea. "I can't help but be amused that ladies' night at the hardware store is an actual thing."

"It's a tradition," Ivan said as he flipped pancakes on the griddle.

"It's true," Leigh confirmed. "The store's been holding this event for more than ten years now. I know it might sound a bit odd at first, but it's really popular. And good fun, too. Aside from having things on sale, they have door prizes, demos, samples to give away, and really good food."

"Free food?" Tommy said as he drizzled melted chocolate over a plate of crêpes. "Are you sure your husband can't sneak me in?"

"Sorry, Tommy," Leigh said with a smile. "You'll have to wait for Customer Appreciation Day in the spring." She returned her attention to me. "It's a good chance for you to get some Christmas shopping done. Maybe you'll find something for Brett."

"Maybe," I said, "but he probably already owns at least one of everything the store has for sale." My boyfriend had his own lawn and garden care company, and during the winters he helped out with his dad's home renovation business. He had a whole workshop full of tools behind his house. "I might get something for myself, though. I'll need a few things if I'm going to make a garden in the spring."

"Don't forget to try the mini cupcakes while you're there," Leigh advised. "Greg already knows he's supposed to smuggle one home for me."

She disappeared through the swinging door. I drank down my tea and followed after her a few minutes later. I spent some time in the office between the breakfast and lunch rushes, but then I was back out at the front of the house helping Leigh.

I carried a plate of bacon cheddar waffles over to a man I'd seen in The Flip Side three or four times before. Prior to that morning, I hadn't known anything about him aside from his name—Adam Silvester—but thanks to my chat with Ed and Gary earlier, I now knew he had once been friends with Wally Fowler.

There wasn't anything about Adam that screamed or even whispered "low-life," but maybe I had a distorted view of Wally. Even if I didn't, the fact that Adam had been buddies with Wally back in high school didn't mean he was a bad guy. They weren't necessarily friends any longer, and I couldn't say that I'd always picked the best people for friends when I was a teenager.

As far as I remembered, I'd only ever seen Adam at The Flip Side on his own. While he was always polite, he kept mostly to himself, gazing out the window as he ate or reading the latest issue of the town's local newspaper. That was what he was doing today, perusing the articles as he started in on his waffles.

I cleared up the neighboring table and carried the dirty dishes into the kitchen before delivering mocha mascarpone crêpes and blueberry crumble pancakes to hungry customers. I glanced out the window on my way back to the kitchen, noting that the rain had stopped and the sun was attempting to peek through the clouds. As I was leaving the dining area for the kitchen, the front door opened, admitting three new arrivals, two men and a woman. I didn't alter my path.

Leigh darted through the kitchen door behind me, grabbing my arm.

"That's him!" she said in an urgent whisper.

"Him who?" I asked as I set down two dirty coffee mugs.

"Wally Fowler," Leigh said, keeping her voice low. "The so-called Waffle King."

"He's here?" Ivan's question boomed across the kitchen. "Why?"

"I don't know, but I guess we'll find out." Leigh hurried out of the kitchen.

I followed right on her heels, ready to finally meet Wally the Waffle King.

Meet the Author

Sarah Fox is the author of the Literary Pub Mystery series, the Music Lover's Mystery series and the *USA Today* bestselling Pancake House Mystery series. When not writing novels or working as a legal writer, she can often be found reading her way through a stack of books or spending time outdoors with her English Springer Spaniel. Sarah lives in British Columbia and is a member of Crime Writers of Canada. Visit her online at AuthorSarahFox.com.

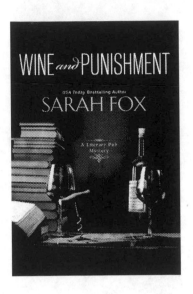

In the first in an engaging new mystery series from **USA Today** *bestselling author Sarah Fox, the owner of a charming literary pub finds her fresh start on the rocks thanks to a case of murder.*

Booklover Sadie Coleman knows that in life, as in fiction, the right setting can make a world of difference. The small town of Shady Creek, Vermont, seems like the perfect place to start over after losing her Boston job to a merger and her relationship to her ex's gambling addiction. She's bought and redecorated the old grist mill pub, transforming the Inkwell into a cozy spot where tourists and regulars alike can enjoy a pint or a literary-themed cocktail, or join one of several book clubs.

Little by little, Sadie is adjusting to the rhythms of her new home. Fall in Shady Creek is bookmarked by the much-anticipated Autumn Festival, complete with a pumpkin catapult competition and pie bake-off. Unfortunately, the season also brings an unwelcome visitor—Sadie's ex, Eric, who's angling for a second chance…

Before Sadie can tell Eric to leave, he's found dead near the Inkwell. When the local antique shop catches fire on the same night, it's clear the town is harboring at least one unsavory character. Now, with her Aunt Gilda, her friend Shontelle, and the pub's patrons all in the mix, Sadie must uncover the truth…before a killer declares last call.

Printed in the United States
by Baker & Taylor Publisher Services